DRUMOSSIE

ECHOES IN TIME - BOOK 1

By M MacKinnon

This book is a work of fiction. Names, characters, places and incidents are either the product of the author's imagination or are used fictitiously, and any resemblance to actual persons, living or dead, events, or locales is entirely coincidental.

Printed in the United States of America
Print ISBN: 978-1-953910-76-9
eBook ISBN: 978-1-953910-77-6

Library of Congress Control Number: 2021910513

Published by DartFrog Plus, the hybrid publishing imprint of DartFrog Books.

Publisher Information:
DartFrog Books
4697 Main Street
Manchester, VT 05255
www.DartFrogBooks.com

Join the discussion of this book on Bookclubz. Bookclubz is an online management tool for book clubs, available now for Android and iOS and via Bookclubz.com.

This book is dedicated to my friend Kathleen Kiel, who read this manuscript almost as many times as I did and was always there to offer support when I faltered.

OTHER BOOKS BY M MACKINNON

The Highland Spirits Series
The Comyn's Curse
The Piper's Warning
The Healer's Legacy

CONTENTS

19 APRIL 1746

An eerie silence lay over the clearing like a cloak. Forest creatures, sensing something amiss, scurried to their burrows and hunched against a menace they could not understand. The dusk settled down, bringing grey mist and a dank cold that owed nothing to the weather.

The quiet was broken by a whisper of sound, a tiny movement against the grass of the clearing. A twitch of tartan, a breath of air. A soft moan emanated from a throat that should never have opened again in this world.

The man groaned and rolled onto his stomach. He could feel the blood dripping from a huge gash above his forehead, and one of his eyes was sealed shut. He raised his head, looked around with the other eye—and immediately closed it against the horror before him. But it was too late—the image was imprinted on his mind.

An immense boulder stood sentinel in the center of the clearing, outlined against the darkening sky. Its sides were gouged by time and smeared with moss and lichen—and something else.

A red, viscous substance clung to the sides of the

rock and trailed down to the trampled ground at its feet, where lay bodies that had once been men. Proud Highlanders, warriors who dared to dream of a better world and who had been willing to gamble their lives for that dream.

The gamble was lost. The rulers of these harsh mountains were destroyed in a single afternoon. Not for generations would tartan be seen in these hills, never again would the skirl of bagpipes lead the clans into battle. The earth would be populated by the descendants of these men, driven far from their land by the wrath and vengeance of the victor.

A rook swooped down and pecked at an eye. There was no one to shoo the bird away, and this was an unaccustomed feast.

Something moved again at the base of the rock. The rook rose into the air with a raucous cry of disappointment and swooped away into the trees.

The man raised his head again, as if compelled to do so by a force greater than himself. He looked at the carnage that surrounded him with his one good eye and let his head drop again. Great gasping sobs welled from somewhere deep inside him, muffled against the dirt. Against the back wall of his eyes, the scene before him replayed again and again.

Dead. They were all dead. His fellow officers—men with whom he had charged into battle, comrades who had spent the past three days languishing together at Culloden House—all sprawled here staring at an unforgiving sky with empty eyes. He lay still and waited to join them.

Pain. His entire body was a seething mass of

it—excruciating agony that defied description. He probed with his mind and followed the pain to its many sources. His leg. His gut. His head. Which would be his death—or would they all conspire together to end him? It did not matter much; death would be a blessing.

But his Highlander's body refused to yield, and after a long time he gave up and struggled to his knees. He kept his eyes screwed tight against the horrific truth at the base of the boulder and rocked back and forth, keening for his comrades. Blood continued to trickle from his head, and his left leg refused to move when he willed it. The pain in his stomach had settled to a throbbing rhythm, reminiscent of the drums that had sent him into battle only days ago.

A new emotion curled its way into his mind, and he felt an anger begin to take root and build. The bastards had stolen his country, but they had miscalculated. There had to be a reason he was still breathing—God wanted something more from him. He would escape this place of horror and tell his story. He owed it to the soldiers who lay before him, and to the thousands who had followed them into Hell. The world could not be permitted to forget what happened on Drumossie Moor.

Slowly, an inch at a time, he crawled toward life.

CHAPTER 1

CAPE BRETON ISLAND, NOVA SCOTIA – PRESENT DAY

I believe in fairies, the myths, dragons . . .
It all exists, even if it's in your mind.
Who's to say that dreams and nightmares
aren't as real as the here and now?"
John Lennon

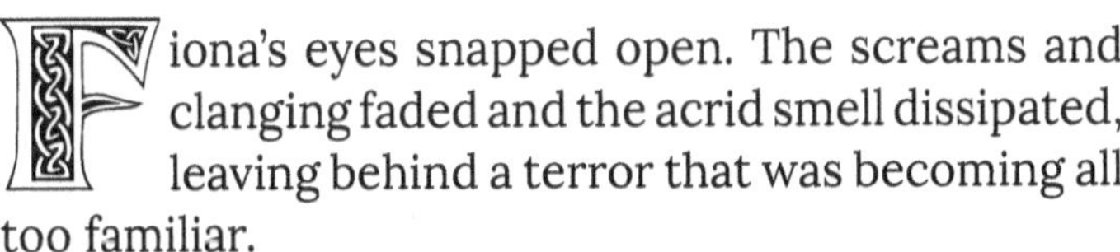

iona's eyes snapped open. The screams and clanging faded and the acrid smell dissipated, leaving behind a terror that was becoming all too familiar.

She closed her eyes again and lay still, waiting for the shaking to subside. A trembling finger found her forehead and trailed across the droplets on her brow. She took a deep, shuddering breath and let it out slowly, opened her eyes and stared into the darkness above.

What the hell? This was the third time she'd had this nightmare—she, who barely ever dreamed. It was always the same. The dream was all smell and sound and shifting shadow—alien sensory images that she had never known and couldn't understand.

Sweat, rancid and pungent in a smoke-filled land-scape. Screams of agony and hatred, grunts and gasps. What was this place? Weren't you supposed to dream about things you'd experienced?

A glance at her alarm clock told her this was going to be another sleep-deprived night. After the dream, it took forever for her heart to steady its beat and her breathing to return to normal, before she could drift off for a couple of hours just before morning.

Fiona thought back over the past few weeks, searching for a clue in the images that swirled in her memory. She didn't watch TV, hadn't been to the movies in years, and her preferred reading tended toward the romantic. There was nothing to point to a reason for the violence that was tearing up her sleep.

Maybe she should see a doctor, though the thought filled her with distaste. Like most people who enjoyed perfect health, she had a natural abhorrence of doctors, hospitals, and the messy stuff that went with them—like blood and bodily secretions. If the doctor could be guaranteed to be young and handsome, now . . .

She sighed. This was Cape Breton Island, after all, where everyone knew everyone else except for the summer tourists. The only doctor she knew was her father's best friend, Caleb MacMillan, and he was sixty if he was a day. Also stumpy, ruddy-faced, and badly in need of a diet. In short, Dr. MacMillan resembled a cheerful Santa Claus in corduroy trousers and tartan bowtie.

Besides, it wasn't a GP she needed. She strongly

suspected that a shrink was called for here, and that was *not* going to happen, because these dreams couldn't last forever. Surely they'd go away in time; she just had to ignore them and wait.

Despite her preference for the sort of novels whose covers sported shirtless, kilted young men with six-pack abs and flowing hair, Fiona MacLean was impeccably practical in her non-reading life. She was not the sort of person to have dreams that jolted her awake and left her quaking in terror. If truth were told, she was boring. She was fine with it and was beginning to yearn for it.

And yet, she was hearing things in her dreams that were alien to her experience in all the twenty-seven years she'd been on earth. She was smelling things she couldn't identify. Things that terrified her and wrenched her awake, shaking as if she had the flu—things that sounded and smelled like death. And that was the worst part, because how would she know what death sounded or smelled like?

There was something else that gnawed at the edges of her mind. Somewhere in that dream was somcone who meant something to her. She remembered blue eyes and wild black hair. Nothing else, but somehow she knew she was supposed to protect this person. Why? From what? His image danced on the surface of her memory, teasing her sleeping self even as it terrified her. When she awoke, he was gone, even as the smells and sounds hung in her memory to torment her long into the night.

She glared at the clock and its stubborn hour hand stuck on the five. Then she sighed and crawled out of her quilt to stand swaying beside her bed. Sleep was a lost cause. Might as well get an early run at the bathroom before her sister Kirsty took it over.

The house was a crisp forty degrees even now in early May, the result of living on an island in northernmost Nova Scotia. Fiona didn't mind the cold—she'd been born here and was used to it. The blood of her Scottish ancestors flowed through her veins, reminding her that her people had once conquered an island much like this one.

Conquered—and then been conquered. The history of Scotland was one of endurance. Highland clans had lived off the land and the sea for hundreds of years, before war, famine, and greed had driven them away from their homeland in search of a better life.

Many of them, like her great-grandfather Angus MacLean, had boarded the great ships bound for the New World, surviving the perils of an unfriendly sea to land here. In Canada they had found a place that reminded them of home, of the Highlands and wild seas. They gave the new land the old Gaelic names and resumed fishing and farming as if they'd never left.

Fiona negotiated the narrow hallway of her family's farmhouse in the dark, confident in her knowledge of every floorboard and corner in the place where she'd been born and raised. Closing and locking the bathroom door, she turned on the light and stared at her reflection in the mirror.

A pale face looked back at her, set off by dark circles under tired green eyes, framed by a tangled mess of chestnut hair. Whatever had been going on in that dream last night, she must have been an active participant.

She rummaged in the drawer for her hairbrush and held it in the attack position. This was going to take some work. The thick knots laughed at her pitiful efforts, and with a growl of frustration she threw the brush back into the drawer and piled it all into a messy bun on top of her head. This look was becoming too familiar for comfort.

The house was beginning to stir. She brushed her teeth and washed her face, dabbed on a bit of concealer and lipstick and called it a job. The concealer wasn't likely to fool anyone, but you had to try. And she didn't want to scare away the customers, after all.

She could hear her mother moving around the kitchen downstairs, humming to herself as she whipped together the usual huge breakfast that would survive about three minutes against the onslaught of her children.

There was a pounding at the bathroom door. Fiona jumped and opened it to find Kirsty just raising her fist to pound again.

"Hurry up! You know Mom'll start nagging if we're late to breakfast—jeez! You look like shit!" Her younger sister pushed by Fiona and turned back to study her. "The dream again?"

"I—"

Without waiting for an answer Kirsty shut the door, leaving Fiona in the hall. So much for concealer. She wandered back down the hall to her room, threw on a pair of black pants and a white turtleneck sweater, and fished her boots out of the closet. She took a last despairing look in her bedroom mirror and clattered down the wooden staircase and into the huge farm-house kitchen.

"You're early," her mother turned from the stove and ran a practiced eye over her daughter. "Bad night?"

Sheesh, did none of them ever miss anything? "I'm fine." Fiona gritted her teeth. "Stayed up too late reading—not to worry."

Her mother held her gaze for a long moment, eyes narrowed.

"Hmmmph," she said, and turned back to the huge pan of scrambled eggs. Fiona's shoulders slumped as she made her way to her seat. No fooling Mom—they'd be revisiting the subject later.

Her brother Brian grinned at her in commiseration from his place across the table and raised an eyebrow. Fiona gave him a wry smile. Brian knew the truth—she told him everything—and he'd have her back no matter what.

She studied her favorite sibling. He was a legend in the family for his skills in the kitchen—and those skills had nothing to do with cooking. No matter how early she might get to the long wooden trestle table, Brian was already there and waiting. He seemed to think that the early bird got the bacon. Despite the fact that they had never yet run out of food, he wasn't taking any chances, and he never seemed to fill up. It was truly a talent.

Tall and broad-shouldered, at twenty-eight Brian was the closest to Fiona in age and looks. All their lives they'd been taken for twins, which astounded his sister because to her he was the handsomest man in the world. No circles under *his* clear green eyes.

They were bright with longer lashes than a girl's, and his wavy russet hair fell onto his forehead in a perfect style that owed nothing to effort.

Twelve-year-old Niall flew into the room and slid into his chair, yelping as he barked an elbow on the edge of the table. Niall was a paler replica of Brian—brown hair, brown eyes, skinny frame that looked as if it would never fill out. But the promise was there. A few more years and Niall would be breaking hearts just like his older brother. Her parents' surprise fourth child, he was twelve years younger than his next older sibling and milked his status as adored baby of the family for all it was worth.

The door opened and Kirsty glided in looking fresh and lovely as a spring rose, as usual. Model thin, her blonde hair perfectly combed and her flawless skin shining under the makeup she didn't even need, Kirsty was the real beauty of the family—and she knew it. At twenty-four, she had the hearts of every man and boy on the island, except one.

Kirsty slid gracefully into the seat next to Brian and looked across the table at her sister.

"Oh dear, isn't Greg picking you up this morning?" There was a smirk in the words. "You'd better put some more concealer on, or he won't recognize you."

"Leave Fee alone, Kirsten." Her mother plunked a huge bowl of eggs next to a platter of toast in the center of the table. "Bacon's coming. Eat, all of you, and try to act as if you like each other."

"Greg likes Fiona," Niall said. "He doesn't care what she looks like. Why do you care—do you like him?"

Out of the mouths of babes, Fiona thought, and a wave

of appreciation for her little brother's loyalty washed over her. He was absolutely spooky sometimes, innocently hitting on the truth without knowing, but his logic was just what she needed this morning.

A cloud marred her sister's perfect brow for just a second, and then Kirsty shrugged and reached for the eggs.

"Of course I don't. Mind your own business, brat."

"Well then, why—" Niall caught a signal from Brian and pressed his lips together.

"Mmm, Mom, the bacon's great," Brian gave his mother a beautiful smile, the dimple on the left side of his mouth deepening. "You're an angel."

"You say that every day," his mother said, but her face broke into an answering smile as she looked at her son. "It's just bacon."

"Brian, can you give me a ride to the restaurant?" Kirsty asked. "My car's in the shop again."

"Sure," her brother said. "Need one home too?"

"No, I'll get Kevin or Gordy to bring me home," she said. "They never say no."

Brian snorted and returned to his eggs. Kirsty never had trouble finding a ride anywhere. Every waiter and busboy tripped over his feet to be her chevalier, and she used them with the practiced artistry of a courtesan.

Fiona's phone lit up. *I'm here*, the text read. She excused herself and carried her dishes to the sink, and then grabbed her purse and her corduroy barn jacket on the way out to the driveway.

"Hello, princess." Greg Ross stood next to his red Mustang. His warm brown eyes crinkled and his face broke into a smile. "Your carriage awaits." He opened the driver's door and climbed behind the wheel.

Shouldn't a princess be helped into her carriage? Fiona thought irritably. Then she gave herself a mental slap. *Don't be bitchy, just because you're tired.* She gave him a wan smile and rounded the car to climb into the passenger seat. She belted herself in and leaned back against the headrest, eyes closed.

Greg maintained a running commentary on the latest acquisitions of his favorite hockey team, the Montreal Canadiens, refusing to believe that she didn't care. Within minutes she was asleep.

Someone was shaking her. Arms went around her and held her close, and she knew in this moment that everything would be all right, because he was here. She allowed herself to sink into his embrace. She stared into his beloved face and put her arms around his warm body, pouring her love and gratitude into him, willing him to understand how she felt.

"Whoa!" A voice came from a distance, and she opened her eyes, startled to see that she had somehow gotten out of the car. Greg stood staring at her, his eyes wide. He peeled her arms off and stepped back, face breaking into a sardonic grin.

"I get it—but try not to break me, okay?"

Embarrassed, Fiona wrapped her arms around herself and stood mute. They were standing in the parking lot of the Gaelic College, and several people were staring. Never one for public display of affection, she felt her cheeks growing warm. Greg, on the other hand, looked thrilled.

"Didn't know you had it in you, Fee," he said with

a laugh. "We'll have to explore this new you later, though, because I have to get to work." He kissed her on the forehead, climbed back into the car, and drove off, leaving her standing in the parking lot staring after him.

She had never been so passionate with Greg—their relationship was only a few months old and they hadn't progressed that far, not for any lack of trying on his part. She just wasn't ready.

But that wasn't what had her rooted to the pavement, rigid with shock. The embrace had felt natural, right. She had wanted it as much as he had.

And that was the problem. The man she had been hugging with everything in her soul wasn't Greg. His eyes had been a brilliant blue, his hair as black as night, and she knew him.

She had seen him just last night, in her dream.

CHAPTER 2

GLENCOE,
SCOTLAND - PRESENT DAY

*Life seems sometimes like nothing more
than a series of losses, from beginning to
end . . . what you make of what's left, that's
the part you have to make up as you go."*
Katharine Webery

"So this is your idea of a relaxing day out? Are we even related?"

Ewan MacArthur turned. His younger brother's forehead was creased and his expression accusing.

"Adam, what are you talking about?" Ewan brushed his black hair out of his eyes and assumed an innocent look.

"You know you love scrambling almost as much as I do," he said. "You've bagged your share of Munros, haven't you? Quit your whingin' and look at this view. It never gets old, does it?" He turned back to the vista spread before them from where they stood atop

Sgorr nam Fiannaidh, the first Munro in the Aonach Eagach ridge.

Adam sighed, and his face relaxed into a grin.

"Aye, it doesn't. And you're right about the scrambling." His mouth twisted. "It's just that when your brother invites you out for a pint, *and* offers to pay, this is not the first place that comes to mind."

Ewan winked one blue eye. "The pint is our reward at the end of the day. Just think how much better it'll taste after we've walked the ridge."

His brother shook his head. "You're definitely more obsessed than I am. You've walked Aonach Eagach how many times now? Five? Is it even a challenge anymore?"

Ewan's look turned serious. "It's always a challenge, and I pity the climber who gets complacent about it. Aonach Eagach is the most dangerous ridge of them all."

He stared into the distance. "Six miles of exposed trail, drop-offs that mean certain death if you make a mistake, paths that lead to impossible rock walls . . . what's not to love?" He clapped his brother on the back, laughing as Adam rolled his eyes.

They had begun their trek early in the morning, when the mist hung almost to the car park, with hopes it would clear by the time they reached the higher levels. Scrambling over wet moss and scree and wading through heather was never a good plan. So far, so good, except for the wind.

Ewan adjusted the collar on his insulated jacket and tied his scarf tighter, glad for its warmth on this cold May morning. The Munros, and especially this ridge, were nothing to attempt alone, even for an experienced scrambler.

He looked at his brother with gratitude. It was true that of the two of them, Adam was the lesser climber in both skill and experience, but he never passed up an opportunity to go along with his older brother. Loyal to a fault.

Why had this brother stuck with him, Ewan wondered, after all that had happened? In a family—if it could be called that, he thought bitterly—of six children, to everyone except Adam he was non-existent. He was the black sheep, the One Who Shall Not Be Named. The oldest son, the one who once had carried his father's hope for the future.

The one who had killed his mother.

Ewan shook his head. Why was he thinking about that now? For sixteen years he had managed to hide the memories of that night and its aftermath away, locked them into a hidden compartment in his mind where only the darkest things lived. He had sent the ghost of his father's hatred away, had managed to pretend that he had no family.

"Ewan." Adam's voice broke into his thoughts, and he turned to find his brother looking at him with an uncomfortable intensity.

"Aye?"

"Um . . . Dad asked about you the other day."

Ewan stiffened.

"*Don't.*" His voice held a warning, but Adam chose to ignore the tension in the words.

"He misses you, Ewan. It's been a long time, and I think he's sorry." A pleading note had entered the younger man's voice, and Adam's brown eyes were damp.

"I said, don't." Ewan's voice was hard, his fists clenched. "I don't have a father. I don't have a family, except for you. Leave it . . . *please*." The flat words fell into the mountain air. Adam looked disappointed, but he tightened his lips and turned back to stare out at the rocky hills.

Ewan knew he sounded defensive, but he didn't care. It was true, and Adam of all people should know it. He hadn't had a family since he was twelve, although he'd lived under the same roof as those people for six more years.

His sister Iseabail, only two years older, had tried for a while, but she'd been so intent on taking on the responsibility left by his mother that she'd had no time left for a grieving twelve-year-old, and she was no match for their father's silent condemnation.

Jonah had been only eight and Daniel five, and three-year-old Sophie had barely understood that her mother was never coming home. Adam was the one who had stuck by him even then, refusing to accept their father's judgement.

Ewan sighed. Like it or not, the memory was there, hanging in the thin Scottish air like a ghost, as strong and as virulent as it had been when he'd awakened with stomach pains in the middle of the night. He remembered it all as if it were yesterday—the pain and the vomiting, and the frightened look on his mother's face. Funny, that was the clearest memory he had of his mother—the beautiful pale face, the wide anxious eyes as she bundled him into a blanket and stowed him into the back seat of the car.

There was a storm that night, and the phone lines had gone down. His father was still at the distillery, so Mum had run next door to the neighbor and asked her to stay with the other children while she drove Ewan to the hospital.

He remembered the lightning, the thunder, and the agony that tore through his abdomen as she drove through rain and darkness. He'd gone in and out of consciousness, lost in a surreal landscape of sound and fury and relentless pain.

They'd almost made it. Only a mile from Raighmore Hospital, the car had skidded on the slick pavement and gone off the A9 and straight into a telegraph pole. As close to the hospital as they were, the ambulance had been there within minutes, and Ewan had awakened a day later to the loss of an appendix—and a mother.

His father had blamed him. He'd never put it into words, but the wall that was erected between them had grown and solidified into something immutable and permanent. The silence grew and swelled and became a living thing, poisoning the family and leaving Ewan alone on one side of an impassable sea of unspoken condemnation. Only Adam had tried to understand.

They were all so different. In a family of six children, you would think that at least a few of them would share interests, but the rest of his siblings were all vastly dissimilar in personality and pursuits—from him and from each other. The only real thing they all had in common was the family distillery, and that was work. Beyond the business, they all went their separate ways.

Ewan was surprised that Adam didn't have more of a bond with Jonah, only a year his junior, but the two had never had much in common. Jonah couldn't have been less interested in scrambling, or anything pertaining to the outdoors, if truth had it.

He was in his sixth year of university, working on an advanced degree in mathematics, and seemed destined to be an eternal student.

Iseabail's husband Aaron was an experienced climber, but Adam had confided to Ewan that their brother-in-law was too intense for his taste and took the fun out of scrambling.

Daniel, at twenty, had no discernible ambition, athletic or otherwise. On the contrary, he seemed bent on drinking the family business into oblivion. He and his friends spent a rather large amount of their free time in the pub, and his exploits were legendary in Inverness.

From what Adam told him, "Danny Boy" attracted girls like midges, and treated all of them with a breezy charm. He was going to rule the world, Adam said, if he didn't pickle himself during his university career.

The youngest was Sophie. She'd be nineteen now, Ewan realized. He remembered her most vividly as a pretty toddler who had everyone wrapped around her tiny finger, but realized with a pang that he knew nothing about his little sister. She was a stranger to him—as they all were. Just one more thing to lay at his father's feet.

Shaking himself out of the memories, he turned to

find Adam staring at him with a look of pity. *Reading my mind again, aren't you?* A surge of annoyance tempered with affection surged through him, and he gave his brother a wry smile. He turned back to the trail.

"Ready?"

"If by ready you mean thirsty, then aye. Lead on; I can taste that pint."

Ewan laughed, and then sobered as he regarded the trail. Ahead of them, the ridge became increasingly exposed. The wind had picked up over the last hour, threatening to blow them off the narrow path if they weren't vigilant.

Aonach Eagach had claimed more than its share of lives. It wasn't only novice climbers that succumbed to the wild terrain and fearsome rock ledges. Just a few years ago, Ewan remembered, a father and daughter team had fallen from the ridge near where he and Adam stood now.

The daughter had managed to climb down treacherous rock faces and through waist high gorse and bracken until she was able to reach help, but it had come too late for her father. They had had the right equipment and plenty of experience in scrambling, but it only took one misstep on this ridge to become a statistic.

There was no room for error here—or ghosts from the past. Ewan, with Adam behind him, made his way down a series of well-worn ledges, careful to test each step on the treacherous rock, until they reached a section where the rocks reared up and blocked their way. The only way seemed to be up.

Above them somewhere Ewan could hear the

sound of boots scraping along the ledge, and knew they weren't alone in this hostile landscape. A lot of climbers traversed Aonach Eagach; he was surprised that they hadn't come across anyone before this.

He didn't feel like meeting other scramblers today, not with the melancholy turn his thoughts had taken earlier. Adam was all the human interaction he could take right now. He narrowed his eyes and studied the ridge before them.

"Here." He pointed to a narrow, zig-zag pathway leading off the ridge. Not much more than the width of a man's two boots in places, the path disappeared under heather and loose stone, winding away and down to disappear around another steep wall of rock.

"You game?" Ewan turned, his eyes glinting in the weak light.

Adam gave an exaggerated sigh and followed his brother down the path. Slightly less experienced in this scramble, he kept his eyes to the ground and picked his way along, leaning away from the precipice and grasping stone and bits of bracken where they existed.

Reaching the wall, Ewan paused before working his way around the stone outcropping. An odd sensation crawled down his spine, surprising him in its intensity. *What the hell?* He'd done this trail more than once; he was an experienced scrambler. He and his brother were only yards apart; he could hear Adam's boots behind him, but the rock wall between them made him feel alone in an alien world. What was going on with him today?

As he turned to wait for Adam to come around

the rock face, Ewan realized he was holding his breath, and forced himself to let it out slowly. He heard the boots again, but this time they were behind him. Someone was coming toward him, going the other way.

He turned back to see how close the other hiker was, and felt one foot slip on the loose stone. In the next second he was flying off the ridge, scrabbling in the air for purchase as he plummeted down the rock wall toward the bushes a hundred feet below.

"Ewan!" He heard Adam's panicked voice far above him.

In desperation he reached out for the wall and grabbed at a piece of rock that jutted out slightly. His right hand closed around the spar and he felt a violent wrench in his shoulder. Pain ratcheted through his wrist and up his arm, but he clenched his teeth and held on, slamming into the wall with a thud that nearly took his breath away.

Ewan clutched the spar and looked down. Just ten feet below him was a ledge, roughly four feet wide and running about eight feet along the rock wall. If he could manage to land on that ledge without going over, he had a chance. If he didn't . . .

No choice. The hand clutching the piece of stone was becoming numb. He was going down, one way or the other, and the ledge was his only hope of survival. With his free hand he loosed the backpack from his shoulders and let it go. The lessening of weight nearly pulled him off his precarious handhold, but somehow he held on.

All or nothing. Ewan took a deep breath and let go.

He hit the ledge and his legs buckled under him. His head slammed against the rock and he felt his vision narrow. He fought to stay above the pain, but it was a losing battle. As he drifted into darkness, a memory slithered into his mind. A whoosh of air, the feel of a thump against his back, propelling him forward.

He hadn't fallen from the ridge. He'd been pushed.

CHAPTER 3

ISLE OF MULL, SCOTLAND - 1745

EILIDH

Sunlight sparkled off the Sound of Mull, lighting the whitecaps and creating a rainbow of color in the clear air. A day to celebrate, to be alive, to plan. A day full of hope for the future.

What a lie. Eilidh MacLean stood and watched the waves chasc cach other across the sound, wondering how they could be so beautiful when her heart was filled with such despair. Why did she have to be born a woman? Why did her family have to be so unfair? Marrying her off to the highest bidder, in this day and age? This was 1745, not the dark ages! She had never been so miserable in all her eighteen years.

She turned and cast a look of loathing at the looming bulk of Castle Duart, rearing over the landscape like an aged dowager gone to seed. She supposed her family home had been elegant once, but those days were gone, and marrying her off for an alliance was never going to make this pile shine.

Eilidh sighed, putting as much drama into it as she could manage. Maybe she should just throw herself off the promontory and meet her death on the rocks below. It would be the ultimate punishment for those who thought to control her life.

She allowed herself to imagine the scene. Her long chestnut hair trailing over her pale face as they carried her lifeless body to the shore and laid her out reverently. Her father would be sobbing, begging her to come back, telling her how sorry he was for not listening to his daughter's heart. Tears rolled down her cheeks unchecked as she relished the horror and grief of those who had professed to love her. Rory would—

She snapped herself back to reality. Rory. She couldn't do that to her brother, even in her imagination. Eilidh choked back her tears. Even thinking about such a thing filled her with shame. Rory was her knight in armor, her partner in all things. He understood her with that mysterious magic that only twins possessed, and she knew he felt the same way about this insane plan as she did.

Unfortunately, they were the only two who felt that way, and, comrade or not, Ruaridh MacLean didn't have any more power over this situation than she did. Their older brother Domnall, the arrogant beast, was the heir to what little they had left, and it was he who had conspired with Father.

"Cullen is a fine man, Eilidh," he had told her in exasperation. "Any woman would be proud to have him. He is going to be laird, for God's sake. You should be thanking me for setting you up for life, instead of being so stubborn and ungrateful!"

Of course he would say that. He was close friends with Cullen MacLeod, after all. She herself had never met the paragon, but to hear Domnall wax on about him, you would think the man invented whisky. They had met in university and bonded instantly over a shared interest in hunting and drinking.

Despite the distance between them, the pair managed to spend an inordinate amount of time together. It was always Dom who did the traveling from Mull to Raasay, and until now Eilidh had been perfectly fine with that. Her older brother was annoying and intrusive, and his absences were more than welcome. Until she found out that he was doing more with Cullen MacLeod than hunting boar and drinking. He was selling off his sister.

When her father had approached her with the "offer"—ha! As if she had a say in the matter—she had reacted with shock, then tears, and then a sullen silence. And Dom? Well, after his lofty praise of the future bridegroom, Domnall had wisely avoided his sister, and within days was back on the road to Raasay. The coward.

Eilidh turned from the churning water of the sound and made her way across the vast lawn to the castle. If they thought this was over, they had another think coming. By the time she was through with him, Cullen MacLeod was going to regret the day he had ever met a MacLean. Her father had apparently for-gotten that she was her mother's daughter!

"Eilidh." Rory stood in the doorway. "Are you all right?"

"No."

"I wish there was something I could do," he sighed. "Maybe MacLeod's not so bad, even if he is friends with Dom."

"You know it isn't that, Rory. I don't care how won-derful or awful he is . . . I do not want to marry. At all."

Her brother stepped forward and took her into his arms. She rested her head on his shoulder and wondered what she would do without him when she left for Raasay. Tears ran freely down her face and soaked his shirt as he stroked her hair.

"I have confidence in you, El. You will never let yourself be someone's chattel, even if you're a wife. You are strong; you will accomplish what you want. And I will be there to see you do it."

Eilidh pushed herself away and looked into his clear green eyes, so like her own.

"What do you mean? I'll be so far away. Raasay is days from Mull."

"You think you know everything, don't you?" Now his voice was teasing. He held her face between his large hands and forced her to look at him. "The fact is, I will be going with you."

"What? How?" Eilidh stared at him in confusion.

"You need an escort to Raasay for the wedding, right?"

"But—"

"I am that escort. Father was happy to let me go

in his place."

Eilidh snorted. "Of course, because now he can stay home and plan how to use all that lovely money he'll get for marrying me off."

Her eyes filled again. "But then you will leave, and I will be left there with a husband I never wanted. A husband who is probably horrible."

"Well, we do not know that, do we?"

She stamped her foot. "He would have to be, would he not? Since he is friends with Dom."

Rory laughed. "Your logic is a little strange, but I do understand it. In any case, there will be no need to face MacLeod alone, because I will be staying on at Raasay House. I've been hired as constable, since theirs died last year and I know a thing or two about horses." He lifted his head in a lofty gesture.

"Oh. Oh, Rory, really? But how? I know there's nothing you don't know about horses, but how would they know that?"

"Well, your brother Domnall, for whom you have so little regard, suggested me to his great friend Cullen, who went to his father, and now I'm to be in charge of all the horses, grooms, and pages at Raasay House. So you should probably be a little nicer to Dom when next you see him, don't you think?"

"Humph." Eilidh gave her brother a militant look. Her brows furrowed. "But do you really want to do that? It's not just for me, is it? Because I'll love you as long as I live, but I don't want you giving up your life here to be some sort of lackey to the MacLeods."

"What life?" Rory arched an eyebrow at her. "I'm nothing more than a glorified servant here, anyway.

Father has no use for a second son—I'm just another mouth to feed. He barely puts up with me as it is. And don't be so full of yourself. It's horses, El!"

Eilidh spun away, executed a little dance, and then rushed back to hug her brother again.

"Oh, Rory, I love you. I love you, I love you!"

His look was smug. "As you should."

CHAPTER 4
EDINBURGH, SCOTLAND - 1745

IAIN

ompany . . . halt! Right face! Present arms! Front line kneel . . . make ready . . . present . . . fire! Recover . . . reload . . ."

Iain felt the sweat running down the back of his neck and into his shirt. Tendrils of black hair straggled from beneath his tricorn and he blinked bleary blue eyes in a futile effort to keep them away.

Lord, it was hot. How much longer was Murray going to keep them out here in the sweltering heat, firing and reloading the muskets? The sun reflected off the stone walls of Edinburgh castle and right back at the thirty men in their red woolen coats. Didn't the bastard notice that the city was gripped in the talons of a heat wave seldom seen in Scotland?

He went through the familiar motions without

thinking about them, wishing he were back home helping his father to build the new Inveraray Castle. Iain pictured the old man at work, ordering his subordinates around as if he were the laird himself, and smiled. Angus Campbell was an institution in Argyll.

Dad hadn't gotten the job because he was a distant cousin to the laird, as some thought. He was simply the best. He was a legend in the area—sought after for his skill and admired for his artistry. With backing and money, he could have been an architect, but he wasn't the "right" kind of Campbell, so it wasn't to be. Angus had never expressed disappointment, choosing to take quiet pride in what his gifted hands could create. But it bothered his son.

Iain twisted the silver ring on his right hand. A gift from his father, it was a simple silver band inscribed with the words *Ne Obliviscaris. Forget Not*—the motto of their clan. He found it comforting—the feel of the ring took him back to days when the world was clean and new, and anything was possible.

As a boy, Iain had followed Angus around, holding his tools and soaking in his knowledge of wood and stone. He'd dreamed of becoming a builder like the old man, but that wasn't in his father's plans.

No matter his skills as a builder, the elder Campbell's dream had been to follow his ancestors into the army. When an accident cost him that dream, he had transferred it to his son. Angus Campbell's unwavering plan for his only son was that he become a career soldier in the British Army. So here Iain was, letting himself be roasted alive for the crown.

"Campbell! What the hell you doing?" A high,

petulant voice rang out over the parade ground. Iain jerked to awareness to find the rest of the company staring at him, smirking. A slight figure stood in front of him, arms akimbo.

"We can't move to swords until I'm satisfied that you lot know what you're doing with the musket," Sergeant Murray barked. "And it looks as if we'll be at it all day, thanks to Mr. Campbell here. D'you think you can get your head out of your ass and bear with us, now?"

"Yes, sir." Iain said. He gritted his teeth but kept his face impassive. It was a bit unfair, really—these men were the best in the unit, and Murray was fully aware of it. The wee arse was just trying to prove his right to the command, and for good reason.

His was one of those promotions handed down to sons because of their fathers' standing, and Murray was desperate to show his men that he was a force to be reckoned with. He was out of his depth—he knew it and his troops knew it, but that was how it worked. Life in the army wasn't always fair.

Iain sighed. Murray's easy path might have been his own, if he'd been born a different kind of Campbell. If his father were the laird of the clan instead of a poor cousin, for instance. He smiled to himself. None of this sweating in the summer and freezing in the winter. He'd be a man of leisure. Maybe a lawyer.

Not that he wished for that life—not in the least. He wasn't the type to sit still, and reading law sounded more like a punishment than a career. His father's dream suited him. Military life came with discipline, but it also offered the chance for a man without antecedents to distinguish himself.

It was a good life, all things considered. The British army was the greatest fighting force in the world, and it was an honor to be a part of it. He was working his way up the ranks, already a lance corporal with five men under his supervision, and doing it without the golden path provided by money and heritage. So why was he standing here whinging about a rare spell of heat? Why was he letting Murray get under his skin?

If he were honest, the reprimand was deserved. He had been distracted, and now the men were going to suffer for his lapse, a fact made quite clear by the glares aimed his way. Iain pulled himself together and straightened his shoulders. He'd stand them all to a pint tonight, to make up for it.

"Hmmph. Well, then. Form up! Forward, march! Right face . . . right face! Present arms! Make ready . . ."

Hours later, Iain squinted into the beautiful amber liquid in his mug and pretended to listen as his comrades ribbed him for his lapse. They didn't hold back, these lads. No matter that the ale they were drinking was paid for by their victim, they would keep it up until they got tired—or too drunk to remember the extra hours of training they'd endured because of him. Tomorrow they'd roll out of bed and face another day of marching, all grievance forgotten.

Iain smiled at the faces around the rough wooden table. It was probably due in part to the ale, but he loved it all. His lads, the army—even the drills. He knew he was lucky to have found his purpose. He struggled to his feet and narrowed his eyes, attempting to look fierce.

"Sorry, you lads'll have to find someone else

to badger; I'm for bed. It's going to be another hot one tomorrow, and I'll need to be rested so I don't embarrass the company again by fainting or killing Murray, nice as it sounds. Anyway, I can't afford to keep pouring ale down your rotten throats. Who's coming?"

"Well, there's no fun when the lad who's payin' runs off, is there?" Hal Erskine swayed as he stood. "Funny you should be talking about Murray, though. If I have to spend a couple of extra hours in the heat tomorrow because of you, it won't be Murray that winds up dead!" He grinned and threw his arm around Iain, and the two made their unsteady way out of the tavern.

CHAPTER 5

CAPE BRETON ISLAND, NOVA SCOTIA - PRESENT DAY

*Once you make a decision, the universe
conspires to make it happen.*
Ralph Waldo Emerson

"What?" Fiona stared at her father, green eyes wide with shock.

William MacLean grinned at his daughter.

"I thought I was pretty clear. How would you like to spend some time in Scotland?"

"Are you serious? Wait. You're serious!"

Amusement colored her father's voice. "Should I say it again? I need someone to go over to Inverness next month to research the roots of the Scottish diaspora to Canada." He took a breath. "Those roots began with the third Jacobite rising and the Battle of Culloden Moor . . ."

"Dad." Fiona's voice was patient. "I know that. I'm your daughter, remember? I was raised on the Jacobites."

"Ahhh, my little know-it-all—but this is different." Her father let his glasses slide down to the tip of his nose and regarded her with a wide, innocent expression. He sat back in his leather chair and let the silence lengthen, tapping his forefingers together over steepled hands.

"Different? How? Different from what? And why—" Fiona stifled the next question, sat back, and mirrored her father's pose. She'd almost fallen into his trap. She of all people knew better than to push him when he had something important to say. The professor had the patience of Job, honed over many years of dealing with the wiles of students.

She tempered the excitement that was beginning to build and forced a nonchalant tone into her voice. "But why aren't you going, Dad? This is your thing. You've never sent anyone else."

He shrugged. "It's usually me, but I can't leave Gaelic College right now, so I need a reliable second, and the only one I trust is you. Besides, this trip is different. You'd be there for about a month, and the university would put you up."

"The University?"

"The University of the Highlands and Islands. It has the highest ranking in Gaelic studies in the UK, and we have a professional relationship with them. You'd be researching while staying in the place your ancestors called home."

Her father laughed, his eyes crinkling the way

they did when he was up to something. Fiona narrowed her own.

"And there's a mystery that might involve our family."

"Mystery?" She sat up straight, the word evoking visions of ancient castles full of ghosts, and mountains shrouded in centuries-old shadows. "What kind of mystery?"

"You'll have to wait until you get there to find out. Just know it has to do with the last Jacobite rising and everything that led up to that final battle."

"The Battle of Culloden?" Fiona sat up straighter.

"Right. That battle ended a way of life in the Scottish Highlands, as you know, and is indirectly the reason that you were born here, in Canada."

"So what's the mystery?" She stole a look at her father's face and knew he wasn't about to divulge anything.

"Sorry, can't tell you. You'll find out when you get there . . . if you agree to go. You'll be meeting my colleague Jeremy Brown at the University, and he'll fill you in. And that's all I'm telling you until you agree." William MacLean sat back and crossed his arms over his chest, jutting out his chin.

Fiona's face fell. "Oh, Dad, you know I'd kill to go to Scotland, but does it have to be next month? Greg has a huge event planned at the distillery, and I promised to help him host it. It's really important to his family, and I know he'd be disappointed if I bailed."

She shook her head in frustration. "Damn. I really want to go!"

Her father's brow furrowed. "I'm sure Greg would

understand how important this opportunity is. He seems like a pleasant lad."

Fiona closed her eyes. Would he? Their relationship was so new. He was fun, and sweet. They never fought. And judging from Kirsty's jealous comments, he was the hottest commodity on the island. She really liked him. Really.

It was just that nagging sensation at the back of her mind. The feeling that there was someone else out there who was waiting for her—someone with hair as black as night and eyes as blue as the summer sky. Someone who came to her in her dreams, and whose kiss was imprinted on her memory.

So, so stupid. An imaginary love was just self-destructive, that's all. It had to be her insecurity trying to warn her that she wasn't good enough for someone as wonderful as Greg. And didn't that prove he was the one?

She shook herself back into the moment, to find her father watching her with concern. He didn't miss much, darn it.

"Well, you have some time to think about it." Her dad pushed his chair back from the desk and stood up. "I'll need to know by the end of the week, though, so I can look for someone else."

A flash of jealousy arced through her. Someone else? Hell, no, she wasn't going to let that happen. This wasn't going to be fun, but somehow she was going to have to convince Greg that leaving him behind in Nova Scotia for a month was a terrific idea, and breaking her promise to help with his project was great romance material. *Good luck, Fiona!*

"I'll let you know, Dad." She stood and walked to the office door, turning back at the last minute to focus on his face. Sure enough, he was wearing that smug look—the one he used when he knew she was caught in his net. Fiona sighed.

She stopped by the gift shop on her way to her next class, a children's beginner workshop in Gaelic. Her young charges ranged from ages ten to twelve and were guaranteed to give her a challenge. Most of them were the children of Cape Breton residents, but some came from as far away as the mid-Atlantic states of the US.

She was proud of the college, and of the diverse students it attracted. Usually, they worked hard and were serious, but this crop was uncommonly feisty, and had more than the usual collection of class clowns. She picked up a few pencils to give out, and armed with her bribes, she stepped into her class-room to face the fifteen eager faces. Instantly a hand shot up, and Fiona groaned.

"Teacher, how do you say, 'I love k-pop' in Gaelic?"

The twelve-year-old's mouth opened in a metallic grin of challenge.

There's one in every class, Fiona thought. These summer workshops had their share of kids who seemed intent on showing off for their peers rather than really learning the language, every one of them intent on causing as much distraction as humanly possible while maintaining a facade of wide-eyed innocence.

"*Tha gaol agam air k-pop*," she said, as if she heard this one every day. The child blinked in surprise. *Ha!*

Thought you got me, didn't you, you little twerp? The hand went up again, and Fiona ignored it. She glanced at her watch. A headache was building behind her eyes—a headache named Greg MacNeill.

Four days later, she'd gotten no closer to broaching the subject of Scotland. Scotland for a month. It was almost as if he sensed something—he had been extra sweet lately, gentler, more affectionate. Or maybe that was just guilt on her part. No, there was definitely something there. Greg wasn't the type for romantic gestures; he thought sentimental things like flowers and jewelry were mushy and un-manly.

Their dates usually involved sailing or hanging out with his yacht club buddies. But last night he'd taken her to the most expensive restaurant in town and switched up his usual beer for wine. She'd opened her mouth twice to tell him—she was sure she had. It just wasn't the right moment. It hadn't managed to be the right moment for four days, and her father wanted his answer. She was running out of time.

Fiona dragged herself back to the classroom full of unruly Gaelic-learners and spent the rest of the afternoon giving them the gift of a language that most of the world thought was dead and gone, like the Highland culture it embodied.

"Let's add some words that we would use right here on Cape Breton," she told them, as she wrote the words on a whiteboard. "*Bàta* means 'boat', and *seòl* is 'sail.' Can you hear how close those words are to English? If you want to *seòl* in your *bàta* on the water, you would say, '*Seòl mi mo bàta air an uisge.*'

"Extra points for the one who can tell us which

word means 'water.' Her students studied the board, and several hands went up tentatively. Surprisingly, the k-pop fan was one of them, and Fiona decided to allow the miscreant to redeem herself. "Sara?"

"*Uisge*," the child announced, and looked around at her audience. "It's in *uisge beatha*, and that means 'water of life,' which is fancy talk for 'whisky.' I know because my dad works at the distillery, and he says that's the only kind of water you should drink." The classroom erupted in giggles.

Fiona gritted her teeth. "Good job, Sara. And you're right—at least about the 'water' part."

A voice piped up. "Miss MacLean *knows* that, Sara. Her boyfriend *owns* the distillery."

Fiona sighed. She loved teaching, she mostly loved children, but sometimes they gave her a run for her money. And now the little monsters had thrown her head right back into the problem of how to tell Greg about Scotland. She looked at her watch. Class was over, and that problem was waiting for her outside in a shiny red Mustang. She rubbed her temples, where the throbbing had taken up permanent residence.

The headache gave her the excuse to put her head back and close her eyes on the trip home to Baddeck, but all too soon they were pulling into her driveway. She steeled herself and turned to face him.

"Um . . . Greg?" He turned his hundred-watt smile on her, and Fiona felt her insides turn to water. Suddenly she found herself in agreement with young Sara's father. What she needed right now was a dram of *uisge beatha*—or two.

"I don't think I'll be able to help out with the event

next month—something really important's come up."

The smile disappeared. "What? You promised—it's been planned forever, and I need you there. You know how important this is to me!" His voice rose in disbelief.

"My dad asked me to go to Scotland to do research," she said, trying to keep the pleading note out of her voice. "You know I wouldn't drop out of the project if it wasn't important."

"Do I?" Bitterness edged his voice. "Your dad goes to Scotland all the time—why do *you* suddenly have to go?"

"I don't have to go—" she stopped. Wrong, wrong, wrong. His eyes narrowed. She tried again. "Just please listen—it's really important to him, and it's just for a month—"

"A *month*? What the hell, Fiona! You're not only running out on your promise, you're dumping me for a month?"

"Greg, I'm not dumping you! I haven't made my decision yet—"

"It certainly sounds as if you have. You're putting a vacation above a promise you made—if that isn't dumping me, I don't know what is!"

"It's not a vacation!" Fiona felt nausea churning in her stomach. "It's a job. It's my work. Please calm down and try to understand."

Greg threw the driver's door open and got out. He marched around to her door and opened it with exaggerated chivalry.

"I guess I don't understand you as much as I thought I did." Now his voice was low, but she could hear the anger and the hurt in the soft tones. "Or maybe I never understood you." He stomped back around the car and slid behind the wheel, not looking at her. "I think you have a decision to make here, Fiona. And it's about more than Scotland."

His knuckles whitened as he gripped the wheel. "Go on your trip. Have fun. Just don't expect me to be waiting when you get back."

CHAPTER 6

INVERNESS, SCOTLAND - PRESENT DAY

*Sometimes the slightest things change
the direction of our lives . . .*
Bryce Courtenay

It seemed as if he'd been falling forever. His arms pinwheeled uselessly as the ground rushed to meet him, and he knew this was the end. A stab of regret—a flash of green—

Ewan jerked awake to find himself in his own bed, covered by a sheen of sweat. His heart pounded and his lungs wheezed from the terror of the dream. He sat up and waited for his body to recognize the truth. He was safe; he had survived.

It had been four months since the accident on Aonach Eagach. The dream was coming with less frequency, but its effects were the same. Always the sensation of falling, the panic and the despair of knowing he was going to certain death. The relief at waking to find himself alive.

But not everything was the same. Each time the dream visited, details were added. Were they pulled from his reluctant memory, or just created from his overactive imagination? Like the corrosive feeling that someone had pushed him?

He had no basis for that feeling. Truthfully, he couldn't remember anything from the time he rounded the outcropping on the narrow trail until he'd awakened in the hospital with his brother's anxious face hovering over him. One minute he was waiting for Adam to follow him, and the next he'd found himself attached to a bed in a white room, with tubes protruding from his arm and a cast on his left leg.

Adam had told him that he'd come around the rock face in time to hear his brother's scream and the thud of his body hitting the ledge twenty feet below. He had almost catapulted over the edge himself, he'd said, but somehow managed to scramble down the cliff face and reach Ewan's unconscious body.

The 999 call had brought a team of experienced mountain rescue workers, and hours later the patient had awakened to find himself in possession of a concussion, three broken ribs, a fractured leg, and a badly sprained wrist. A miracle, they'd told him—that he'd managed to land on the only ledge along that cliff face, and also that his injuries had been surprisingly minor for such a fall.

You're lucky, the doctor and nurses had said, like bobble-head sages. It reminded Ewan of a cartoon he'd once seen where a man was encased in plaster from head to foot, and the doctor congratulated him on his good fortune. He remembered thinking it was funny then—now, not so much.

The concussion was responsible for his memory loss, they'd told him. The memories of those few moments would likely return, but it could be dangerous to force them. Not a problem—doing so did nothing but bring on an excruciating headache. The memories could wait—he wasn't sure he wanted to remember, anyway.

It was only in the dream that details of that day assailed his senses. The feeling of free fall, the smell of fear, a sense of fury at such a stupid end to his life. Those sensations had been there from the beginning, but now there was more.

Two weeks ago, the dream had gifted him with the pain of landing. He saw himself reaching out for something—what?—and watching as it eluded his outstretched fingertips and he crashed to the stone ledge. Real, but not real. Adam had told him a blood smear on a rock jutting from the cliff face proved that he had grabbed it and held on for a few seconds, long enough to truncate his fall and save his life. An aching wrist was proof of that truth.

And this time, a flash of green. There was nothing green on a cliff face; could it be clothing? Ewan lay still in his bed and tried to bring back the flash, but it was gone into the abyss that captured dream images.

What in the world could it have been? Not vegetation—it reflected light like a jewel. There was a feeling of recognition just beyond his senses, as if whatever possessed the green had been watching him. Warning him. But there had been nothing near him on the trail—surely he would have noticed if something had gotten that close.

An animal, perhaps? He snorted. An animal wearing a green jacket? Now he was being ridiculous. Anyway, Adam would have seen if something was with them on the trail, wouldn't he?

The headache was back, reminding him not to press for memories within a fantasy. He'd remember when his brain was ready, and there was nothing he could do about it until then. He sighed and pushed himself up and out of bed.

The dream with its mysteries receded as he dressed in jeans and a sweatshirt. Work was calling; there was no time to waste on such a frustrating puzzle. Ewan slung his camera into his backpack, added his laptop, and grabbed a cup of coffee on his way out to the car.

He drove out of Inverness, heading for Culloden Battlefield. This would be the third time visiting this month; he sensed that the answer to his latest problem was just on the horizon. He was always seeking, always looking for the next great idea in a profession with prescribed rules and fixed ways of doing things.

Ewan's tour company, Wild Scotland, primarily dealt with hiking and scrambling adventures, and this was where his heart lay. The company was his baby—his family, really. Started after he'd left college with a business degree and no idea of what to do next, the idea of making money doing what he loved best had seemed foolish and whimsical, but at the same time it offered the promise of a future. He'd spent the first year working harder than he thought possible, existing on little but hope.

To his surprise and delight, the venture had been a success from the start. Who knew there were so many people out there who wanted to experience the mountain culture of the Highlands under the guidance of an expert who was in love with his craft?

There were a lot of those brave explorers—but not enough. Three years ago, he'd bitten the bullet and decided to reach out to the more traditional tour venues, hoping to add a twist to the ordinary bus tour with its canned presentation and stale history. He'd looked with interest at the success of the Outlander tours, based wholly on popular books, and was sure he could do as well. He just needed a niche, a hook of his own.

He found it in his country's colorful history. Ewan had always stepped off the beaten path and searched for the unique in his business, and he realized that the Scottish Highlands, in all their wild glory, were the key.

Sure, the market was saturated with tours. Buses and vans crowded the main roads, headed for the well-known attractions. Tourist shops littered the streets of Inverness, offering trips to castles and monasteries, graveyards and pubs with storied pasts. Cruise ships docked at Invergordon and disgorged hundreds of excited visitors intent on being the first to spot the Loch Ness monster.

Ewan appreciated the need for tourism, and some of the offerings weren't all that bad. But he hated the idea of being shoved onto a bus to listen to a guide rehash the same tired tourist tripe to visitors who would take hundreds of photos and put them on Facebook, and then forget everything when they went home. He wanted to appeal to another kind of tourist, one with imagination and courage.

Scotland's history was too important to be spewed out in a scripted travelogue. People needed to *live* the history, experience period dress and cultural mores; they needed to feel a part of what had made Scotland the rich tapestry it was.

He arranged with reenactment groups and actors hungry for work, so that every tour was met by Highlanders in full regalia who spoke in Gaelic and Scots and invited the delighted guests to be a part of the past with them. He searched for the off-highway secrets that would appeal to the serious searcher. His groups were limited to eight or fewer, so his small vans could travel the single-track back roads where the real history lay.

Within two years, his company's stock had risen to new heights. Adventurers scrambled to sign up for Ewan's Highland Magic, as he called this branch of his business. They were different from his hikers who cared only for the mountains and the wild beauty of the Highlands and thought little about history, but brave explorers nonetheless. These were the people who secretly wished for a time machine to be built during their lifetime, people who bought books and went home and read them—people who came back. And there were a lot of them.

He'd left the most difficult and yet most important until now, wanting to give it the benefit of experience, but now he was ready to tackle Culloden. The battle that had ended the last Jacobite threat was the most famous tour venue in Scotland, and it had roadblocks that stymied Ewan in his search for a unique approach.

There was a limit to what could be allowed on the battlefield itself, as it was also a graveyard to the two thousand Jacobite and three hundred English soldiers who had fallen on a day that changed the face of Scotland forever. So, no Highland charges, no reenactments of that fateful forty-five minutes. He was glad of that—his own ancestors had fallen on that soggy moor and he owed them his respect.

He pulled into the car park and took a moment to study the modern structure before him. The National Trust for Scotland had done a masterful job with the Visitor Centre, with a timeline walkway, better-than-average cafe, and a gift shop that offered books, tartans, and an array of tasteful souvenirs.

The highlight of the experience, though, was the holographic video of the battle itself, and this was where he began his visit every time. What could Ewan's tour offer, that wasn't already explored? He wanted inspiration.

The centre was relatively quiet today; it was raining and few people wanted to venture out onto the battlefield. Ewan wondered what his country's history would have been if the Jacobite and government forces had thrown their hands up at the rain and just decided to go out for lunch instead. He grinned to himself. There was something to be said for modern tourism.

Ewan signed in and made his way to the video presentation room. About twenty people stood in the center of the empty space, looking around with hushed curiosity. He walked to the center of the room and waited.

The lights dimmed, the sound came up, and he was lost, as always, in the events of April 16, 1746. The video played on all four walls of the room, placing him in the middle of the battle. He watched the desperate Highlanders as they rushed straight at and through him to meet the government forces in the middle of the field, heard the screams, the clashing of swords, the moans of dying men. He was there, watching his fellow soldiers die.

But who were his fellow soldiers? Ewan had seen this video so many times, yet it was always different. Sometimes he watched from the perspective of the doomed Jacobites, and at others he felt as one with the British soldiers who had triumphed after only forty-five minutes of fighting. He wondered if anyone else had that experience.

It was all over so quickly. The lights came up and he blinked. Across the room, an attractive auburn-haired woman stood in a daze, and Ewan smiled in understanding. No one walked away from that video untouched.

He turned and made his way out of the centre, bypassing the information desk and the gift shop on his way out to the battlefield. As he reached the path, he realized that he'd forgotten his notebook and detoured toward the car park. Retrieving the book, he began to walk back, looked up—and froze.

The woman from the video room was walking toward the car park. She still seemed to be in a fog, and as he watched, she stepped off the sidewalk without looking—right into the path of a vehicle which was traveling much too fast for the car park and for the misty conditions. Ewan's eyes widened in horror as he realized that the driver wasn't going to see her in time to stop.

In the next second, he was sprinting across the pavement toward the woman. He reached her seconds before the car did, wrapped his arms around her, and sent them both flying. They rolled across the sidewalk and into an ornamental bush.

As his heartbeat struggled to return to normal, he focused on the pair of shocked green eyes staring into his own and realized two things simultaneously. They were the most beautiful eyes he'd ever seen—and they were the flash of green from his dream. He felt himself sinking into those eyes, and for some reason it made him furious.

Ewan rolled over, scrambled up and offered a hand to the woman, yanking her to her feet with perhaps a little too much force. His chest heaved and he took a deep breath to calm himself. It didn't work.

"What were you thinking?" he gasped.

"Wh—what?" The woman seemed to be trying to focus.

"You almost got yourself killed—what the hell's wrong with you?"

"I'm sorry, but—" The voice was low and husky with an accent. American?

"Don't they have cars where you come from? I'm pretty sure you have traffic there, right? Maybe you should pay attention so you make it home to the States in one piece, aye?"

The woman stood still, her hands on her hips. The green eyes narrowed as she stared him down.

"Are all Scottish people as rude as you?" she asked, in a deceptively polite voice.

The voice rose.

"And for your information, I'm Canadian, you buffoon!"

CHAPTER 7

EDINBURGH, SCOTLAND - 1745

IAIN

A half-moon bathed the cobbles in weak light. Shadows hunched in the doorways and openings to the closes that ran off the High Street into the myriad courtyards of the city. A cool breeze drifted down the street, teasing of a break in the unusual weather.

As the two soldiers emerged from the pub, Iain took a deep breath, feeling the air of his homeland sink deep into his lungs.

"This is the best place in the world, aye?"

"Aye, 'tis," Hal said. "Mind you, I haven't actually been anywhere else in the world, but it can't be better than Scotland. If you have to be marching around in wool all day, you might as well do it here. And my home is just down the road two days, so there's that."

He turned his eyes to the west. "Not that we ever get a chance to visit, mind ye. Wee Murray sees to that, right enough. It's just nice to know it's so close, aye?"

"Aye. Even though Argyll's a bit further north, it's still like going to the moon. There's only my da to visit, but I miss the old man." A wistful look passed over Iain's face.

"Is it just you and your father, then? Strange, we've known each other for a while now, but we've never talked about family. Don't you have brothers and sisters?"

"Not so strange, really. Guess it's because the army is our family," Iain said. "Anyway, no. My mam died having me, so it has always been just the two of us."

A smile creased Iain's face, and pride lit his blue eyes. "My da is a builder. A damn good one too. Right now he's in charge of building a new castle that was burned out years ago. If I was not in the army, I would be up there helping him."

"Why'd you join, then?"

"It was Dad's dream to serve. He got hurt when he was young and couldn't join up, so he wanted me to take his place. He used to tell me stories about all the Campbells that served in His Majesty's army, all the acts of bravery performed by my grandfather and great-grandfather."

Iain shrugged. "I always suspected half of it was nonsense, but I never said so. And the army suited me, so it's all to the good." He paused, then went on in a soft voice, "You should have seen the old man's face the first time he saw me in uniform. Thought he was going to cry."

"Must be odd to be an only child." Hal gave his friend a look of wonder. "In my family, there's eight of us, and I'm the oldest. I joined up to help put food on the table, to tell you the truth. But it's a good life, as you say, and the pay's steady. If it weren't for the marching, and the heat, and the damned Jacobites . . ."

Iain raised his eyebrows. "If it weren't for the damned Jacobites, we might be marching around in the colonies, knee deep in swamp mud. So be careful what you wish for, laddie—there's worse things than Highlanders, ye ken?" He clapped his friend on the shoulder. "And now I'm sober, dammit, so let's get back, aye?"

The two men made their way up the street toward the barracks, keeping a wary eye on the shadows that huddled in the corners. Only a fool would believe that there was no danger in this posting. Scotland's history was one of violence and bloodshed, whether between feuding clans or against the king down in London, whoever might be sitting on the throne.

And now it was the Jacobites—again. There were rumors that Charles Stuart, son of the Pretender, was raising an army in France and would soon be descending on Scotland in hopes of rallying the clans for his father. It was a romantic cause, to be sure, supported by hotheads and brigands, but no one was taking it lightly.

Thus the enhanced presence by the British Army up here. It had been drilled into them all time and time again that the Jacobites were a real threat, a powder keg that could erupt at any time. Even the shadows held danger.

As if answering Iain's thoughts, two of the shadows resolved themselves into human figures. The patterns of their kilts were muted in the near darkness, but there was no mistaking the swagger. Highlanders. Iain swore under his breath, suddenly wishing he hadn't had that last pint. You needed your wits about you when you were facing Highlanders.

"Well, look what we have here—two of His Magesty's finest, walking up the street as if they have every right to be here!" The taller of the two men spoke, his tone derisive. "English pricks, all dressed in their pretty red frocks."

"We're as Scottish as you are!" Hal snapped, rising to his full height of six feet and some inches and glowering at the speaker. "I was born in Dumfries, you eejit, and my friend, here—he's a Campbell. A Highlander as much as you lot."

Iain groaned and punched Hal in the arm. "Shut up!" He pushed the words through gritted teeth. "You're not helping!"

Their kilted adversaries snorted. The other man stepped closer and hissed, "A Highlander my arse! Your uniform says you're a traitor to the true king." He spat on the ground in front of Iain and stepped back. "Let's go, Dùghall. It stinks around here."

Iain and Hal watched them saunter up the High Street, their kilts swishing from side to side. Sweat dripped down his neck and under his shirt. For some reason, he felt as if they had just been in a pitched battle—and that his side had lost. He wanted to run after them—grab them by the collars and shake some sense into them.

"The true king, my arse!" Iain stood in the middle of the street, hands fisted at his sides. "As if that foreign fop is a Scot just because his name's Stuart. Bonnie Prince Charlie. What a load of shite."

He shook a fist after the departing Jacobites. "Don't these people realize that Scotland is better off united with England? There's a reason that both countries signed the Acts of Union thirty-five years ago. Those hotheads just want another Catholic king, no matter that he's a nitwit."

"Iain." Hal's voice was soft. "Let it go. You won't change their minds. They think that Charles Stuart is the rightful king, and nothing you or I can say will ever change that. It's why we're here, aye?"

"I suppose you're right, but it shouldn't be necessary. I was born and raised in the Highlands, just like them. I'm proud of my country, but I don't believe in some romantic notion about the 'king across the sea,' now do I? And where do they get off calling me a traitor? They're the traitors. We have a king—we don't need someone that's spent his whole life in Italy to come gallivanting over here decked out in his Stuart tartan and take the place over!" He heaved a frustrated sigh and jammed his hands into his pockets.

As they walked the rest of the way up the High Street. Iain tried to put his anger away. The Highlanders hadn't meant violence; their words were just bluster. If these men were a sample of the dreaded Jacobites, the unrest wouldn't last long. A few bar fights, maybe a skirmish or two, that would be it—right?

So why did he have this feeling of foreboding? An icy hand ran down his spine and he shivered despite the heat.

Jacobites—damn them all.

CHAPTER 8

ISLE OF RAASAY, SCOTLAND - 1746

EILIDH

Eilidh peered at the imposing facade of Raasay House with trepidation. Grey walls, grim against the cloudy sky, four turrets with roofs like witch's hats. She felt again the foreboding that had grown during the months of anxious waiting and the arduous two-week journey to the island that would be her home from now on. Her headache intensified and her muscles had long since given up and settled into a dull, throbbing pain.

The place looked like a prison. This was worse than she had imagined, even for Eilidh's vivid imagination. The castle glared back at them as if to say, "What on earth is this? Must I really put up with these lesser humans?"

And then, as the horses moved toward the huge double doors in the center of the grey facade, a shade was suddenly yanked down in an upper room, making it seem as if the building had just winked at the newcomers.

The image was so ludicrous that it snapped the tension like a bowstring. Eilidh began to laugh. The laugh bubbled up from her stomach and into her throat, and then spilled out into the courtyard, startling the grooms who were waiting to take their mounts.

Rory gave his sister a warning shake of his head, but there was no stopping the torrent. Eilidh's shoulders heaved, and her laughter climbed and spread, rolling forth like the ocean waves that could be heard beyond the castle's gates. Tears poured down her cheeks and plopped onto the horse's neck, and her mount turned his head and gave her a patient, tired gaze.

"Mistress . . . are ye all right?" The shocked voice of Alice Gunn gasped. The maid's eyebrows had risen almost to the edges of her crimped brown hair and her eyes were the size of saucers, giving her the appearance of a ruffled owl.

The look on the girl's face set Eilidh off again. Rory sighed and dismounted. He handed the reins to a groom and came over to stand beside his hysterical sister. He reached up both arms and she fell into them, burying her head in his shoulder as the laughter diminished into wheezing, hiccupping sobs.

He set her on her feet and gazed into her green eyes with concern.

"Are you all right?"

"Yes—no. Please, it's not too late. Let's make a run

for it."

"Hmm. Do you think we'd get past those guys?"

Eilidh turned to follow her brother's pointing finger, and saw the guards closing the gate they'd just passed through. She was trapped.

"Sister!" a loud voice called, and she snapped her head around to face the castle. A group of people had just emerged and were bearing down on them. Domnall came to a halt in front of his sister and studied her with an exasperated glare. He moved closer, and Eilidh squirmed under the gaze.

"Do you have to look like you're going to your execution?" he hissed between pursed lips. "Achh, you are such a trial."

"Hello, Dom. So nice to see you too." Eilidh put as much honey into her tone as she could and forced a sickly smile.

Her older brother gave an aggrieved sigh and turned to face the rest of his group.

"My dearest sister, please meet your new family. This is Lord Malcolm MacLeod, your laird."

A distinguished grey-haired man stepped forward and took Eilidh's hand in both of his own. Soft brown eyes regarded her kindly.

"You are lovely. I am so very glad to welcome you to your new home." He squeezed her hand and turned.

"This is Lady MacLeod, who will be your mother-in-law. I am sure you two will get along well."

Eilidh looked from the laird to the woman at his side. She was tall, her height emphasized by perfect posture. Black hair swept back into an elaborate chignon accented a face that seemed to be all sharp angles, dominated by a long, patrician nose. The scent of lavender surrounded the woman and hung in the air like a cloud.

Gunmetal grey eyes pierced the younger woman and held her rigid. "Well," Lady MacLeod said. The word came out like a bark. "We shall see."

The laird cleared his throat. "Ahem. This is my son Hugh."

A slender young man stepped forward. "Welcome to the family. It's a delight to meet my sister-in-law to be."

Eilidh studied Hugh MacLeod. He couldn't be much older than twenty, but his carriage was that of a much older man. He was almost ascetic in appearance, a bit stooped, and his face was pinched and sallow. His eyes were the same soft brown as his father's, but these eyes were luminous in the narrow face, and his smile was warm and natural. A word popped into Eilidh's mind—*trustworthy*. She gave him a grateful smile. An ally?

The laird looked again at the group. His smile faltered, and a look of irritation came over his features.

"Where's Cullen?" He looked at his wife. "He was with us in the hall a moment ago."

Lady MacLeod shrugged, a gesture that plainly stated, "Maybe he didn't want to be here." A small smile twitched at the corner of her mouth. Eilidh felt her heart drop. *Oh, dear.*

"Ah, here they are." The relief in the laird's voice was palpable. Two young men came out of the front door and approached the group gathered in the courtyard. The shorter and stockier of the two sauntered up to stand next to Hugh.

"Well, she's not bad to look at." His eyes raked over Eilidh's body, lingering on her breasts a second longer than necessary. A chill spread through her as she met the man's eyes. Cold, like a snake's eyes. They were so dark as to be almost black, set in a handsome, swarthy face that seemed familiar. Had she met him somewhere before? Then it hit her with a thud. He resembled the pirates in the books back home in the library.

She stared at the ground, wishing she could melt into the stones of the courtyard. This was the future bridegroom? She was doomed.

Another man shouldered his way between the laird and the pirate and stood before her.

"Hello," said a low, cultured voice. Eilidh's head snapped up and she found herself staring into a beautiful pair of hazel eyes set in a face straight out of a Renaissance painting. Thick, wavy dark brown hair, straight classical nose that was saved from being feminine by the small bump on the bridge. His skin was flawless, his lips full and sensual. He was the most beautiful man she had ever seen . . .

"Hello," the voice said again. "Welcome to Raasay House. I'm Cullen."

CHAPTER 9

INVERNESS,
SCOTLAND - PRESENT DAY

True things are destined to repeat themselves.
Suzanne Young

cotland. I'm in Scotland. It's . . . so old.

Fiona's pulse quickened as she stood in front of the guesthouse that was to be her home for the next month. To her eyes, the building seemed impossibly ancient, but she knew it dated from the mid-1700's, which made it almost a modern house here on Ardconnel Street. The oldest house on Cape Breton had been built in 1787, and it was an anomaly on the island, but here the entire street was filled with mansions at least as old.

The sign on the old iron post next to the gate read, "*King's Arms, est. 1756.*" Who was the king then? It was only ten years after the Battle of Culloden, so it would've been George II—*the jerk.*

Fiona laughed at herself. She felt the blood of her Jacobite forebears heating up at the name, but as a historian she knew that the feeling was rooted in romance and nostalgia for a past that was long gone.

She'd bet that not one of these modern Scots ever batted an eye at the name as they passed by the guesthouse. King George had made his mark on history, and no one was complaining anymore.

It was the diaspora, the Canadians and Americans whose ancestors had made their way across the sea after the clearances, who held onto their heritage with an iron will. They took the Highland culture with them, and when they landed in the New World, they strove to recreate what they had left behind.

Cape Breton Island was a conclave for these weary remnants of the mountain clans. The island was sprinkled with towns whose names evoked a homeland that was lost: Inverness, Shunakadie, Oban. The Glenora distillery proudly proclaimed its status as the first of its kind in North America, stubbornly calling its single malts *whisky*—without the "e," thank you very much—even if they couldn't by law call it Scotch. And the Gaelic College where Fiona worked proclaimed itself the only institution of its kind in the Western Hemisphere.

Maybe that was why, as she stood looking at the old stone guesthouse, her shoulders went back and her spine felt a little straighter. Fiona MacLean was fiercely Canadian, but the Jacobite roots went deep. She had earned the right to be here, in the land of her ancestors, and woe be it to anyone who suggested otherwise.

She laughed at herself. Standing outside wasn't going to get her anywhere. She pushed the gate open and made her way to the double front doors, painted a bright white to contrast with red sandstone walls. Bay windows of the same weathered stone held white framed windows, and pots of hanging flowers hung on either side of the doors.

Fiona stepped over the threshold and sighed in delight. This place had figured out how to marry the past and the present without stealing from either. A tartan cloth covered an antique sideboard in the foyer, and a Victorian lamp shed soft light onto the massive guestbook.

To the right was a sitting room with comfortable, well-used couches, and to the left a library, arched moulding showcasing books in varying states of wear. At the end of the wide-planked hallway, Fiona could see a room with round tables covered in white cloths and surrounded with serviceable wooden slat-backed chairs.

"Hello."

She turned to see a woman dressed in a navy blue business suit relieved by a soft tartan scarf.

"I'm Mrs. MacDonald," the woman said, giving her guest a wide smile. "You must be Fiona, aye?"

"Aye . . . I mean, yes. You have a lovely house."

"Thank you, it's been in my family for two hundred and fifty years." Mrs. MacDonald studied her new resident. "You're from Canada, aye?"

Fiona nodded. "Yes, Nova Scotia."

"Well," her hostess said, "at least you're on the east coast. My niece lives in the States, in New York, and I visit once a year. That's a long plane trip you had, overnight, and it's so hard to sleep on the plane, aye?

Did you drive up from Edinburgh?"

"No, I took the train. I have a rental car waiting at the Inverness airport, but I'm not picking it up until tomorrow. I suppose I'll have to take the bus to get there, but right now I don't even want to think about it."

"Ach, you must be exhausted, poor thing—such a long day. Well, let's see you to your room, and you can rest. Dinner starts at five."

Mrs. MacDonald led her down the hall to a small elevator—*lift*, Fiona reminded herself—and pushed the button for the second floor. They walked down a hallway carpeted in another tartan pattern, soft shades of blue and forest green, and the landlady produced a skeleton key and opened the door to reveal a lovely two-room suite with a tiny efficiency kitchen and windows overlooking the back garden.

"We keep two of these suites at the back of the house for our longer staying guests," Mrs. MacDonald told her. "I'm sorry I can't give you a view of the castle—" she grinned. "We have to save those rooms for the short-term guests, you know—and believe me, they pay for the privilege." She chuckled as she handed the key to Fiona.

"This is lovely! And since I'm here for the month, I'm sure I'll see plenty of the castle. Thank you, Mrs. MacDonald. I'll see you at dinner."

Fiona rolled her suitcase over to the closet. *I'll unpack later*, she decided. She sat down on the oversized bed, just for a minute, and then lay back on the white comforter . . . just for a minute.

Fiona did not see Mrs. MacDonald at dinner. She

didn't see anyone, because the second her head hit the pillow she was out.

She heard the clanging of metal on metal, and the acrid stench of smoke filled her nostrils. A thick pall of the stuff hung before her eyes, obscured her vision and brought tears to her cheeks. Her feet sank into the boggy ground as she tried to make her way forward, and wet grass whipped at her legs. The screams of dying men rose on all sides, and she felt the familiar terror clutch at her throat.

A hand grasped hers and she found herself pulled against a hard male body. She looked up, struggling to focus in the smoky landscape. Wild black hair straggled into blue eyes that held her frozen where she stood. Eyes that she knew.

She awoke gasping for air. Despite the fatigue of the day, sleep did not return, and she tossed and turned until the early light stole through the window of her room on Ardconnell Street. It was all depressingly familiar. The dream had followed her to Scotland.

Fiona drifted down to the dining room in a fog. Lack of sleep, jet lag, and remnants of the dream danced behind her eyes and teased the edges of her mind.

"Good morning, lass. Missed you at dinner—goodness, are you alright?" Mrs. MacDonald's concerned grey eyes swam into her field of vision, and Fiona summoned up a weak smile.

"I'm okay. Fell asleep too early, I guess. I'll be fine when I get used to the time change."

She pulled herself together and mustered a more

genuine smile for the landlady.

"Now, what is that amazing smell?"

Mrs. MacDonald laughed. "That, lass, is the best medicine Scotland has to offer. Come with me."

She steered Fiona to a small table next to a window overlooking the garden and gave her a menu.

"Cape Breton is very Scottish in some ways," Fiona said. "My ancestors brought so many traditions with them, but I think they might have been running away from the food, because we don't really have many good Scottish restaurants on the island. We're known mostly for our seafood, for obvious reasons."

She scanned the menu. "But my mom sometimes cooks haggis, and I've had black pudding. This menu is making me homesick, really.

"My boyfriend likes—" She snapped her lips shut. Mrs. MacCullen gave her a curious look but said nothing.

Fiona sat back. "I think I'd better just go with the porridge today. Not sure my stomach is ready for the onslaught of meat and beans."

As she ate her breakfast, Fiona's thoughts wandered back to the last meeting she'd had with Greg. It had been anything but pleasant. For the three weeks after their argument, he hadn't called or texted once. Nor had he answered her calls. She tried not to be hurt by his behavior, but now she could admit that he had made the decision to go to Scotland easier.

I never realized how petty he can be. Couldn't he even talk about this—try to understand how important it is? I would have listened.

She tried to ignore the small voice in her head that

kept saying *Would you? You were going to go anyway, weren't you?*

And that, she told herself as she sat on the plane to Scotland, was the crux of the problem. Neither of them had cared enough to give in. It was a harsh way to find out, like cutting off a limb to make sure it hurt. She missed his humor, his smile, the companionship. On the surface, they had seemed the perfect couple.

Underneath, though, insane thoughts swirled through her mind. His eyes weren't blue. His hair wasn't black. Her pulse didn't race when she saw him. The fact was, he wasn't the man she needed.

Time to get on with things, she told herself. She changed into jeans and a white summer sweater and threw on her trusty rain jacket before following her phone's GPS the short distance down to the High Street. From there it was a couple of blocks to the bus station. So far, so good.

An hour later, Fiona was seated behind the wheel of a small red Vauxhall. She congratulated herself on her cleverness in practicing ahead of time back home, sitting in the passenger seat of Brian's Honda in the driveway, working the gears with her left hand until it felt normal. Now all she had to face was driving on the left side of the road.

When she was ready, she pointed her new companion toward the highway and brought up the GPS for Culloden battlefield. Dad had told her to go there first, to visit the saddest place in Scotland before she did anything else.

"Just go, walk around by yourself—and make sure you watch the video presentation. You'll never be the same, Fee, I promise you. It's your history."

It was raining by the time she reached Culloden Moor, which somehow seemed appropriate. Fiona parked the car in the huge lot of the Visitor Centre and went in to buy a ticket. Grateful for the hooded rain jacket, she spent the next hour wandering along the paved pathway through the battlefield, reading the stones that marked the resting places of the Highland clans who had given everything for a dream—and lost.

Cameron, MacGillivray, Donald, Fraser, Macintosh. Many of the names were common in Cape Breton, and it made the experience all the more personal. She paused at the marker for Clan MacLean and said a prayer for her ancestors before moving on.

The rain had chased most of the visitors off the battlefield, and the Visitor's Centre was crowded. She worked her way through the throng and took her place in line for the presentation her father had told her not to miss.

The doors opened, and several tourists flowed out of the room. All had shocked looks on their faces; some were crying. Every single person was silent. Fiona felt a strange sensation in her stomach as she entered the room and made her way to the center.

The lights dimmed. The sound of bagpipes filled the room, and Fiona found herself looking across the moor at the Government lines. Union Jacks flew in the wind. The video was in black and white, which lent a stark feeling of timelessness to the scene before her.

The perspective shifted, and now she was standing

at the British lines staring at the Highland clans across the moor. Where the British Army had been organized, the Jacobite lines were chaotic. Men shouted, waved the saltire, beat on their targes with swords as they prepared to face the government army.

Shots rang out. Smoke began to fill the landscape, but still the lines held. More shots, more smoke, and suddenly the Highland lines began to charge. The men, shouting and screaming, ran straight at the tourists who stood frozen in place in the modern Visitor Centre.

An entire front row of men went down, and howls of agony rose over the bagpipes as the Highland clans continued their mad rush toward the enemy. The screams and the clanging of metal were deafening.

Now Fiona could see the individual men racing toward her, resolution etched on set faces. She stood transfixed as the kilted men met the British officers and began hand-to-hand fighting. Bodies littered the boggy ground.

A soldier turned suddenly. He was British Army; even in black and white the iconic uniform was obvious. He had lost his tricorn. Wild black hair flew in the wind as he stopped and stared straight at her, and Fiona felt her blood run cold. In the monochrome vista of grey, somehow she knew that his eyes were blue—the color of a summer sky.

She stared into those eyes, rigid with shock. They might have been alone on the battlefield; everything else had receded into the smoke and clamor.

Then he was gone, melted into the chaos as if he'd never existed. The sounds of battle diminished and finally stopped altogether, as the ramifications of the day's slaughter began to dawn on both sides. The scene was oddly quiet, the clanging gone, bagpipes silenced. The moans of dying men were all that could be heard in the harsh landscape.

The lights came up and the room returned to the present. Nearby, a woman was crying softly, the only sound as people began to wander out of the room. Fiona stood alone, transfixed by what she had seen.

The man in the video—the British soldier—was the man in her dream. His eyes were the eyes she had seen countless times. But that wasn't what was keeping her rooted to the floor, unable to move.

The eyes had blazed with recognition. He *knew* her.

She found herself out on the sidewalk, uncertain how she had gotten there, and began to step into the parking lot.

Suddenly she was swept off her feet onto the ground, a pair of strong arms holding her as she rolled across the sidewalk into a bush.

The pain of the branches penetrated her daze, and she found herself looking up into angry blue eyes. She mumbled an apology and scrambled to her feet to face the man.

He was sputtering. "Maybe you should pay attention so you make it home to the States in one piece, aye?"

She felt an answering anger building.

"Are all Scottish people as rude as you?" she asked. "And for your information, I'm Canadian, you buffoon!"

CHAPTER 10

INVERNESS, SCOTLAND - PRESENT DAY

And that is how change happens. One gesture.
One person. One moment at a time.
Libba Bray

What the hell? Ewan stared at the woman who stood, hands on her hips, glaring at him. Glaring at him! He'd just rescued her from serious injury, and she was angry? A buffoon? Weren't Canadians known for being polite? Someone should have told this one. Okay, maybe his crack about her nationality had been a bit boorish, but did it deserve an outright insult? He'd been shaken too, damn it.

Auburn hair straggled onto her forehead, nearly obscuring one green eye. She brushed the hair back with an impatient hand, and a leaf came loose and fluttered to the pavement. He felt a pang of guilt—he was responsible for that leaf—had he hurt her?

He took a closer look. No, the gleam in those

green eyes held no sign of pain, nor was it anger, despite her harsh words. What he saw reflected in those depths was something else—fear. Which was understandable, given her narrow escape a moment ago. But there was something else there, something unsettling.

"I'm sorry," Ewan said again. "Maybe I was a little too rough. Are you all right?" She swayed, and he placed a tentative hand on her arm. She shrugged it off and backed away from him, still glaring. He felt a stab of irritation. What was wrong with her? Did she think he was some barbarian who attacked women in crowded car parks?

Well, somebody had to be civilized here. He took a steadying breath and tried again.

"I'm sorry if I insulted you—I didn't mean it. I guess it was the adrenaline. I don't usually have to rescue tourists as a part of my job, you know." *Go for a touch of lightness, Ewan. She's just scared.*

It worked. The woman's face softened a tiny bit, and she sighed. "No, it's not your fault. I just had a shock, and I reacted badly. I'm the one who's sorry. And . . . thank you." A watery smile made its way onto her face. *Her beautiful face.*

Ewan brought himself up short. *Pretty sure this isn't the time and place to be thinking about her looks. But . . . achh.* He struggled for coherency.

"This is one of the most crowded tourist venues in Scotland, even on a draich day like this one," he said. "Even the car park can be deadly."

"I feel like enough of a fool, without you rubbing it in, you know," she said with some asperity. "I said

I'd had a shock."

"Well, almost getting run over can be pretty shocking . . ."

"It wasn't that—"

"And I suppose being accosted and rolled into a shrubbery wouldn't help." Ewan gave himself a mental pat on the back. In the spirit of chivalry, it might be time for a bit of humor.

"I said, it wasn't that!" The edge was back in the voice.

Maybe not the time for humor. This woman! Prickly as a gorse bush.

"What then?"

Her eyes evaded his. "I mean, yes, almost getting hit by a car and being manhandled by a total stranger was a little . . . surprising, but that's not why I was distracted." Her voice was low now, and shaking.

Ewan said nothing. It wasn't his place to pry into a stranger's affairs.

The woman shook her head and sighed. "Never mind. It has nothing to do with you. Again, thank you, and I'm sorry for causing you so much trouble."

She turned to go, giving an exaggerated look both ways before stepping off the curb. But it was almost as if she were forcing herself to pay attention, just going through the motions, and her walk was unsteady as she headed for the second row of cars. For some reason, he wanted to go after her— beg her to stay and talk to him. Make sure she was okay so he could gaze into those gorgeous eyes again. *What the hell?*

A red Vauxhall pulled out of a spot near the back

of the lot, and Ewan watched as the woman made her way to the access road, correcting her lane as most tourists did. She turned left toward Inverness and in another moment was gone. He wondered at the sharp pang he felt at the loss of her company—and at the feeling of sadness.

He shrugged off the feeling and turned back toward the battlefield. Well. That had been interesting, to say the least. Not something he wanted to work into his tours, for sure.

Tours—he'd almost forgotten why he was here. He'd never see the woman again, so it was best not to dwell on it. But something about the encounter niggled at the edge of his brain and wouldn't let go. Best to lose himself in work.

He wandered out to the battlefield and spent the next hour pretending he'd never seen it before, trying to look at the moor through the eyes of a tourist. What could he add to the experience that would cement that forty-five minutes in 1746 into the minds of his clients?

How could he make people who had never been to Scotland before understand those who had fled in hope of a better life, and those who had been left behind, their culture destroyed, their homes owned by an oppressive government?

So many had gone, forced off their lands by the clearances, driven in desperation to find hope in a new world. Australia, America, Canada . . .

And she was back. The Canadian tourist who had decided to lodge herself in his brain like the beginnings of a headache. What was wrong with him? He'd seen his share of beautiful women before, for heaven's sake. She wasn't even the prettiest, and she damn well wasn't the nicest—so why was he still thinking about those green eyes, and that brown hair—no, not brown—auburn?

Because he'd seen those eyes before. Not once, but many times. They were the eyes he saw every time he fell into his nightmare—the flash of green he'd seen just before his flight off the ridge at Aonach Eagach two months ago. And that made no sense at all.

"It wasn't that." What had she meant by that? He'd been so busy trying to apologize for assaulting her in the name of rescue that he hadn't paid attention to what she was saying. Ewan sat on a bench along the paved walkway and reached into his memory.

Something about a shock. And now that he thought about it, why *had* she been in such a daze that she'd almost walked in front of a car? Something had to have happened in the Visitor's Centre. Had someone said something to her?

She'd been in the video presentation room. Ewan sat up straight. She'd had that same look on her face when the lights came up—an expression of stunned surprise.

It wasn't the look people usually wore after viewing the video of the battle. The presentation was certainly vivid and compelling; that was why it was his favorite part of the Culloden experience. People often reacted emotionally; many came out in tears. But the look on the face of the Canadian woman had not been awe or sadness.

In fact, now that he thought back on it, she'd

looked sick. Her face had been white, and she had seemed to be struggling to remain erect. Something in that video had caused her to react in a way he'd never seen before.

On an impulse, he returned to the Visitor's Centre and took in the video presentation one more time. Nothing—it was, of course, exactly the same as always. Watching the reenactment of the Highland Charge, that military tactic that had worked so well in the past, evoked the same feelings as always.

His ancestors ran straight at him, sure of another victory, unaware that their reward today was death and the destruction of all they held dear. It was an emotional punch in the gut, the same as always, but nothing to explain that weird look on the Canadian's lovely face. Maybe she was crazy, after all.

He snorted as he walked out of the centre. *Sure, you don't understand, so she has to be crazy. Nice job, MacArthur.* He shook his head in disgust and headed for the front doors.

This day, at least as far as creativity, was a wash. There was no point in staying longer when his mind was virtual mush, his thoughts swirling like a cyclone. What he needed was a drink, and he knew just the person who could get him out of his funk.

His brother Adam was only too happy to be his companion, since it involved one of his own favorite pursuits, and soon the two were sitting at the bar in Gellions Tavern on the High Street. Ewan had no intention of telling his brother about his experience as the savior of truculent damsels in distress, so it was some surprise when, after the third beer, he heard his own voice doing just that.

"The wee eejit stepped right off the curb, and it was just lucky that I was right there and able to grab her," he said. "And what did I get for my troubles, besides a scraped arm?" He brandished his injured arm, and Adam squinted to examine the tiny scratch.

"Hmm," he said, sounding unimpressed. He studied his brother's face for a long moment and took another swig of beer. "Was she pretty?"

"What the hell does that have to do with it?" Ewan said. "She was . . . just a woman. A rude tourist," he raised his voice in a falsetto imitation of the offender's tone, "a *Canadian*, thank you very much! And she called me a buffoon!"

Adam choked on his beer. "Well, you can be an arse and you're stubborn to a fault, but I never heard that one before." He sat back and studied his brother. An evil grin appeared as he cocked his head and swirled the contents of his beer glass.

"So...she was pretty. I say this because you seem to be quite worked up about her, and you don't usually give women the time of day. But a pretty woman who hurts your wee feelings, now..."

"Shut up," Ewan growled. He stared into the depths of his mug for a moment.

"She was scared," he said. "I mean, even before the accident. Something had frightened the hell out of her, and that just doesn't make any sense at all."

"Could someone have been following her?" Adam sat up straighter, intrigued. "A stalker, maybe?"

"A stalker, at the Culloden Visitor's Centre?" Ewan gave his brother a look of distaste. "What movies have you been watching, anyway?" At Adam's shrug, he sighed.

"I don't know why I'm telling you about this. It was a five-minute interaction, and it's done. I don't know her, and I don't want to know her."

Liar. The voice in his head mocked him.

"Whatever." Adam threw his hands up in the air. "Just trying to help. I didn't start this conversation, you know." He held up his mug. "One more?"

"No, I'm done," Ewan said. "I'm going home. This day started out with a headache, and it's looking to end the same way. I think I'll write the whole thing off and start over tomorrow." He stood.

"Want to share a cab?" Adam joined him on the street.

"No, I think I'll walk. I need air. Thanks for listening, and for your sympathy." Ewan gave his brother a sarcastic grin and started up the High Street toward his house on Charles Street. By the time he reached Ardconnell, he felt the beauty of his city working its magic on his soul. Inverness Castle loomed on the right and bed-and-breakfast inns sat like stately old dowagers along the road. The rain had stopped, and a weak sun was trying to make its last stand.

He came to a sudden stop. A red Vauxhall sat in front of one of the guest houses that lined the old street, and Ewan stared at it in disbelief. He'd seen that car before, very recently. If he was not mistaken, it had been driven by a woman with auburn hair and green eyes, as she exited the car park at Culloden Visitor's Centre.

As Ewan stood still, wondering what to do about

this astonishing coincidence, a black sedan glided down the street and came to a stop next to him. The driver's window rolled down, and a voice spoke from the shadowed interior.

"Ewan."

All thoughts of red cars and beautiful tourists were driven from his mind at the sound of that voice. He cursed under his breath. His heart quickened and a sweat broke out on his brow.

It was a voice he had sworn he never wanted to hear again.

"Son."

CHAPTER 11
INVERNESS, SCOTLAND - PRESENT DAY

*Grief makes a monster out of us . . . and
sometimes you say and do things to the people
you love that you can't forgive yourself for.*
Melina Marchetta

Ewan felt as if someone had nailed his feet to the sidewalk. Frozen, he stared at the man he hadn't laid eyes on for ten years. Unblinking blue eyes, mirrors of his own, stared back at him. For what seemed hours the two remained in a tableau, the world passing unnoticed around them. Then Ewan turned his back on the black car and began to walk away.

"Son . . . please."

It was the quaver in the voice that turned him back around. His father had always had a commanding tone, the deep baritone utilized to keep employees in their place and to lend authority to meetings with whisky vendors and craftsmen. A voice whose venom could slice through the heart and soul of a young boy and leave him in helpless tears.

This voice belonged to someone else. It was thin, reedy, and filled with something he'd never associated with his father: fear.

"I *think he's sorry.*" Adam's words came through the fog in Ewan's brain.

He blinked. "What do you want?"

"Would it hurt to use a little respect?"

There, that was more like it. Here was the real man. Ewan snorted in derision. He knew this version of his father; it hadn't changed in all those years.

"Are you serious . . . *sir?*"

"I—I'm sorry." The trembling was back, and the fierce blue eyes held something suspiciously like moisture.

Ah, shite. He felt his resolve begin to crack.

"Please—will you give me a few minutes?"

"And why should I want to do that . . . *sir?*" But Ewan's resolve was draining away in the face of that plea, and his own words sounded petty to his ears. He rubbed his temple where a headache was taking root, then sighed and made his way around to the passenger side of the car, wondering if this was the first step to a descent into Hell.

He sat still and stared straight ahead out the windscreen. Damned if he was going to be the first to speak.

"How have you been?"

"Fine."

"You seem to have recovered from your accident."

"Yes."

"Did Adam speak with you?"

"About what?"

His father sighed and cleared his throat. *Is he nervous? Good. This can't be over soon enough.*

"Ewan . . . I've been thinking a lot about you lately."

Ewan turned and regarded his father with astonishment. "What? Why?" He knew his voice sounded bitter, and he didn't care. How dare the man say such a thing? Duncan MacArthur had had sixteen years to be a father. Instead, a twelve-year-old boy had had his entire family stolen from him through no fault of his own. And now this pitiful excuse for a parent was *thinking* about him?

It was so absurd it was almost funny. So why was his throat constricting with the effort to stem the tears that had sprung to his eyes? Ewan turned and looked out the window. His hands were clenched into fists to stop them from shaking, and his heart felt as if it might explode. Damn! He could feel that twelve-year-old taking over his emotions. He hated this so much.

"Father—I suppose I must call you that—I don't think we have anything to talk about."

"I'm sorry," his father repeated. The voice was low, filled with some deep emotion that Ewan couldn't identify. Didn't want to identify.

"I was wrong."

"About what? Our relationship doesn't have enough basis for such things."

"Please—hear me out. Just give me that."

Ewan turned back from the window. His father looked as if he'd aged years in the last few minutes. His face was grey, and his bloodshot eyes sagged as if with extreme fatigue. A sudden fear seized Ewan and for a moment his adult self fell away, ceding the field to the small boy he had been.

He didn't want this, didn't want to spend another minute in this toxic atmosphere, but he didn't want to be the reason for his father to collapse. Had wanted it, many times . . . but not now.

"Okay."

His father's expression didn't change. He turned and looked at his son, who looked back at him with as little emotion as he could muster.

"I loved your mother so much. When she died, I think I went a little crazy." The naked pain in the man's eyes startled Ewan. Well, of course he'd loved his wife—the whole family had suffered unspeakable loss that night. But was that an excuse to shun his son, to shatter his own child into a thousand pieces?

"You blamed a twelve-year-old boy who had just lost his mother. You cut me off from my own family. You abandoned me!" Ewan's voice rose and he could hear the trembling. The tears that had gathered in his eyes betrayed him, spilling down his face and dripping onto his shirt.

"I know. It was unforgivable." Duncan's own eyes were bright with unshed tears, as if his grief had dried him up from the inside out.

"Good, because I can't ever forgive you." Ewan swiped at the tears and fisted his hand in his lap. "You stole sixteen years of my life, turned my family against me. I hate you for that."

His father's shoulders slumped. "I know. I'm not making excuses. I have none. I don't mind if you hate me, but I needed to tell you that I'm sorry. There wasn't a day went by after you left that I didn't regret how I treated you. I wanted to reach out so many times—to tell you how proud I was of the job you were doing with your company, to talk with you about the distillery. I missed you."

"How does that even make sense?" Ewan made a supreme effort to keep his voice level. "You had so many chances, but you didn't care. Even when I nearly died—"

"I was there."

"What?"

"I came every day of that first week in the hospital. I slept on a cot through that first night. After you regained consciousness, I left, because I knew you wouldn't want me there."

Ewan stared at him, eyes wide. "But, why didn't Adam tell me you were there? He was pushing me to meet with you, just before the accident."

"I told him not to tell you. I didn't want to have our first meeting be at your hospital bedside, when you were weak and helpless. It wouldn't have been fair."

Ewan was silent, trying to take it in. His father had been there. He'd kept a vigil at his son's bedside—had stayed beside the son he'd let go so many years ago. It didn't fit into the neat pattern of hatred and anger that Ewan had constructed to explain his father's rejection, and it rocked him to his core. How the hell could he handle this?

"None of this changes anything," he said, after a long pause. "It's too little, way too late."

He fumbled for the door handle and nearly fell

in his haste to exit the car. He walked away without a backward look, thoughts swirling in his muddled head. After ten steps, he whirled and looked back.

The black sedan was still there. Its driver sat motionless behind the wheel, head bowed.

Ewan watched, but there was no movement. He turned to go again, turned back, and sighed. He walked to the car, opened the door, and slid into the seat he'd vacated a moment ago.

"Why?" He asked the silent figure in the driver's seat.

"I told you." His father's head remained bowed over the wheel. "I wanted to see you."

"No. I mean, why did you visit me in the hospital, when I didn't even know you were there? Why did you stay by my side? And why did you really leave before I woke up?" He heard the plea in his own voice, but couldn't stop. "Why, after all these years?"

"You—you are my son. My oldest son. I let myself forget that for a long time." The older man's bleary blue eyes found Ewan's.

"Your mother's death nearly killed me. It was such a stupid reason to die, and I needed to blame something or I would have lost my mind. I guess I did lose my mind, because the something I blamed was you."

He stopped and took a shuddering breath. "I hated you, my own child, because I told myself you took my wife away from me. It was your fault. She was in that car, on that road, because of you. I told myself that, and I made myself believe it. I couldn't even look at you, the grief and the guilt ate at me until I wanted you gone more than I wanted anything else."

Ewan said nothing.

"And then you *were* gone. For ten years I was convinced that you'd left on your own because you wanted to, that it was for the best and we'd both be able to get past it as long as we never saw each other again."

He looked at his son, and now the tears came, rolling down the ravaged face without stopping. He began to cry great heaving sobs that shook his body.

Ewan reached out a hand without conscious knowledge and patted his father on the shoulder. Duncan MacArthur looked up, a flash of hope crossing his face before he lowered his head again and covered his eyes with both hands.

A muffled voice came from behind the veined hands. "There's more. I need you."

And just like that, the thin cord connecting them was snapped. Ewan pulled his hand back as if it had been stung.

"What? You need me? Why?" The anger was back, dark and vicious in its strength. "I should have known you'd have some ulterior motive for all this." His voice was a sneer. "Please do tell—this should be rich."

His father flinched. He sat for a moment longer, staring ahead out the windscreen. Then, "I think someone is trying to kill me."

It was the last thing Ewan had expected to hear. The anger drained out again, replaced by incredulity. For a long moment he was unable to muster up words, and when he finally spoke it was in a voice he barely recognized.

"Someone is trying to kill you? Seriously? And

what—did you think it might be me?"

His father jerked upright in the seat. "Of course not! Don't be an arse!"

The reaction went some distance in calming Ewan's frayed nerves. The corner of his mouth twitched, and he put his hands up in defense.

"All right—calm down. Tell me what you mean by that ridiculous statement, then."

"There have been—incidents—at the distillery, things that by themselves seem coincidental but when put together challenge that idea. Some records missing. A mild case of food poisoning, a minor gas leak in my office. Little things. I wasn't sure if I was just unlucky or careless, but then you—"

"Me?"

"Your accident on the mountain. I've followed your adventures, and I know that you're never careless when climbing. So when you fell and nearly died, I started thinking."

"But how could there be a connection? We're not even family anymore."

Duncan's head jerked up and Ewan saw the pain reflected in his eyes. He steeled himself.

"Sorry, but it's true. We haven't seen or talked to each other for years. How could my accident be related to the things that have happened to you?"

"Are you so sure it was an accident?"

"Don't be dramatic." Ewan snorted. "Of course it was an accident. Yes, I'm careful, but climbing is dangerous. A fall can happen to anyone.

"And you haven't answered my question. How could it be related to your incidents?"

"Because I want to make you the heir to the distillery."

"What? Why the hell would you do that?"

"Because you're my eldest son, and because you've the best brain in the family. I told you I've kept track . . . and because I miss you, and I want to make amends." His voice took on a petulant tone. "What's so hard to understand?"

Ewan sat immobilized by shock. Never in a million years . . .

"What about Aaron?" he said, when he could speak. "He's your vice president. And as far as I understand, the distillery's doing quite well under him."

"He's not blood. Yes, he's married to your sister, but Aaron Grant is right where he should be. He doesn't have what it takes to run the place alone, and he knows it."

"Well, I can certainly see how popular I would be in certain circles," Ewan said, sarcasm evident in his tone. "You've cast me in the role of the prodigal son, without asking me. Thanks for that, too. And no thanks—I already have a job."

Duncan ignored him. "So, you don't have to forgive me, but will you give this some thought? Think of it as saving your own hide, if you want."

Ewan opened the car door and stepped out without a word. He closed the door with slightly more force than necessary and stood on the sidewalk as the black sedan pulled away.

Did his father really think that an apology was enough, after all these years? Did he think that would erase the pain, the anger? Well, he could forget that.

Images whirled through his head, crashed into each other, and spun away. Accidents. Too many accidents had woven themselves into the fabric of his life. His mother. His father. And two months ago on Aonach Eagach.

He remembered his thoughts from the day of his fall and wondered. *Had* it been an accident?

CHAPTER 12
ISLE OF SKYE,
SCOTLAND - 1746

IAIN

How did I get myself into this?

Iain sat back in the plush velvet chair and gazed around at the luxury that was Castle Dunvegan. The first stones had been laid in 1200, and now the castle was a jewel adorning the northern-most corner of the Isle of Skye. It stood in majestic glory above the sea loch for which it was named, proclaiming to all that those who lived here were a clan to be reckoned with.

The original tower house had been embellished through the centuries by each generation of MacLeods and reflected the differing tastes that could be indulged by the owners' vast wealth and privilege. Dunvegan was truly an architectural marvel, inside and out. Iain wished his father were here to see this.

The MacLeods were still doing well, by anyone's standards. Working for king and country paid off, as long as you were already high-placed. Which left him and his family out, of course. No matter how the war panned out, their fortunes would remain the same.

Not that he was complaining. The rich and entitled risked everything by their political choices. If the war went as expected, the MacLeods would reap the benefits of their alliance with the king. The rich would get richer. On the other hand, if the worst happened and Charles Stuart succeeded in taking the throne of England and Scotland, those Scottish clans who backed the government stood to lose everything.

It meant little to Iain, beyond his pride and loyalty to the army and to his government. He would be paid as usual. He would go on to fight the next war in an endless stream of conflicts in which the British army embroiled itself in its never-ending quest for world supremacy.

Iain couldn't deny that he sometimes questioned his country's motivation—there was an undeniable taint of arrogance and elitist snobbery in the British army's dogged determination to establish roots in far-flung lands that thought they had been doing just fine by themselves.

Those who wore the red uniform were known throughout the world for their fighting capabilities and their confidence. They would win, because they always had. This latest rising in Scotland would be no different.

He studied the people who sat at the table with him and wondered for the tenth time why he was here. The MacLeods of Skye had welcomed him with warmth, given him the grand tour and shared their finest wine. They were proud to entertain a member of his Majesty's great army, even under these strange circumstances.

Iain thought back to the day last month when his military life had been turned upside down. He'd been called in by his superior officer, Colonel Buchanan, and given an order that both surprised and baffled him.

"You will be making a trip up to Skye to investigate the growing concerns with the Jacobites," Buchanan began. "You know that Charles Stuart spent most of last year in France, making a nuisance of himself at court. Louis probably wished he could pack the man back to Italy and be done with him. It was never a secret that he was planning his rising, and that he was looking for money to fund his efforts."

Iain tried to stifle his impatience. All this *was* no secret. He sighed and settled back in his chair to wait. The colonel was well known for his love of talk—he thrived on the sound of his own voice. Also, he had the ability to make even something mysterious and dangerous seem boring. It had to be a gift. Sooner or later, he'd get to the point—the question was, could Iain manage to stay awake that long?

". . . .harles is winning." The words jolted Iain out of his mental fugue, and he sat up abruptly.

"As you know, he has been here in Scotland for six months. He landed in the Highlands last July, on Eriskay Island, and since then he has been busy. Edinburgh fell to the Jacobites in September, followed by the disaster at Prestonpans. We were simply unprepared there—we underestimated Charles and we've paid dearly. The Jacobites are making inroads, and it doesn't take much intelligence to figure out that they're preparing for something big—enough to concern the highest levels of his Majesty's army."

Buchanan continued in his slow, measured drone. "The Jacobite clans are working with Stuart. We have lists of the clans, but precious little information on their movements or their plans. And that is where you come in."

"Me?" Now Iain's attention was on full alert. "Why me, sir? I'm only a lance corporal. Does something like this not require someone of higher rank and more experience?"

"That is not what is important here. I see how you are with your men—they like you and trust you." The colonel smiled at the startled look on Iain's face. "Oh, you did not know how you are regarded by your superiors?" There was a touch of humor in his voice. "We have been watching you, and we've talked to the soldiers in your section. They would march into Hell for you, you know. You have the ability to pull men to your side—to make them yours. That is a gift."

Iain shook his head to dispel the wash of pride that went through him. Pride was dangerous. Distraction could be fatal.

"But—the Jacobites aren't my men, sir. They're the enemy. They are not going to listen to me—more likely they'll shoot me on sight."

Buchanan leaned forward, his arms folded on the desk.

"You are a Highlander—one of them."

Iain leaned back again in his chair. Now he understood the flaw in this plan.

"I'm a Campbell, sir. The Campbells have sided with the government in every Jacobite rising since 1715. No Jacobite would ever accept me. It would never work."

"You will not be going as a Campbell." Buchanan's voice was smug. "You are going as a MacCrimmon."

"The pipers?" Iain tried to mask the astonishment that surely must be reflected on his face. Never would he have thought—

"The MacCrimmons have been pipers to the MacLeods of Skye for generations," the calm voice of the colonel found its way through his fog. "They have no political agenda and are revered throughout the Highlands for their artistry. A MacCrimmon can go anywhere and is welcomed everywhere." Buchanan sat back and regarded Iain with the happy smile of someone who has won a major battle.

"Ahh . . ." Iain cleared his throat. "There is just one problem, sir. I am sorry to have to tell you this, but I'm barely passable at the pipes. I would be discovered the moment I tuned up."

"Pssh," the colonel waved his hand in the air. "You are not going to actually *play*, Campbell—er, MacCrimmon." The smile never wavered. "The MacLeod will know who you are, and he will provide you with safe passage anywhere you need to go in the Highlands. You are piper to that clan only; no one else would have the audacity to ask you to play."

"But, why the MacLeods?" Iain felt as if he were swimming through mud. "They're not Jacobites. Never have been. How are they going to help me to get in with the rebels?"

"You will begin your mission on Skye, at Dunvegan. But your ultimate destination is Raasay—specifically Raasay House. You will ingratiate yourself with the MacLeods of that island—" he paused for a long moment.

"—who are avowed Jacobites."

Buchanan cleared his throat. "They are planning something decisive—and you are going to find out what it is."

CHAPTER 13

ISLE OF RAASAY, SCOTLAND - 1746

EILIDH

Eilidh crept along in her future husband's wake as he walked swiftly along the halls of Raasay House. It didn't really matter if he saw her, since in another two months they would be married. But being caught hovering like a lovesick puppy would be embarrassing. A girl had pride, after all.

In the three weeks since her arrival at Raasay, she had been beset with conflicting thoughts. She did not want to marry—that was still true. But . . . how could a man be that handsome? She studied Cullen out of the corner of her eye at dinner, looking for something—anything—that could be considered a flaw. But there was nothing. Unless it was the growing sense that he seemed to avoid her as much as possible, but surely that would change once they were married. He was simply shy, that was all.

She watched out the window when he practiced swordplay with Dom and his friend Godfrey Lewis and noted that he was as graceful as a dancer. Of course, he seemed to be an expert horseman as well, almost one with his mount.

He spent a lot of time in the library, which meant he was smart, too, and that was where he was headed this morning. She knew because it was the one place she could find him without his two shadows. She already knew Dom was an idiot, and she had a slithering feeling that Godfrey's intelligence tended toward the sinister.

Besides the stables, where Rory could be found most of the time, the library was Eilidh's favorite place. There were hundreds of books there, and they weren't just for show. She had already found some of her favorites, like *Gulliver's Travels* and *Robinson Crusoe*, as well as two full sets of Shakespeare's works. On days when she wasn't stalking Cullen, she could be found curled up in one of the big armchairs, lost in another world.

She had to admit that Raasay wasn't turning out to be as bad as she'd feared. For the most part she was left to her own devices, allowed to explore to her heart's content. Her maid Alice had befriended two of the other maids and left her alone during the day, and the castle's cook seemed to think Eilidh was a waif who needed fattening up, as she always had treats at the ready, as well as a warm smile.

And there was Rory. At least once during the day

she visited him in the stables or tracked him down where he was monitoring the activities of the pages, and he always stopped what he was doing to spend time with her. There really wasn't much to complain about at Raasay, she had to admit.

Only two things. Two people, to be exact.

Lucretia MacLeod, Cullen's mother, hated her. Eilidh was sure of it. The woman rarely looked at her directly, as if somehow that would be acknowledging her presence as anything other than a bug to be squished at the first opportunity.

Eilidh was sure that her lower financial standing was behind the disdain, but there was nothing she could do about that. After all, it certainly hadn't been *her* idea to get married! Now that she'd met the bridegroom, things didn't seem as dire as they had back home, but still . . . she wished she had the courage to sit that woman down and tell her exactly what she thought of her. Not a likely scenario, though. If she were honest with herself, Lady MacLeod scared her to her bones.

Her future mother-in-law was the real power behind the throne here, and Eilidh knew without a doubt that things would not change for the better after the wedding. She was going to have to keep her wits about her with that one. It was fortunate that the woman's approach was preceded by that cloying scent of lavender. Who could have foreseen that a fragrance Eilidh had learned to hate would give her an opportunity to avoid meeting the laird's wife?

It was different with the other fly in the ointment here. Cullen's odious friend Godfrey was the one who'd given her that reptilian gaze the day she'd arrived —the one she'd mistaken for her future bridegroom. Her first impression of a dangerous pirate had not abated in the days since her arrival.

He seemed to show up often when she was alone, raking her over with those heavy-lidded dark eyes that she was sure were a doorway to Hell. He never said anything—just stared. She needed no fragrance to know he was near. It had gotten so that she could *feel* him coming, a slow, cold dampness that crawled up her spine and left her shaking.

A rustling sound stopped Eilidh's mental meandering. She turned around and scanned the shadows, but she was alone in the corridor. A rat, perhaps? Madame would certainly not approve! The thought cheered her, and she moved on and into the vast library.

She scanned the space for her quarry, but Cullen was nowhere to be found. Curious—she was sure he had been bound for the library. Why did she have to lose herself in her thoughts all the time? Now she'd lost him.

Another sound filtered through the silence of the room. Eilidh turned in a circle, looking for its source, but there was nothing. There were three doors that led off the main room of the library, but as far as she knew those led to small empty rooms that were presumably used for study, and they were always locked.

The noise came again, and this time she was able to target its source. Yes, it was definitely coming from one of the small rooms. She crept toward the door, holding her dress to keep it from rustling. She put her hand on the knob and turned it slowly. As expected, locked.

In the next second she was jerked backward, and a rough male hand clamped over her mouth. She was dragged away from the door and into the center of the room, unable to release the firm grip of her captor.

The hand over her mouth was removed, but the one grasping her wrist remained, holding her in place. She swung around to find herself staring into the glinting black eyes of Godfrey Lewis. A look of something she couldn't identify resolved into a sardonic grin.

"My lady." The smooth voice oozed honey. "So nice to find you here."

"Let. Me. Go." Eilidh tried to keep her voice steady, but she knew it sounded more like the gasp of a landed fish. She yanked hard, and her hand was released.

"I'm sorry," Godfrey said, sounding exceedingly un-sorry. "I never meant to frighten you."

"I wasn't frightened," she managed, but that was a lie. Everything about this man shouted *Run!* She forced her face into a semblance of calm and faced him. "You just startled me, that's all. I'm not used to being manhandled while I'm reading."

He laughed. "You didn't look as if you were reading, my lady. I don't see a book." He directed a pointed look at her empty hands.

"I was getting one. I just got here, and I didn't have time—" *Why am I explaining myself to this person?* She backed up a step, toward the nearest shelf. "Anyway, I was busy, and you—"

"It seemed to me that you were busy listening,"

the smooth voice interjected. "Snooping, one might even call it." Godfrey crossed his arms over his chest and smiled his pirate smile. "Pardon me if I was in error."

"Snooping? How dare you?" Eilidh straightened to her full height. "You are no gentleman, sir."

"I never pretended to be a gentleman, my lady." Godfrey's gaze roved over her body, lingering on her chest for a second. "You must have me confused with your sainted bridegroom. Please, go on with what you were doing." He sat down in one of the armchairs, never taking those black eyes off her.

Eilidh realized that she was very much alone with this man, and the cold dampness turned to ice.

"I think I'll come back another time," she said, trying to sound haughty. "I've lost the urge to read." She managed somehow to look away from him and crossed to the library door on stiff legs.

There was no answer behind her.

At the door, she turned once more. The room was empty.

Her eyes shot to the door from which she was sure she had heard a sound—in time to see it close.

CHAPTER 14

INVERNESS, SCOTLAND - PRESENT DAY

The past is never where you think you left it.
Katherine Anne Porter

"And this is what your father was so interested in." Jeremy Brown indicated a small piece of wrinkled yellowed paper with letters in faded Gaelic script, encased between two panes of glass held in place by a simple metal frame. The paper was dirty and blotched, and the left corner had been torn away, taking some of the words with it.

"This? Just this little bit?" She felt a pang of disappointment go through her. "It's so small, and almost illegible."

She looked from the paper to Dr. Brown. The historian was much younger than she'd thought, probably still in his late thirties. Soft, intelligent brown eyes, made larger by the wire-rimmed glasses that kept sliding down his nose, gazed back at her. Brown flyaway hair that needed a trim and a shy smile that was like the sun coming out on a cloudy day contributed to the youthful image and gave him an unconscious charm.

She'd liked him from the first. His self-effacing manner hid a droll sense of humor and a sharp intellect, and Fiona understood immediately why her father had trusted him so completely with his Scottish research. Brown spoke Gaelic fluently, the words interspersed with English creating an effortless and unconscious melody. His love for his country and its history was palpable, and she instinctively felt that he could be trusted and he would not betray that trust.

"Doesn't look like much, does it?" he said. "It's been through a lot over the years—you can see where this bottom corner and some of the message has been lost. But it's these seemingly inconsequential notes, written by everyday people, that sometimes yield the most fascinating information or present the best puzzles." He grinned at her dubious look.

Fiona arched her brow. "Hmm, I guess. Dad said it has some mystery connected to our family, but I can't see what he means. There's so little of it left," she said, as she bent over the glass again.

"He's never seen it, has he? All he told me was that there was a mystery and that you could enlighten me about it."

Brown chuckled. "Your father is a hopeless romantic, as I'm sure you know," he said. "I sent him a photo, but it didn't translate to modern technology well. He's never seen the letter itself, no. Still, he agreed with me that it might contain a link to something in your family's past history."

"Look," he said, pointing to a word. "This word, *mo grà*—is cut off, but it could very likely mean *mo ghràidh*, which I'm sure you know means 'my darling.' And these words up here, *Feumaidh mi rabhadh*, mean—"

"'Must warn,'" said Fiona. The professor beamed at her.

"I wonder if the recipient ever got the letter. It seems romantic, but at the same time mysterious." She looked up. "But wait—why do you and Dad think it has something to do with my family?"

"This." Brown pointed to a name. "—*acIllEathain*. It's in the top left corner, all by itself. It's not a stretch to think this is the recipient, and of course you know that *MacIllEathain* is the Gaelic for MacLean. So it's possible that someone was trying to warn someone named MacLean about something."

"But there are hundreds of MacLeans in Scotland, Jeremy." Fiona knitted her brows. "Why does Dad think it's our branch?"

"Ach, William was right about you. You're more of a cynic than he is, which is why I suspect he sent you instead of coming himself. You're going to need convincing. You'll have to be a detective to solve this one. It might be nothing—just a note from a clansman to his lover—but then again, it could mean more."

"More?"

"Look here, the date under the name. 12 A 'Ghiblean, 1746. Does that tell you anything?"

Fiona thought for a moment. "The Battle of Culloden was fought on April 16, 1746. Just days after the date on this letter."

"Right. Some researchers think that this letter writer might be warning someone about something to do with the coming battle." He grinned. "Your father is one of them."

"Well, seems like a stretch, even for my dad," Fiona said, a dubious look on her face. "Maybe it's just a love letter, and the date is coincidental. Where was this found?"

The historian gave her a mysterious smile. "It was discovered in one of the books removed from Raasay House, a castle on the Isle of Raasay. It was pure luck that the message was found at all, since the castle was torched right after Culloden, and even more amazing that this much has survived all this time."

"I still don't see any connection to the Jacobites or Charles Stuart," Fiona said.

"See this name here?" Brown pointed to a faint scribble in the middle of the note. "This name—*MacLeòid*—can you see it there?"

Fiona squinted at the scribble. "If you say so. That's MacLeod, right? Just another Highland clan."

"Ahh, my wee Canadian friend—not just another clan. There were two branches of clan MacLeod back in those days. The MacLeods of Skye fought on the side of the government during every Jacobite rising, including the last. They reaped the rewards of being on the right side of history, so they kept their lands and castles and their wealth after the battle. You should visit Dunvegan Castle on Skye while you're here—it's a masterpiece, and the family still lives there."

"So, maybe the sender of the letter was a MacLeod, from Skye?"

"I doubt it—everybody knew what side they were on—it wasn't a secret. But there's another branch of the MacLeods, and they were Jacobites. There is historical documentation that they sheltered the prince when he first arrived in Scotland and then again, when he was in flight after the Battle of Culloden."

"I don't know much about the MacLeods," admitted Fiona. "There are some on Cape Breton, but I've never followed their history."

"Maybe you should." Brown sat back and folded his arms across his chest. "You might be related to them." His eyes sparkled with the excitement of a detective who has found a clue. She recognized it from spending so much time as her father's assistant, and knew it was contagious.

"Really?"

"The Jacobite MacLeods' seat was on the Isle of Raasay. The clan was never as big or as wealthy as the Skye branch, even before Culloden, but they did well enough." He paused for a long moment, eyes boring through Fiona's.

"And one of the sons was supposed to marry a MacLean—in 1746."

She felt her heart speed up. "And you and Dad think this woman might be an ancestor? Why?"

"Take a trip up to Raasay House. The castle runs tours. You'll understand after you go."

"Can't you tell me now? Why the suspense?"

"Because it's fun." Brown laughed. "Come back after you visit and tell me what you think. What do you have to lose?"

She realized that it was becoming harder to hear

him. Brown's words seemed softer, farther away. His voice receded into the distance until it was a whisper, lost in the howling wind. Wind? Where had the wind come from?

Her thoughts were lost in the rising cacophony that invaded the quiet of the room and drowned out all other sound. Clanging of metal, screams and moans. Smoke-filled air swirled around her, and in the distance she could hear the sound of bagpipes. She knew this place.

She felt the grip of a hand on her arm and was pulled into a hard embrace. A pair of intense blue eyes stared into her own. She could see fear reflected in those eyes. Fear for her.

Fiona stared, mesmerized, into the face of the man from the video presentation at Culloden Visitor Centre. Wild black hair flew in the wind, and she saw her own hand reach to brush the strands away. Her hand disappeared and a sharp pain lanced through her body. Vision narrowed to a pinpoint of light as she felt herself fading.

"Fiona! Miss MacLean! Are you all right?" The noise receded and silence returned to the room. She opened her eyes to find Jeremy Brown's hand on her arm, supporting her as she sagged in the chair. His worried brown eyes studied her. "You're so pale. Are you ill?"

"N-no. What happened?"

"You just froze and stared into the distance, and then you started to slide out of the chair," he said. "Has this happened before? Do you want to go to hospital?"

"No. No, it's never happened before, and no, I don't want to go to the hospital. Probably just delayed jet lag or something." She covered her face to avoid Brown's gaze and forced herself to straighten in the leather chair. "I'll be fine. Let's just get back to work, okay?"

"If you're sure," he said, shaking his head. His brows furrowed. "But if that happens again, I'm taking you straight to Raighmore, understand? I'm responsible for you—can't have you getting sick on my watch. William would kill me." His tone was light but the brown eyes had narrowed and he looked nervous.

He's worried about me. If I told him what just happened—what's happening—he'd be even more concerned—probably send me back to Nova Scotia on the next plane. And why isn't that what I want? It's what I should want.

Her voice came out in a squeak. "I'm fine. Where were we?"

For the next hour they spoke in generalities of clans, battles, and castles. Brown kept it light, but Fiona caught him giving her a sideways glance more than once. They didn't mention the letter again.

With a date to meet next week and a promise from her to visit Raasay House, Fiona left the historian's offices and drove the short distance to her guesthouse on Ardconnell Street. She needed to shut herself up and think about what had happened back there.

She let herself into her room and threw herself down on the bed. Scotland was doing something to her. The dream was no longer confined to the time she was sleeping; it was a daydream now. If it was even a dream at all.

Dreams were fleeting, ethereal things, with elusive fragments that changed and flowed. This one felt too real. The images were solid, and they weren't changing. It was more as if the picture was being enhanced and clarified. Details were being added to the picture—emotions, clarity, physical sensations. Sounds, smells, the feeling of fear and pain.

Fiona sat up suddenly. Pain. This time she had felt pain, as if her stomach was being ripped in two. Just for a second, and then it was gone. But it wasn't her imagination, she was sure. She'd never experienced a pain like that one, and it filled her with fear. Was this going to keep happening?

That wrist grab, and a hard male body. She had *felt* that, in the video room at the Visitor Centre and just now. It wasn't something from memory, because Fiona had never been manhandled like that in her life. Greg at his most petty had never touched her that way.

She lay back down and tried to think. The touch hadn't been aggressive, just shocking in its suddenness. The hand on hers, the arms around her, had felt protective, not dangerous. No, the threat had come from outside. Because even with the horrible noise and the awful stench, she had felt safe in those arms. She had looked into those amazing blue eyes and known she was loved.

She scrambled off the bed and began to pace. She had lied to Jeremy Brown. She wasn't okay. Not by a long shot. She was having visions of a place she'd never seen in her life, and was being held by a man she'd never met . . . Fiona stopped short in the middle of her room, and felt the gorge rise into her throat.

A man she'd never met.

But she *had* met him. The wild black hair, the worried look in those blue eyes . . . she had seen them before. Not just in her dream, or in the video, or in the vision in Brown's office.

The eyes were the same. The arms that had wrapped around her and pulled her out of harm's way were the same arms. It was insane, but it was real.

She had dreamed of this man months before, back home on Cape Breton Island. He was the one she'd kissed in the parking lot of Gaelic College—not Greg. Even then her body had recognized him, although she had never met him and didn't know his name.

And she had seen him again, more recently. The man in her dreams and visions was the man who had rescued her from being run over in the parking lot at Culloden Battlefield.

CHAPTER 15
INVERNESS,
SCOTLAND - PRESENT DAY

*Everyone has that moment I think, the moment
when something so momentous happens that
it rips your very being into small pieces.*
Kathleen Glasgow

Where to start? Fiona sat in the library of the University of the Highlands and Islands and stared at the remains of the note in its glass frame. *Mo ghràidh. Feumaidh mi rabhadh. MacIllEathain. MacLeòid.* Names and words that had been lost in the mists of time. These were people who had lived and died almost three hundred years ago—people who had cared about each other, loved each other. What had happened to them?

Four days after this letter was written, the Highland clans had met the army of the Duke of Cumberland on a spongy moor known then as Drumossie, and had been utterly destroyed. The hopes and dreams of generations of Scots, gone in the space of forty-five minutes and never to return. It was beyond sad.

Her mind forced her back to that video at Culloden Battlefield, and she shivered. The Mackenzies, the MacGillivrays, and her own ancestors had joined other clans intent on returning their homeland to what they thought was its rightful ruler, only to be betrayed by a prince with clay feet who hesitated too long and then ran away to save his own skin.

She took a deep breath, and a wry smile creased her face. *Whoa, lassie! Remember—you're a historian. You're not supposed to get emotional.* But it was hard not to, with the blood of so many generations of displaced Jacobites running through her veins. And since she couldn't decide whether she'd rather punch the Bonnie Prince or "Butcher" Cumberland first, that had to count as being impartial, didn't it?

Fiona dragged herself back to the job at hand. The note had been written in Gaelic, so it was reasonable to assume its author had been a Highlander, and very likely a Jacobite. Writing in the Highland tongue meant that the contents wouldn't be deciphered as quickly were they to fall into the hands of the government forces.

Of course, there were Highlanders in the government army who spoke Gaelic. Contrary to popular belief, the last rising wasn't a contest between the Scots and the English. The Jacobite army hadn't only been made up of Highland clans, or even Scots.

"Only half of the Jacobite Army at Culloden was made up of Highland clansmen," Fiona could hear her father telling his students. "The rest were Lowlanders, French, Irish, and even English regiments, not counting the deserters from the British army who risked more than anyone else if caught."

Fiona smiled, imagining the look of frustration on her father's face every time an innocent student insisted that the Battle of Culloden was about the Scots versus the English.

"Why can't people understand that history is not like the movies," he would sigh. "It's much more complicated, and much more amazing, than anything dreamed up by Hollywood. The government army wasn't all English, either. Lots of Scottish clans supported King George, and they were well rewarded for it. The MacLeods, the Grants, and the Sutherlands kept their lands and became wealthy beyond reckoning."

Fiona returned her attention to the ragged piece of paper under the glass. *Feumaidh mi rabhadh*— "must warn." Who must be warned, and about what? It was so little to go on, but she had always trusted her instincts, and they were telling her now that there was more to this small fragment of frozen history than appearances might indicate.

The note had been found at Raasay House. Her father had told her that his research on the family had led him to the Island of Mull, not Raasay. It was unlikely that a MacLean from Coll could be her ancestor, so why was Jeremy so sure that the writer of this note might be related to her? She'd have to make a trip up to the Isle of Raasay soon to see what had him so excited.

MacLeans of Coll. MacLeods of Skye. MacLeods of Raasay. It was hard to keep track of the participants in this quest, and she was getting a headache. Too much thinking, too little evidence. She grabbed her sweater and backpack and left the stuffy library, intent on clearing her mind with a walk along the river.

Fiona walked along the western side of the Ness away from the center of town. Inverness Castle rose on its hill across the river, and she stopped to admire its red sandstone towers. Fiona knew that this building, by Scottish standards, was barely able to be considered old. It wasn't the first castle to have been built on this hill; the previous structure had been burned down by the Jacobites in 1746 during the Siege of Inverness.

This castle was now the home to mundane government offices. To the eyes of a woman from the New World though, it was old enough, and retained an elegance and beauty unsurpassed by anything she had seen back home.

She continued on past the large hotels that fronted the river and crossed to the other side by the bouncy bridge. She left the river and walked up to the castle to admire the statue of Flora MacDonald, heroine of the last Jacobite rising.

Flora's story was one of Fiona's favorites. Her family supported the government during the rising, but Flora risked everything to give aid to the fleeing Charles Stuart, dressing him as her maid and helping to smuggle him to Skye. For her efforts, she was arrested and held in the Tower of London, but ultimately pardoned due to her family's connections.

She married a British officer and later emigrated with him to North Carolina, and never again wavered in her support of the British government. Fiona had always wondered if her decision to help Prince Charles had been a flash of teenage rebellion or a yearning for adventure, but whatever the reason, she had stepped into the pages of Scottish history and would never be forgotten.

Fiona continued onto the promenade of the High Street, passing shops that sold everything from tartan scarves to keychains sporting goggly-eyed sheep and Highland cows. A young busker stood near the steps that led to Ardconnel Street, playing a spirited version of "Highland Cathedral" for an admiring crowd of tourists who threw coins into his bagpipe case. She closed her eyes and stood for a few moments allowing the music that had moved the Highland armies into battle for centuries to seep into her soul.

A prickling sensation crawled up the back of her neck, and Fiona opened her eyes. She studied the crowd that surrounded the young piper, and stiffened.

Across the circle of listeners stood the man who had pulled her out of the path of a car at the Culloden Visitor's Centre last week. The man who had called her an American—the one to whom she had been unspeakably rude. She had thought she'd never see him again and told herself she was glad. And now here he was, only thirty feet away from her, and he was staring at her in recognition.

She found herself unable to tear her eyes away from that gaze. The black hair tumbled onto his forehead, and he seemed as frozen to the spot as she. Blue eyes locked with green for a long moment, and then he moved around the circle of tourists to stand next to her.

The sound of the music receded into the distance, replaced by a drumming in her ears as Fiona stared at the man. Then he smiled, and she was lost.

Neither spoke. It seemed as if time stood still, like those movies where everything rushes around and past and the protagonists are unable to move. Slowly, the sounds of the High Street began to filter back into her consciousness, but still she stood immobile. The man cleared his throat.

"Um . . . hello." He seemed surprised at the sound of his own voice, and Fiona felt a small smile work its way onto her frozen face. He was as nervous as she.

"Hello," she returned, and then they stood for a while longer, saying nothing. It was enough.

"My name is Ewan. Ewan MacArthur."

"I'm Fiona MacLean. From Canada."

He smiled again. "I'm not likely to forget that, lass."

She could feel the heat rush into her face at the memory. "I'm sorry . . ."

"For what?" The voice was a purr, coated with innocence, but the smile had morphed into a grin.

"For—for calling you a buffoon." His grin grew wider, and Fiona felt a surge of annoyance. She sniffed and raised her head to look him straight in the eye. "I mean, you may very well *be* a buffoon, but I don't know you well enough to judge. I shouldn't have been rude."

At that, he threw his head back and laughed, a deep, throaty chuckle that was the sound equivalent of caramel coated with whisky.

"Aye, you don't know me. But since I don't want

you to feel burdened, I supposed the only thing is to come to know me better. Would you like to have a wee bit of lunch with me?"

No, she didn't want to have lunch with him. She wanted to jump him right here on the street and kiss him until they both melted. She wanted to stare into those amazing blue eyes for all eternity. She wanted to ask him why he was in her dreams, why he had appeared in the video at the Visitor's Centre, why . . .

"Lass?" The soft brogue reached through her mangled brain.

"What? Oh, I'm sorry. I was just—"

"It's true then, what they say." His eyes were dancing. *Did he just read my mind? Oh, shit.*

"W-what they say?"

"That Canadians have a habit of apologizing all the time. How could I ever have missed that?"

"You're making fun of me now, aren't you?" Fiona put her hands on her hips and tried to glare at him, but gave it up as a lost cause because he was smiling again—damn it.

"Of course I am. It's fun. Do you want lunch?"

"Yes." She heard a robotic version of a voice that might have been hers. "I would like to have lunch. Thank you."

Something told her that this was a bad idea—that it was too soon, that she should not be so drawn to him, but she knew it was all just posturing. Her heart had gone over to the enemy, dragging her brain behind like a toy wagon. She could run away later.

They walked in silence back down the High Street until they reached a tavern whose sign proclaimed,

"The Gellions—oldest pub in Inverness." A chalkboard sign next to the ancient door stated, "Freshly caught haggis served here," above a whimsical drawing of a pig-like creature wearing a tammie and lipstick.

"It's not much, mind you, but the food is good, and this is where the locals go," Ewan told her, as he ushered her into the dark interior of the pub.

It was disappointing. No frills, nothing special in the way of decor—just utilitarian tables and two bars. The place was empty except for the two of them.

"Are you sure this is where the locals go?" Fiona said, her voice dubious. "Are the locals sick today?"

"Humph," said Ewan. "You should see the place on Saturday night. Not even standing room. I'll take you sometime and prove it."

Fiona cocked an eye at him, but he was making a study of the bar in the back of the pub. Then he grabbed her hand, and an electric current arced through her at his touch. She pulled her hand away without thinking and tucked it into her sweater pocket.

He pulled out an old metal chair and Fiona sat, numb. She stared into the beautiful blue eyes and wondered how she understood that he drank Talisker whisky, that he was artistic, that he loved books and reading. She didn't know him at all, and yet she did. Time was blurring at the edges, and she felt an excitement building inside her that battled a fear for this man so strong that it took her breath away. She felt tears welling and was at a loss as to their origin.

This is moving too fast. What the hell is going on here?

CHAPTER 16

INVERNESS,
SCOTLAND - PRESENT DAY

I live my life until I start the cycle of my dreams,
then I leave and search for you until I die.
Molly Bryant

Five drams in, he was telling her everything. About his business, his love for scrambling, his estrangement from his family, even about his mother's death. In sixteen years, he had never told anyone about the darkness that resided in his heart. He'd held it close, wrapped it in gauze, but here he was spilling everything out to this stranger.

And she was listening. He had never met anyone before who could give every bit of her attention to another person the way Fiona MacLean was doing right now. Her body stilled, her hands intertwined on the table, and her only movement was the occasional blinking of those incredible green eyes.

Those eyes. He had seen them before; he was sure of it now. As his body plummeted off the cliff edge at Aonach Eagach, he had seen that flash of green in his mind. A part of him had known since that day at Culloden what that flash was, but the impossibility of it had kept the knowledge safely tucked away.

And now she was here, like a tether to his memories. They flooded back like the waves in the North Sea. The sound of boots on the trail, the sensation of something just behind him—the hard push against his back that sent him flying out into the air.

"I *was* pushed," he said, in wonder. "Someone pushed me off that cliff. It wasn't an accident."

"And you didn't remember this until now?" Fiona's question was soft, but he heard the slight tremble in her voice and was strangely comforted. *She cares.* It was strange, knowing that someone else besides Adam worried about him. He hadn't felt anything like this for a long, long time, and it left him slightly dazed.

"No, not until just now. And the strange thing is . . ." he hesitated, wondering if this would prove to her that he was insane, and decided it didn't matter. He had to tell her.

". . . .he strange thing is, I felt as if you were there, in my mind. I didn't know it was you then, but it was. We hadn't met, but you were there. Maybe you even saved my life." He stopped, and then went on, his voice thick. "I know, I sound crazy. Are you going to run for the hills now—what? What's wrong?"

She was staring at him, his shock mirrored in her eyes. It wasn't caused by his fanciful confession—there was something more here. She took a sip of her whisky with a shaking hand and put it back down, holding the glass with both hands to keep it from spilling.

"I have something to tell you, Ewan. And when I'm done, we'll see who runs for the hills. Will you hear me out without judging?" There was such a plea in her eyes that in that moment he would have promised her anything.

"Aye, lass, I'll hear you out. It can't be any stranger than what I just told you, now can it?" He kept his voice light and registered her nervous laugh as she sat up straighter in her chair and leaned forward.

"You might be surprised." She took a long breath and told him. About the recurring dream, the blood, the bagpipes, the cacophony of sound and the screams of dying men.

"It's been going on for months now. I've never seen war, I don't even watch that stuff on TV. I'm a historian, so of course I know in an academic way what happens during a battle, but this was different. I could hear it, feel it, *smell* it. The blood and the sweat. I was there—and so were you."

"What?" He'd thought he was prepared for anything, but this was nuts. And yet he believed her. After his own experience, how could he not?

"Tell me."

"You appeared in front of me in the middle of the battle. I could see you clearly—your eyes, your hair—it was longer, but it was the same. And I think you were protecting me."

"Do you know where this was? Could you tell when this happened?" Ewan heard himself asking questions about things that should have seemed ridiculous, and yet were as real as Gellions, as real as the whisky in the glasses before them on the table.

"I know exactly where it was. And when." Fiona took a shuddering breath, and without thinking Ewan reached across the table and took her hands in his.

"It was the Battle of Culloden. And I don't think it was a dream."

He stared. "What?" His hands tightened. "Why do you think that?"

"Because I saw you again—that day at the Visitor's Centre. In the video." She let out her breath, and suddenly she was crying, soft, helpless sobs that were more air than substance.

Ewan ran a thumb under her eye to wipe away the tears, and she looked at him with a watery smile.

"There's more," she said.

"Of course there is," he muttered, and then they were both laughing. *We're drunk, that's what it is. Tomorrow we'll realize what eejits we're being right now. Fanciful eejits. We'll go our separate ways and forget all about this. I'll never see her again.* As he thought the words, he knew them for the lies they were. No amount of alcohol could explain this away, and there was no way on earth he was letting this woman go. That ship had sailed.

"You were dressed as a British soldier," Fiona told him.

"Achh, what?" Ewan sat up straight.

Fiona laughed. "So, were your ancestors Jacobites, then? Have I insulted your clan?"

Ewan grinned, looked at the table for a moment, and then met her eyes again, all mirth gone. "Well, we were hereditary pipers to the MacDonalds of the Isles, and they were Jacobites. To be honest, though, the MacArthurs are a sept of clan Campbell, and the Campbells fought with the British army during every Jacobite rising. I suppose it's not that surprising that an ancestor would've been wearing the British army's uniform." He stopped and thought over what he'd just said.

"I think we're getting ahead of ourselves here." He squeezed the hand he was still holding. "Assuming you're right about the time and place of your dreams, or visions, or whatever they are—why does a dream about a time three hundred years ago have meaning for us, now?" He captured the green eyes with his own gaze. "Why do you see *me*?"

"I don't know," she said, holding his gaze with her own. "All I know is that before a couple of months ago, I never in my life had the same dream twice. I rarely dream in color, and I absolutely never smell and hear anything like the things I've experienced in these dreams."

"But why you?" Ewan wrinkled his brow. "Why are you dreaming about *me*? I've never had a dream like that."

"How should I know?" Fiona blew out a frustrated breath. "I'm just telling you what has happened to me. People don't decide what to dream, you know."

"Do you think . . ." Ewan stopped. "Never mind."

"No, tell me. I need all the help I can get here."

His look was measured. "Do you believe in past lives?"

"You mean, like reincarnation?" Fiona thought

for a long time. "I'll be honest. I've thought about it since the dreams . . . a lot. But no, I don't believe in reincarnation."

"Just because you don't believe in it, doesn't mean it's not true," Ewan said. "Let's look at the facts that are indisputable. I saw you before I met you—okay, just once and just your eyes, and I thought I was going to die so I don't know if it counts—but it happened. Fact."

Fiona was quiet for a moment. "I've seen you in dreams, and again at the Culloden Visitors Centre. That's a fact."

"I recognized you when I did finally meet you, in the parking lot." Ewan's mouth quirked into a wry smile. "Maybe that's why I reacted the way I did."

"I didn't recognize you at first—sorry about that," Fiona said. "But later, when I was in a meeting with my father's friend Jeremy Brown—he's a historian at the University—I had a vision and almost passed out. That's when I realized it was you I'd seen in the video." She shuddered at the recollection. "The video is in black and white, but somehow I knew your eyes were blue. And that's another fact."

"So what does it mean?" Ewan stood and began to pace the empty tavern. "I mean, it seems like a lot of work for the fates to go through just to get a lad to meet a lass."

"Professor Brown told me to go up to Raasay House. He said I'll understand more after I go on the tour," Fiona said. She hesitated. "Would you—would you go with me?"

His answer was immediate. "Of course, on one

condition. You have to come meet my family and do a tour of the distillery. I told you about my father. He wants me to 'let bygones be bygones.'" His tone was bitter. "After sixteen years of rejection, he wants me to come home." He gave Fiona an imploring look. "I don't think I can do it alone. Will you be my shield man?"

"Ugh. You want me to crash a happy family reunion?" Fiona shuddered. "From what you've told me, *you* meeting your family will be problematic enough. Explaining me will make it even more complicated. But hey, sure, sounds like fun. Anyway, you're going to Raasay with me, so fair's fair."

Ewan had never realized how much he'd been counting on her answer, or how much he'd dreaded meeting his family again. Up until now, he hadn't seriously considered following through with his father's request, no matter how shocking the old man's breakdown had been.

But with Fiona's support, things that had seemed impossible were entering the realm of normalcy. He didn't know how he was going to introduce her, but he'd face that when the time came. She would be by his side—that was enough.

He looked across the table, wondering at the vagaries of fate. Two hours ago, he never would have believed that they would be sitting here in his favorite pub, talking about past lives and reincarnation as if it were something bandied about every day.

She looked back at him, and Ewan felt as if her green eyes saw right into his soul. This stuff had to be real. Living proof was sitting right across from him.

Fiona removed her hand from his and laced her

fingers together again. She gave him an even glance, paused, and then spoke in a low tone. "There's something else that we need to think about."

"Aye?"

"If your memories of that day on the mountain are correct, your life may be in danger. People don't just throw other people off cliffs on a whim. You need to be thinking about people who have an axe to grind with you. Have you crossed someone in your business?"

Ewan paused, startled. "I don't think so. The tour industry is competitive, but it's not cutthroat. I don't think I'm a threat to anyone. My company is kind of unique, really. No, I'm sure it's not that." He tried a weak grin. "I'm actually kind of a nice lad, you know."

Fiona ignored the attempt at levity. "Then, who's left? Your family?"

"They've left me alone for sixteen years. I was dead to them already, why would they decide to off me now?"

"I don't know, but you need to take this seriously." Fiona's look was stubborn. "You were pushed off that trail. If you hadn't caught onto that rock spar—if there hadn't been a ledge below you, if you hadn't been lucky—" She looked at him, her face serious.

"We would never have met. That's a fact. No matter how we look at it, your fall was no accident. Someone was up on that trail for a reason. They came up there for one thing.

"Someone wanted you dead."

CHAPTER 17

RAASAY, SCOTLAND - 1746

EILIDH

This was going to kill her, there was no question about it. It was only the third day of sitting in front of this beast of an artist, but every muscle in her body felt like screaming from being held captive.

She would never look at a portrait again without thinking of the torture those poor souls had gone through to be up on that wall. She hoped the limner was good enough to avoid painting the excruciating boredom that had to be fixed on her face.

At least this was a step further toward the wedding. Her portrait would hang in the great hall with the others—the latest MacLeod bride, wife of the future laird. She wasn't sure how she felt about that—for one thing, the thought of hanging out on the wall with Cullen's mother was somewhat nauseating.

Lady MacLeod had changed her tactics recently; where before she had ignored her future daughter-in-law, now she favored her with what Eilidh assumed were supposed to be smiles. More like grimaces—a crocodile would have been impressed. She was probably up to something; there was no earthly way the woman could be softening.

She tried to ease the cramp in her back without moving and searched for a bright side. All right. The sittings would be over at some point, she wasn't really likely to die, and there would be a wedding eventually. It wasn't as if she had a choice, and at least the bridegroom was presentable. More than presentable—so why did she feel depressed?

Her confusion was building again at thoughts of Cullen. He was like a work of art. He seemed to have no discernible flaws at all—almost *too* perfect. It was ridiculous, but there was something worrying at the edges of her mind, playing games with her emotions. Was it her fault? She had been adamant about not marrying—was that the problem? Did Cullen perhaps sense that reticence in her? People here, with the exception of Lady MacLeod and Godfrey Lewis, had been nothing but kind. She was permitted the run of the castle. A new wardrobe was being commissioned—beautiful gowns that should have sent her to the pinnacle of happiness. So what was the problem?

"Miss MacLean," the exasperated voice of the limner told her that *he*, at least, was not interested in her dilemma. "Only a few minutes more, and then you can rest. Please?"

"I am sorry." She forced her face back into the mask that she was sure was going to crack soon and tried to rein in her thoughts. No use. The thing was, she had nothing to do here but think.

I'm lonely. I have never been so lonely.

It was the truth. She rarely saw Cullen. When she did, he was charming and kind, but there was a distance there that she could not breach. She had initially assumed he was shy, but now she wasn't sure. He was lively enough around Godfrey and Dom, laughing and joking, but with her he seemed always on guard. He was like two different people, and she was beginning to realize that she wasn't as fond of either as she had once thought she was.

That was how infatuation worked. She'd been mesmerized by his beauty, awed by his power and prestige. The real Cullen, the one she was going to spend the rest of her life with, was . . . boring.

He treated his parents with respect, his brother Hugh with affection. Even Rory received more attention than she did. But the lion's share of Cullen's attention went to that loathsome friend of his.

Avoiding Godfrey was a full-time job, and since that day in the library last month she never went anywhere without looking behind her at every other step. She checked the hallways before stepping out of her room, never made eye contact with him at dinner, and had stopped following Cullen because Godfrey was so often his shadow.

Where did the man live? Did he not have family—a

job of some sort? He seemed to be at Raasay most of the time. Her curiosity, which had been growing since that day in the library, was only matched by her fear of the man. In order to find out more about him she would have to get close enough to ask, and *that* was not happening.

Who had been talking in that locked room? She had no doubt that Godfrey knew. And she was equally certain that he'd pulled her back and away from that door on purpose. He had frightened her so that she would be afraid of him—and it had worked.

It might just have been a business meeting, but everything about that incident had screamed secrecy, and the more she thought, the more she wanted to find out why. It was a mystery, and Eilidh loved mysteries. She straightened her shoulders. When this evil painter released her, she was going to investigate that room.

A smile crept over her face at the thought of something to do. She had a mission. She would watch out for Godfrey, and she would listen. Something odd was going on here, and she was going to find out what it was.

"My lady," the painter's tired voice said, "I can't work if you keep changing your expression. It is quite obvious that you are tired. I think we will continue tomorrow, if that suits you."

Eilidh almost bounded out of the chair in her eagerness to escape. Tired? Little did the man know. She was anything but tired, and it was time to stop being a milkweed and do something.

She made her way toward the library, scouting

every corner and alcove for signs of the hateful Godfrey. As she approached the double doors to the room that she knew better than any other in this castle, she stopped short. The sound of voices came to her from within. She stepped inside to find two men seated at the round table in the center of the library.

One of them she knew. Hugh MacLeod gestured to something in a book that lay open between the men, his grey eyes shining the way they always did when literature was involved. His thin face was animated and held an unusual trace of color, and Eilidh's heart warmed.

Hugh was such a dear. He was shy and reserved, and at first she had thought him standoffish, but when the subject turned to his books he became another person—witty, outgoing, and charming. He was the most important person to her here next to Rory, and they had begun to form a bond shared in the love of words.

Eilidh's eyes followed Hugh's gesturing hand and focused on the other man. Tall, she could tell even though he was sitting, and lean rather than muscular. She registered a plain brown suit that should have been dull, but on this man seemed to give him an air of authority. Untidy black hair stuck out all over his head as if he had been running his hands through it. She found herself chuckling at the sight.

The man looked up at the sound. Brilliant blue eyes found hers, and time stood still. She felt her heart stop and then quicken, and she knew that, were she to look into a mirror, her cheeks would be flushed.

She had never seen this man before, and yet she felt somehow as if she knew him. The feeling was strange, and frightening, and suddenly she wanted nothing more than to flee the library and hide in her room.

Hugh looked up and smiled at her.

"Eilidh! I am glad you are here. Please meet our house guest, Mr. MacCrimmon." He has come over from the MacLeods of Skye, and you will be happy to know that he *reads*. Is that not wonderful?"

Eilidh forced her feet to move forward. She placed her hand in the outstretched one of the stranger, and a jolt of electricity ripped through her. She was sure she saw an answering shock reflected in those sea-blue eyes.

"Hello. I'm Iain," a husky voice said.

A single thought made its way through her muddled brain.

I am in trouble.

CHAPTER 18

RAASAY HOUSE, SCOTLAND - 1746

IAIN

"Ach, she's a beauty!" Iain's tone was reverent. "An Eriskay, is she no?"

"Aye." Rory looked at his friend with surprise. "You know your horses."

"We've had a few Eriskay ponies over the years, in Arg—back home." Iain took a deep breath and turned to study the horse to cover his slip.

This espionage was hard. Trying to be a MacCrimmon from Skye was stressful when you didn't play the bagpipes and you'd never been to Skye. He just wasn't cut out for subterfuge. Under his breath, he cursed Colonel Buchanan for choosing him, wondering for the hundredth time why it had to be him.

He liked Ruaridh MacLean and hated lying to him. The young constable was open and friendly, and Iain had been drawn to him immediately. Curly red hair framed an open, honest face with astonishing green eyes that sparkled even in the dim light of the stable. In another world, another time, Iain knew they could have been good friends, despite the differences in their politics.

Rory was a staunch Jacobite, passionate and forthcoming about his beliefs. The true king was coming, he told Iain, and when he did, Scotland would be free from the oppressive rule of the usurper in London. Rory MacLean should have been a preacher, Iain thought; from his lips the heretical assertions seemed rational. Or maybe he'd been here too long.

For once Iain thanked God that he was supposed to be a MacCrimmon; it was like having a free passage card anywhere. People told him of their own political beliefs and expected none from him.

Not everything about him was a sham, he assured himself. He did know his horses, and this one was an exceptional animal. Eriskay ponies were rare and valuable. Good mounts, with wide heads and deep chests, they were intelligent and easy to train. This one was black, with a shiny coat and long, flowing tail.

"What's her name?" Iain asked.

"Mirain," Rory told him, patting the horse's gleaming flank with affection. "His lordship bought her to be his new daughter-in-law's mount. Name means 'beautiful,' which makes her a perfect match for Eilidh."

"Eilidh? You call your mistress by her first name?" Iain was taken aback. Surely this was inappropriate.

Rory chuckled at the look on Iain's face. "Sure I do. What else am I going to call my sister?" The laugh was cut off as he added in a tight voice, "And she's not the mistress yet."

The clipped words caught Iain's attention. The constable's face had darkened. Gone was the open, carefree look, replaced by a hard set to the jaw and narrowed eyes.

"You don't like your sister's betrothed?" Iain asked, keeping his tone even.

"Nothing not to like," Rory said. He shrugged and turned away to brush the horse with rapid strokes. "Cullen's a paragon. Handsome, rich, smart. Has it all."

"But you don't like him."

Rory sighed and put down the brush. He turned to face Iain and crossed his arms over his chest.

"Aye. I don't like him. I can't say why, but I don't think he's right for my sister."

"And what does she think?"

The lad shrugged. "I don't know. She says he's fine, but her eyes say something different. I don't think he pays her enough attention, and if he doesn't do it now, it's not likely to get better when they're married." He picked up the brush again. "Don't mind me. Probably nobody would be good enough for my sister as far as I'm concerned." He gave Iain a strained smile.

"You're close?"

"Aye. We're twins. There's this bond between us—always has been. We can sort of read each other, ye ken? And I think she's trying to block me, which means she's hiding something. She just seems . . . sad."

He laughed. "Listen to me, going on like that when we've really just met. You'll think I'm daft."

"No, it's fine," Iain assured him. "I envy you, having a relationship like that. I don't have any brothers or sisters to worry about—it's just my father and me."

"Listen," Rory stopped currying the pony and gave Iain a steady gaze. "I don't know you very well—I mean we've just met, but I feel as if we are already friends. I think I can trust you."

Iain hoped the red flush that rose up his neck was not as visible as it felt. If the lad only knew! He felt a stab of disgust at the situation his colonel had put him in.

The young constable seemed not to notice. He lowered his voice and moved closer to Iain.

"Can you do me a favor while you're here? You being at the big house and all."

"Of course," Iain assured him, hoping that this 'favor' wasn't going to get him in even deeper than he was now. He hadn't found anything to report back, or even anything interesting, during his visit to the MacLeods of Raasay. They were Jacobites, but none of them seemed particularly passionate about it, and they weren't about to share any secrets with a stranger anyway. This all seemed like a huge waste of time.

Still, when Rory voiced his concern about Cullen MacLeod, Iain had felt a cold sensation slither up his spine and lodge in his chest. Because he felt the same about the future laird. There was something off about Cullen. He bore watching.

Maybe it wasn't Cullen. That friend of his—Godfrey Lewis—now there was a snake in the grass if he'd ever seen one. He seemed to be made of darkness—dressed entirely in black, said little in company, and there was a hooded set to his face that was impossible to read. No matter how hard Iain tried, he could not get past the shadows that surrounded the man.

A part of him knew that Cullen, and even Godfrey, were not the real problem for him—or at least not all of it. The truth was something he could not share with Rory, because it concerned his friend's beloved twin sister.

Ever since he had met Eilidh MacLean in the library, he'd been unable to concentrate. When he tried, the image of Cullen MacLeod's future wife rose up and drove everything else away.

Brilliant green eyes, curling auburn hair, pale skin with a scattering of freckles across her small nose. He found himself looking for her everywhere, listening for her soft step and lilting voice with its island accent. They had exchanged a total of ten words, but every one of them was engraved on his mind.

"Iain?" He turned to find Rory staring at him. "Did you hear what I said?"

"W-what? Oh, sorry. Mind was wandering for a moment there. You were saying?"

"Will you keep an eye on my sister? See that she's all right? Talk to her—see that she's not so lonely. Let me know if there's a problem."

"Uhh . . ."

"You'll like her. I promise. I know it's asking a lot, but I do trust you. Just be her friend. Will you do it?" Rory's face shone with sincerity.

"Of—course. I don't know what I can do, but I'll try to help."

As he stumbled out of the stable, he was reminded of a fox who has been cornered by hounds. Standing alone, surrounded by enemies, waiting for death and hoping it's a quick one.

I trust you. Just be her friend. Oh, you eejit.

CHAPTER 19

HIGHLANDS,
SCOTLAND - PRESENT DAY

Moments, when lost, can't be found
again. They're just gone.
Jenny Han

Wild Thyme Distillery was, in the Highland tradition, a white brick building with black lettering in Celtic script on the front. It sat back from the single-track road, surrounded by fields of placid sheep and framed by heather-covered mountains.

"It's like a painting," Fiona said. "I've never seen anything so beautiful."

"Aye, I suppose." Ewan's smile seemed forced. "It's a bonnie place. Better on the outside—I prefer the sheep to the people."

She laughed. "Tell me how you really feel."

He flushed. "Let's get this over with, aye?" He moved to the large wooden door in the front of the building with obvious reluctance. "We're meeting with my father in an hour, so I'll give you the tour first. And remember to take notes for your book."

It had been Ewan's idea to create a cover story to explain the reason for her presence. She gave him a dubious look that said, "*do you really think that will fly?*" but grabbed a notebook and went along without complaint. This was his show; she was only here for support.

A few heads turned in their direction when they walked into the sales room of the distillery. Behind the counters, one or two employees stopped what they were doing and glanced at the new arrivals, before returning to the business of packaging whisky or arranging tours. No one seemed to recognize the oldest son of Wild Thyme Distillery.

One employee proved the exception. An elderly man dressed in the MacArthur tartan hurried over and extended his hand. Ewan took it gingerly, as if it were a snake that might bite him at any second.

"Albert. It's been a long time." His voice was flat, but Fiona could hear the tension underlying the words.

"It's good to see ye again, lad," the man said. He gave a vigorous nod. "Your father told me ye were coming. And who is this lovely lady?"

"Ah," Ewan blinked. "This is Fiona MacLean, visiting from Canada. She's a writer, doing research on whisky for her next novel. This is Albert Drummond, my father's assistant. He knows more about the distilling business than anyone on Earth."

The older man gave Fiona a courtly bow. "Nice to meet ye, ma'am. Hope I can be of some help with your book. Master Ewan is exaggerating some, but I suppose I do ken a wee bit about whisky."

Ewan snorted, and the tension was broken. Fiona smiled at the older man and was rewarded with the sweetest smile she had ever seen on a human being.

"I used to chase this young rascal around the distillery when he was a small lad," Drummond said, and sighed. "It took everything I had to keep him from falling into the wash tubs." He looked at Ewan, an anxious look on his weathered features. "Ye aren't planning any such shenanigans today, are ye?"

"We'll see," Ewan told him. He gave the old man a level stare. "It's been a long time since I was a small lad, Albert."

Albert Drummond's eyes misted and he cleared his throat.

"I'm sorry, lad. I should've kept in touch. Ye deserved better."

There was silence for a minute. Then Ewan patted him on the arm. "It takes two. I didn't try very hard, either."

"Ach. Well, c'mon, then. What're ye waiting for?" Drummond turned and moved quickly toward a doorway leading from the showroom. Ewan nodded to Fiona and they hurried to catch up.

"This, lass, is the wash room, where the distillation begins. You know how water evaporates and then cools and returns to earth as rain? It's the same procedure, only we make it do what we want," the old man told Fiona. "These are the pot stills," he added, pointing to four huge copper vessels that resembled Hershey's kisses with tall chimneys. She felt her eyes glazing.

"Hehmm," Ewan cleared his throat. Fiona looked over to see him gesturing at her forgotten notebook. She nodded and began to scribble in the booklet: "pot stills," "distillation," "look like gnome hats," "how the hell did I get myself into this?" She gave Albert a look of rapt attention, and he beamed.

"Come here," he motioned, and guided her to where a man stood looking through a small oval window in the pot. "Hello, Sam," he addressed the employee, who nodded and stepped aside. Drummond directed Fiona to take Sam's place. "What do ye see?"

"Um, bubbles?" She ventured and was rewarded with another beatific smile.

"Aye, lass. This is the wash, otherwise known as beer. Hot steam comes in up here—" he pointed to the cylindrical chimneys, "and the wash heats and bubbles. Sam's a 'still man.' It's his job to keep a watch on the wash to make sure the temperature doesn't get too high. If it does, liquid can get into the con-denser, and . . ."

Fiona looked down at her notebook. Her nonsense syllables had become squiggles that meandered over the paper like worms on the sidewalk after a heavy rain. She sighed and tried to pay attention.

Who knew a distillery tour could be so boring? People on cruises paid a lot of money for this, but for the life of her she couldn't figure out why.

She found out the reason at the end of the tour, when Albert Drummond finally ran out of words and led them to the tasting room. People stood around in groups, listening to a young man in a MacArthur kilt wax on about the various whiskys created here while they sent longing looks at the small glasses in front of them.

"Wild Thyme is one of the smaller distilleries in the Highlands, but that's on purpose," Drummond whispered. "Quality over quantity, ye ken." The old man sounded reverent, as if drinking whisky was akin to worship. And maybe it was, for those who liked the stuff.

Fiona looked over at Ewan to find him staring off into the middle distance. She moved closer and tapped his arm.

"Are you all right?"

He looked startled for a second, as if he'd forgotten she was there, and Fiona remembered that, despite the dream connection and immediate attraction, they were virtual strangers.

What am I doing here? Why am I so impulsive? She backed away, creating a distance between them.

Something in her face must have alerted him to her mood because Ewan reached out to take her hand—and there it was again, that jolt of power that raced through her body like an electric charge.

". . . .nd this is our twelve-year whisky. It's our most popular and is a staple in many pubs and taverns around the world." The sommelier's voice filtered through the haze and into Fiona's consciousness. She turned to find a small wooden tray before her, containing four small tasting glasses, one of which was filled with an amber liquid. People around the tables eyed the glasses in front of them but waited patiently for the signal from their guide.

Without coherent thought, Fiona reached for her glass and downed the stuff in two gulps. She looked up to find the young sommelier gaping at her in surprise and mustered up a weak smile.

"Umm. It's good." That was a lie—it burned its way down her throat as if she had inhaled fire like a circus performer. The way people were staring at her, maybe they were visualizing the same thing. Water streamed from her eyes and she struggled to keep a cough at bay.

A soft chuckle came from behind her, and she turned to find a pair of clear blue eyes sparkling with mirth.

"Are you all right?" Ewan said, in an echo of her earlier words. "That's . . . um . . . a very interesting way to taste whisky. You must really like it."

Fiona flushed scarlet. She lowered her head and stared at the table, only to see that another glass in her tray had been filled with whisky.

"Now I want you to taste one of our prize brews, the Wild Thyme Distiller's Choice," the sommelier said, pride evident in his tone. "It's not readily available outside Scotland and the price is a bit of an adventure, but I think you'll enjoy the experience. Take just a sip, like this—" he demonstrated, and eager hands reached for the glasses of whisky. "Now you can see why I have the best job in the distillery. Sláinte!"

Ewan took his own sample and held it up toward Fiona. With a grimace, she picked up the glass from her tray and followed his example. He tapped his tiny glass against hers.

"Sláinte!"

She took a minuscule sip of the whisky this time, and let it slide over her tongue as the sommelier had demonstrated.

"Oooh. It *is* good!" Amazed, she took another sip.

"That's the way, lassie," Albert Drummond told her. "Ye've got whisky in your blood, ye do!"

"Don't get too used to it, lass, not many can afford this one," Ewan cautioned her. "It's Dad's pride and joy."

He sighed and put his own sample down. "Speaking of which, it's time to meet my father. Are you ready?"

"Are you?" she asked him, studying his face. "You look like a man going to his execution. Is he that bad?"

Ewan's face was tight. "Probably won't seem that way to you. Anyway, how would I know? I hadn't seen him for sixteen years, until last week."

He shrugged. "You haven't met him, but you probably know him almost as well as I do. Lead on, Albert." He turned without another word and followed the assistant out of the room and down a hallway.

Fiona watched the set of his shoulders and felt a surge of anger toward the man she was about to meet. How could a father abandon his own son without a backwards glance, over something that wasn't even his fault?

She thought of her own father—of the trust and pride that shone from his eyes every time he looked at his children. She was one of the lucky ones, for sure. She wished she didn't have to meet this sad specimen of parenthood at all. He must be a horrible human being, and her heart ached for the small boy Ewan had been.

A protective feeling flooded her, and she fought

to keep her anger at bay. No, she didn't know Ewan MacArthur well, but she knew one thing. She wasn't going to let anything—or anyone—hurt this man, no matter what she had to do. The strength of that feeling took her by surprise, but she held onto it like a talisman. Whether it was the dream, or fate, or any of the silly superstitions that flooded the world, she was bonded to this man for better or for worse—and his father be damned.

Albert Drummond took them down a long hallway past doors that gave no clue to their purpose in the running of the whisky business and stopped outside a door at the end of the hall. "I'll leave you here, sir," Drummond said, as he stepped back into the hall-way. "He's expecting you." He held the door open and stepped back.

Fiona looked around. They were in an outer recep-tion area, from which two doors with frosted glass panes led to further rooms. The desk to the left of the doorway where they stood was untenanted at pres-ent. The glass in the door to their right was unmarked, but the one across the room bore the words "Duncan MacArthur, President" etched into the glass. A simple proclamation that here was the real power behind the workings of Wild Thyme Whisky.

They stepped into an opulent office. Bookshelves lined two walls, and framed certificates dominated the far wall. The floor was covered with an orien-tal carpet in shades of red and gold, the colors of the labels Fiona had seen on bottles of Wild Thyme Whisky, and a glass case displayed individual bottles in their own cases. Fiona noticed trophies in the case on the north wall, honoring excellence in whisky achievement. It was a room that exuded success and understated elegance.

The room was silent—the quiet that pervades a space empty of human life. In the center of the room was a huge walnut desk, and behind the desk, in a high-backed leather chair, sat the owner and president of Wild Thyme Whisky. The only thing that stood out in the tranquil tableau was the posture of the man slumped back in the chair, and the blue eyes that stared sightlessly at the ceiling.

CHAPTER 20
GLENCOE,
SCOTLAND - PRESENT DAY

And that is how change happens. One gesture.
One person. One moment at a time.
Libba Bray

Ewan rubbed bloodshot eyes and stared unsee-ing at the mountain, unable to process what had happened two weeks before. Two weeks in which he hadn't had a single good night's sleep.

Dead. His father was dead.

A heart attack, the doctor said. Just one of those things that came out of nowhere and struck down the strong and the feeble with equal indifference.

Ewan shivered and zipped up his jacket. Was he partly to blame? Had the stress of his father's effort at reconciliation been too much to bear after all these years? If Ewan had accepted his apology, would his father be here today?

I can't ever forgive you.

You stole sixteen years of my life, turned my family

against me. I hate you for that.

I hate you.

I hate you.

He stood at the base of the Aonach Eagach ridge, staring up at the ledge that had saved his life. Such a small difference, between life and death. Hatred and love. Anger and forgiveness.

Three months ago, someone had pushed him off that ridge, intending him to die. And now . . .

I think someone is trying to kill me.

Cryptic words from a man who abhorred mystery. Duncan MacArthur was practical and ruthless in business, a no-nonsense leader who had no patience for fantasy. And yet, he had been sure that something was wrong, that his life was in danger.

There have been—incidents—at the distillery.

Ewan shook his head to clear the swirling thoughts. What were the facts? Why was his brain telling him there was more to this story? His mind began to construct a list.

Fact. Someone *had* tried to kill Ewan, twice—had almost succeeded.

Fact. His father had thought someone was trying to harm him. Food poisoning, a gas leak. Things that didn't add up.

Fact. His father was dead.

We're not even family anymore.

Ewan flinched. He had seen the pain in his father's eyes at his words, thought he didn't care, and now it was too late. But it was true—they hadn't been family for a very long time—so what was bothering him?

I want to make you the heir to the distillery.

The distillery. At the center of everything was Wild Thyme. Ewan had no interest in the family business; he'd been on his own for so many years, found his own niche in the world and become successful in his own right. But his father had had other ideas.

He felt a pang of grief arc through him, the stronger for being so unexpected. He'd thought he had nothing in common with his father, had made his peace with a life without family. So why did it hurt so damn much?

That day two weeks ago, a day that was marked on his brain like a brand. He was going to tell his father that he would not accept it—neither the distillery nor any kind of reconciliation with a family who had walked away from him and never looked back.

He had walked into his father's office intending to put an end to the ridiculous idea of inheriting a business he had never wanted. He would look into those eyes and tell Duncan MacArthur where he could shove his eleventh-hour attempt at fatherhood.

Instead, the eyes into which he'd looked were vacant, lifeless shells that mocked his righteousness and stole his anger. Even now, staring up at the cliff ledge, all he could see were those eyes. Blue like his own, staring at nothing. All that was left of a man who had created one of the most successful distilleries in Scotland—a man who had it all and gave away what was most important.

What had changed? Why, after all these years, had his father sought him out? Was it fear?

I think someone is trying to kill me.

Was that it—fear for his life? Or was there something

more? Did he know there was something wrong with his heart? Had he been trying to make amends knowing that his time might be running out? Ewan remembered the pain in those eyes as Duncan MacArthur sat in the car beside his son and said he was sorry.

It's too little, way too late.

That had been his answer, to a man who had mustered his courage and overcome his pride to approach his son and apologize. Self-disgust swamped him where he stood on the trail, and he leaned against the rock face for support.

He was a grown man. Yes, he'd been a child when his mother died, an innocent. There was no reason he could have understood the betrayal of the person he had looked up to as a god—not then.

But now he was an adult, and had been one for some time. At any time in the last ten years, he could have taken that first step—made the effort to reconnect, to understand. Fear and anger had held him back, and now it was too late.

It takes two to destroy a relationship. Ewan let the knowledge sink in, his head bowed, and then he turned and made his way back to the car park.

Adam was waiting for him beside the car. His brown eyes were damp and his young face creased with concern.

"Are you all right?" he asked.

"No."

"You don't have to do this, you know," Adam put a hand on his arm. "We can tell Mr. Arbuthnot you're not well. Reading Dad's will is just a formality, anyway. He always said the distillery would go to Iseabail as the oldest, and the rest of us would be provided for—" He stopped and looked away. "I'm sorry."

Ewan patted his brother on the shoulder. "It's all right. I never expected anything from him. But Arbuthnot called me and told me to be there, so I don't see how I can avoid it, aye?" He mustered a thin smile. "As you say, it's just a formality."

"Do we have time for a dram before we go?" Adam's voice was hopeful. "Or maybe a bottle?"

Ewan laughed, a short, bitter sound. "That would seal the deal, wouldn't it? The black sheep comes staggering in guttered? Maybe I could pass out in the middle of the floor, or throw up on Aaron's impeccable shoes."

He sighed. "No, much as I don't think of them as family, I don't hate them. Or at least I'm trying not to. How's this for a happy face?" He leered at his brother, and Adam flinched.

"Practice on the way there, aye?" He climbed into the driver's seat and waited for Ewan to get in and buckle up. Then he turned his head to regard his brother. "I—I know you wouldn't, but there's no chance you'd make a scene, is there?" He looked almost hopeful, and Ewan was struck again with gratitude that this brother was by his side.

"Well, we'll have to see, won't we? For now, just leave me be so I can practice my smile, aye?"

The lawyer had chosen to hold this meeting in the conference room at Wild Thyme Distillery. Ewan paused in the outer office and let Adam go ahead of him while he pulled himself together. The office smelled of old leather and furniture polish, overlaid with a familiar floral scent. That would be Miss Beck, Ewan thought, and smiled despite himself.

Ariadne Beck had started as his father's secretary when she was just out of college and had never worked for anyone else. Nor had she ever married. Duncan MacArthur and his wife and children were her parents and siblings, Wild Thyme Distillery her only child.

It was funny—as a young boy Ewan had thought her old, but she couldn't be more than forty now. He remembered the flowers she'd brought every week after his mother died. She had made an effort to seek him out and spend time with him, on every visit.

He couldn't recall anything they had talked about, but he looked forward to her visits like a starving dog looks for treats. Would've wagged my tail if I had one, he thought. Looking back from the vantage point of age, he realized that it wasn't what she said, but the fact that she had talked to him, asked him questions and listened to the answers.

And then, a year after his mother's death, she had stopped coming. He had wondered if maybe she'd quit and moved away. He mourned her loss and added her to the growing list of people who had forgotten about him. When he found out, years later, that she was still firmly in place in the outer office of Wild Thyme, he'd been hurt—he could admit that now.

"Ewan, lad!" A soft voice brought him back to the present. A woman stood before him, hands on her hips. Her black hair was arranged in a neat bun. Ewan felt transported back in time as he gazed at the face of the woman who had been the backbone of the business for as long as he could remember.

With his adult eyes, he saw that Miss Beck was an attractive woman—trim and athletic in her brown tweed suit that brought out a hint of bronze in her dark eyes. She stood for a moment longer and then moved to stand in front of him.

"Achh, laddie." Her arms went around him in a hug. Tears flooded his eyes. She smelled the same—he couldn't have named the perfume, but it was uniquely her. Ewan hugged her back as the years fell away and suddenly he was twelve again.

They separated and stepped away from each other, and they were adults again, living in a world that no longer contained the man who had shaped both their lives.

"They're all here," Miss Beck told him, and gave his arm a sympathetic squeeze. "Best to get this over with." She led him through the door to the conference room, where the members of the MacArthur family sat around a huge table. At the head of the table stood Simon Arbuthnot, the family solicitor.

"Thank you for coming, Mr. MacArthur. Please be seated and we'll begin."

Six heads turned and regarded Ewan. Expressions varied from bored indifference to mild interest. His sister Sophie's blue eyes regarded her brother with undisguised curiosity. Of course, Ewan thought with a pang, he was almost a stranger to her. She'd been nine when he left home.

What a beauty she's become, he thought. Her blonde hair was cut in a fashionable bob, and the simple black sheath set off a slim figure and flawless complexion. She gave him a polite, distant smile and turned back to the solicitor.

Ewan's brother Daniel reclined in his chair and gave him a cursory glance before he resumed staring at the ceiling. Everything about him said, "*Let's get on with it; I have better places to be.*"

Jonah was busy scribbling in a notebook and didn't bother to look up at all. His face was creased in concentration. His tie was askew, and his hair showed definite signs of having had hands running through it recently. Ewan found his lips twitch despite himself and made an effort to straighten his face.

Adam signaled to a chair next to him, and Ewan gave him a grateful look before sinking into it. He felt eyes on him and looked across the table to see his older sister Iseabail watching him with a guarded expression.

Izzy. He remembered her as a typical bossy older sister and a know-it-all, until her mother's death had ripped the rug out from under her existence and plunged her into adulthood at the age of fourteen. Then she'd been just . . . sad.

He felt a stirring of something long suppressed for the girl she'd been, trying to be a mother to them all—even him. It wasn't Izzy's fault that her father's anger had suffocated her and pulled her away from the disgraced sibling. At least she'd tried.

Next to Iseabail sat her husband, Aaron Grant. He watched Ewan with a disinterested look that plainly said, "*If he's not into whisky-making, he doesn't count.*" Aaron nodded and turned back to focus on Mr. Arbuthnot, who had cleared his throat.

"Thank you all for coming. I'll begin by saying that

a formal reading of a will is highly unusual—not generally done, in fact, except in the movies."

No one spoke.

"However, as the executor of your father's will it is my duty to follow his wishes. I will not actually 'read' the will, but as it is a recent one, I have been instructed to inform you of the changes with each beneficiary in attendance."

"Recent?" Jonah spoke up. "You mean Dad wrote another will?"

Simon Arbuthnot nodded. "Yes. This will was written only two weeks before his death."

"Are the changes significant?" Jonah asked.

Ewan looked around at his siblings. Jonah seemed the only one with any real interest here—as Adam had said, everyone knew the general contents of their father's will. His estate would be divided amongst his children—with one obvious exception. The distillery would go to Iseabail as the oldest, and her husband Aaron would move from vice-president to president. All neat and tidy.

The solicitor spent the next few minutes listing in brief Duncan MacArthur's bequests to his children, with a sizable sum to Miss Beck. Ewan was not mentioned.

"Now, to the reason your father wanted you all present." He paused and looked around the table.

"The distillery and all its business is to be given to the oldest son, Ewan MacArthur."

Gasps sounded around the table, and every head turned to stare at Ewan.

"What?" Iseabail said in confusion. "Dad always

said it would come to Aaron and me. What happened?"

"He changed his mind, Mrs. Grant." The solicitor's voice was calm. "All he told me is that he was rectifying a mistake."

A laugh rang out. Daniel straightened his long form, stood up, and looked around at his siblings.

"Well, that's fun. Good on you, brother!" He saluted Ewan. "Better you than me, I say. Are we done here?"

Jonah and Sophie said nothing. Jonah's scribbling had intensified and a bead of sweat stood out on his upper lip. Sophie regarded her oldest brother with increased interest, and a small smile played about her mouth.

Aaron looked across the table. "Congratulations, Ewan. I think he did the right thing." His voice was level. "Will you be able to meet with me later to go over the accounts and such? There's a lot."

Ewan stared at the table in front of him and mumbled an affirmative.

Simon Arbuthnot cleared his throat again. "I'll be contacting each of you individually in the next few days, and of course you know I'm always available to answer any questions you may have. Ewan, can you stay for a few minutes?"

Half an hour later, Ewan found his way out of the building and stood on the sidewalk. His brain was a confused mass of contradicting thoughts.

I want to make you the heir to the distillery.

And damn if he hadn't done it, even before they'd met on the street. What the hell was he going to do now?

He stumbled to the car park and flopped into

the driver's seat. He had things to do, decisions to make—but first he needed to see Fiona.

CHAPTER 21

INVERNESS,
SCOTLAND - PRESENT DAY

If you watch close, history does
nothing but repeat itself.
What we call chaos is just patterns
we haven't recognized.
Chuck Palahniuk

"What?" Fiona stared across the table at Ewan.

"Aye, you heard it right." He was bent over with his elbows on the table, fingers lost in the mass of black hair that stuck up all over his head like a small boy's. She forced back a grin.

"You own a distillery? Isn't that a good thing?"

Ewan looked up. His brows were furrowed and his eyes bleary from lack of sleep. He gave her a sour look.

"You'd think so, right? It's a damn good business—one of the best family-run distilleries in the Highlands. Anybody would be over the moon to inherit such a prize."

"But—"

"Anyone but me." Ewan's voice was pitched so low Fiona could barely hear the words. "I never wanted it. I have a business I love; I don't need another one. What the hell am I supposed to do now?"

"Can't you just give up the inheritance?" Fiona asked. "I mean, you said it was a surprise to the rest of your family too—wasn't your sister expecting to inherit? Why can't you just give it to her?"

"Because my father was smart as a fox." Ewan sighed. "The whole point of gathering us all together, which is never done in real life, by the way—was to lock me in so I couldn't refuse. The solicitor asked me to stay behind to explain the terms, and they're just perfect." He spat out the word. His hands ran through his hair again, and he groaned.

"If I give up the inheritance, the distillery goes out of the family. The terms state that it'll be given to *Teine Whisky*, our biggest competitor."

"Given? Not sold?"

"Right. The old man knew just how to seal the deal. We'd get nothing, and it would be my fault. Not that I care if they hate me, but he knew I'd never do that to the family."

Fiona studied him from under her lashes. She'd just met this man a month ago, but already she knew certain things about Ewan MacArthur. One of those things was that he most certainly did care if his family hated him.

He had spent half of his life in a sort of limbo, an orphan whose family lived only minutes away. Now he had been given brothers and sisters again. He had begun a tenuous reconnection with the father he once adored, only to have him ripped away, this time for good.

There was no way he was going to lose that tether, no matter how raw and fragile it was at the moment. And the man she knew he was would never allow his family to suffer pain on his account. His father had to have known that. A fox indeed.

Ewan stood up and began pacing the floor of the small pub. Two men at the bar watched him with bleary curiosity before turning back to their pints.

Fiona stood up too. She gathered their coats and pulled him out the door and into the street, where a fine misty rain had begun to fall.

"Let's go across to the museum. You need to take your mind off this for a while, and I haven't been yet. It's on my Scottish bucket list, and I'll be ashamed to call myself a historian if I don't go soon."

He summoned up a wan smile and allowed himself to be led across the High Street to the Inverness Museum and Art Gallery. The modern building was tucked behind a row of shops under the shadow of Inverness Castle, as if paying homage to the edifice that anchored the ancient city.

Inside, the museum was warm and inviting. Recessed lighting bathed the open space with a soft glow. Strategically placed glass cases held fossils and relics from the distant past, creating the effect of a world within a world.

Fiona and Ewan added their donations to the acrylic box filled with cash of all denominations, signed the guest register, and took the stairs to the second floor where the Jacobite artifacts were housed.

Every name and description was in both English and Scots Gaelic, and to Fiona's delight she found that she could understand almost all of the words. Somehow reading about the Highlands in its own definitive language lent a feeling of immediacy to the scene, as if these events had happened just yesterday instead of two centuries ago.

"My dad would be proud of what the college has accomplished," she told Ewan. "He's so particular about the way Gaelic is taught, even so far away from Scotland. Sometimes the other board members complain that he's too much of a stickler, but when I read these signs, I just want to hug him and tell him he was right."

"You might be surprised to know that there are a lot of Scots who don't see the point in learning Gaelic," Ewan told her. "They complain that tax money is wasted by putting all the public signs in both English and Gaelic, saying that it's a language that is almost as dead as Latin, spoken by only a few in the Hebrides." He shook his head. "Just because this country is ancient compared with yours, it doesn't mean everyone appreciates the history."

They were the first words he had uttered since they'd left the pub. Fiona looked sideways at him and smiled to herself. He was improving; the light was back in his eyes and he no longer trailed behind her like a listless puppy.

He turned to face her, and again she felt the charge of power from those brilliant blue eyes. Eyes she knew as well as her own. Eyes that said *I have known you before. I have followed you through time.* She shivered.

Silly, she knew, but there was no denying her heart. She was falling in love with this man, no matter that they'd met in a parking lot only weeks ago. She had loved him for centuries, and somehow she knew she would love him again and again, as long as time lasted.

I'm going to protect him. From whom or what she didn't know, but she knew she would do whatever it took to keep him safe.

"Have you noticed anything odd?" Ewan said, startling her out of her reverie. At her look, he shrugged. "I get these feelings, not dreams like you have, more like a sense of déjà vu. I got one when we came into the museum, and another just now. As if we're being watched."

Fiona gave him a startled look. "I don't feel any-thing!" she said, and turned away abruptly to study the glass case next to them. It was a collection of weapons from the last Jacobite battle—swords, musket balls, and cannon shot that had been recovered from the mire and muck of Drumossie Moor, now known as Culloden Battlefield.

The description, written in flowing Gaelic and English script above the case, gave the story of the battle. Fragments of metal were evidence of vicious hand-to-hand fighting, pieces of muskets shot away or smashed off by the stroke of a broadsword. A coin dropped by a charging Highlander, buttons and belt buckles torn off in the struggle, all provided proof of the close contact of seething masses of men desperate for victory.

Next to each object in the case was a card that detailed where the find had been made and the possible relation to its former owner. Fiona's eyes fell on a circular bit of metal. It was bent out of shape, blackened by time and the elements. The card next to the frame read, "A *silver ring found on the battlefield. The inscription on the ring reads 'Ne Obliviscaris,' Latin for 'Forget Not'—the motto of clan Campbell.*"

"It looks like a man's ring, which makes sense if it was found on the battlefield," Fiona murmured. "I wonder who wore it and what happened to him."

"Likely died in the battle, otherwise he wouldn't have lost it," Ewan said. "Probably a Jacobite, since they accounted for most of the dead."

"He might have been a government soldier." Fiona read the inscription aloud. "You said clan Campbell fought for the government during the risings. And maybe he survived. If it was found on a body, wouldn't they have said so? It just says, 'found on the battlefield.'"

She sighed. "We'll never know, and that's the historian's frustration—the not knowing."

Tears glazed her eyes. "As long as human beings have walked the earth, normal, everyday people have been forced into unspeakable situations because of politics and other people's ambitions. Farmers, coopers, shoemakers—ordinary men who left those they loved to follow a cause."

Ewan didn't answer. He was staring at the ring with an odd look on his face.

"What is it?" Fiona asked.

"This is it," he said softly. "This is where the feeling is coming from."

"The feeling of déjà vu?"

"Yes. Can't you feel it?" he asked her. "A feeling as

if you've seen it before?"

Fiona tried to stifle the shudder that ran through her. "No. It's so damaged it's hard to tell what the original looked like." She turned from the case. "Anyway, they say déjà vu is probably just a memory of something you've seen or heard before. A similar occurrence or thing that you just can't fully remember. So maybe you've seen a ring like this in another museum."

Ewan turned to look into anxious green eyes. "What's wrong, Fiona?"

"Nothing—why?" She turned away and stared across the museum.

"Something's bothering you."

Her shoulders slumped—there was no fooling this man. She turned back and fixed haunted eyes on him. "All right. There is something. And yes—I felt it when I looked at that ring. It wasn't déjà vu, I've had that before. But this is different. It's stronger, and it's not going away. I can't explain it, and it scares me."

Ewan took her into his arms, and she put her head on his shoulder.

"It'll be all right. Whatever there is to face, we'll face it together, aye?" His voice was a low murmur, and Fiona felt herself begin to relax. She took a deep breath and backed up.

"Well, something here affected both of us, so I just need to suck it up and be an adult about this." Fiona turned and studied the battered remnant of the ring again. "I can't afford to let fear get in the way. I am a historian, after all, and it feels as if this ring might be a part of my story."

She turned green eyes on Ewan. "Maybe yours, too. You felt something, and the ring has the motto of Clan Campbell. Didn't you say MacArthur is a sept of that clan? Maybe your heritage is responding to the connection.

"Let's make sure." She tugged him away from the display case. They moved to a case featuring more buttons, more musket balls.

"Is it gone?" Fiona asked after a moment. She didn't need to elaborate.

"Yes. For you too?" She nodded. Ewan turned and stared at the case with the ring. Then he walked back to it and stood where they had been a moment before, but this time he closed his eyes. When he returned to Fiona's side, he was pale.

"It's real," he said, his voice low. "It wasn't my imagination. Something in that case is pulling at us, and I'm sure it's that ring. I can't explain it, I just know. What can it mean?"

Fiona took a deep breath and summoned a smile. "I have no earthly idea. I'm not the one who comes from a country that has a unicorn for its national animal."

He laughed, and the tension broke. "Ach, it's not just me—you felt it too. And I'm not the one who dreams about sexy Scotsmen, now am I?"

"I never said he was sexy!" She cocked her head and the smile widened. "I said he looked like you. You must have an elevated opinion of yourself, sir."

Ewan burst out laughing. "Touché." He grabbed her hand. "Let's get out of here, I've had enough spookiness for one day. I want to do something entirely modern and normal."

She arched an eyebrow. "In Scotland? Good luck with that."

They left the museum and walked toward the High Street in companionable silence. A busker wearing a tie-dyed tee shirt turned up his amplifier and began to wail out the lyrics of a sixties rock song. At the souvenir store, bagpipe music blared from a speaker as if trying to compete with the electric guitar, and plastic Nessies on sticks waved from a display stand on the sidewalk.

They watched a blue-haired girl in ripped denim jeans walk by with two shopping bags from Morrison's grocery store. The McDonald's on the corner was crowded with customers vying to buy Big Macs and fries, and across the street the Poundland advertised the lowest prices in town for aspirin and deodorant.

Fiona sighed happily. The scene could have existed in any city in the free world. Modern and normal, far from Culloden battlefield and its ghosts. It was wonderful.

As they walked up the steep hill leading to the staircase that would bring them out on Ardconnel Street, tempting smells wafted out from Little Italy and the Fig and Thistle. Fiona stopped suddenly, turned to Ewan and grasped his hand.

"What?" His eyes widened in alarm.

"Pizza! I smell pizza!"

"Aye, lass," Ewan said. He grinned and took her hand. "Pizza. All modern and normal." The blue eyes glinted with humor.

"Have you ever had haggis pizza?"

Fiona smiled. "Hasn't everyone?"

DRUMOSSIE

CHAPTER 22

RAASAY HOUSE, SCOTLAND - 1746

EILIDH

The three riders crested the hill and paused at the edge of the sea.

"It is truly something, is it not?" Rory said to his sister. "So wild and untamed—like a steed that refuses to be ridden."

Eilidh laughed. So like her brother—everything ended up being about horses. She looked at him with affection. An outing with Rory was rare. Despite the fact that they lived in the same place, his duties and hers were worlds apart. It was comforting to know he was nearby, but she wished she could see him more often. Until recently, she had thought she might die from loneliness.

Until recently. Eilidh glanced over at the other rider, and as if he sensed her regard, the man turned to meet her gaze. Blue eyes locked onto green, and she felt a shiver go through her that owed nothing to the stiff wind that swirled over the clifftop. The man's black hair had come loose from its queue and flew in wild disarray around his face.

It wasn't a beautiful face—not like Cullen's flawless visage. The features were angular and his nose maybe a fraction too long for perfection. That is, if anyone noticed his nose when those amazing eyes lit up the world.

He smiled, and she could have sworn rays of sunlight spread outward from where he sat straight and tall on his mount, as if an angel had deigned to visit these lower beings for just a moment before returning to Heaven. White teeth flashed and a dimple appeared in the corner of his mouth. Ahh, it was too much.

Iain MacCrimmon turned away, and the sun went back behind the clouds. Eilidh was grateful—she could sense that being too close to this man could be disastrous. There was something about him—something dangerous. He was friendly, cheerful, and she could tell already that Rory had fallen under his spell.

She should trust her brother; she always had before, hadn't she? If he found Mr. MacCrimmon worthy, then what was the problem?

It is me. I am the problem. I am having feelings I should not have.

Rory's voice broke into her thoughts. "I have to go back—Lady MacLeod wants her afternoon ride, and woe be unto me if her mount isn't ready. Can you make sure to get my sister home in one piece, Iain?" He winked. "She is a bit clumsy."

Eilidh gasped in outrage, "Why, I ought to—" but Rory was off, waving one hand in the air.

Iain moved his mount closer. "He's a funny lad, that one. And I know you're not clumsy."

"Oh?" She tried on a lofty tone, which sounded stiff and artificial to her ears. "And how would you know that?"

"I've watched you." Color came up into his face and he turned quickly to look at the sea. Eilidh could feel the heat in her own face and knew how red it must be.

"Oh." This was ridiculous—she wasn't usually this tongue-tied. Maybe she should just tell him she had a headache, and end this before she made a fool of herself.

"I mean," he had turned around again, and those amazing blue eyes found hers. "You seem to be able to walk without difficulty, and I haven't seen you break any crystal."

"What?" Eilidh said, and then narrowed her eyes at him. His lips twitched.

"Ahh, so you're teasing me. Do we know each other well enough for that, sir?"

"Well, I don't know. I suppose we do not. Let us remedy that then, aye? Come on!" He spurred his horse away from the cliff top and down the path that led into the woods. Eilidh shook her head and followed, determined to show him what she could do.

She and Rory had been raised on horses, and she knew she could keep up with any man. Besides, the back of this one was almost as pretty as the front, so that was something.

They pulled up in a small clearing. Iain jumped off his horse and came over to help her down. As his hands grasped her waist, Eilidh was rocked by a tremor that coursed through her entire body. Her eyes went wide and she stared at the man, her own shock mirrored in those clear blue eyes. He had felt it too.

Iain pulled his hands away as if he had touched fire, and she tumbled the rest of the way to the ground. He grabbed her hand and pulled her up to stand shaking before him.

"I am sorry!" His voice seemed unsteady, as if something had caught in his throat. The next minute, he spun away and stalked over to stand near his own horse, his back to her.

Without a coherent thought, Eilidh mounted her horse and rode out of the clearing at a gallop. She refused to look back—no, nothing on earth would make her look back—until she spied the castle in the distance. Then she sneaked a glance behind her.

Nothing. He had not followed her. And why would he? He had apologized—for what, exactly?—and she had responded with unspeakable rudeness. Her embarrassment was complete.

She slowed to a walk and approached the outbuildings that stood on the edge of the castle yard. She slid off her mount and led the horse around the corner and between two of the wooden buildings, putting the nearest one between herself and the stable.

Fortunately, the deep grass muted her horse's footsteps, because the last person she wanted to see right now was Rory. He always saw right through her, and he'd ask questions to which she had no answers.

If she was lucky, he'd be out and she could stable her horse without being seen.

"*It is almost ready,*" a low voice said.

It had come from inside the building to her right. Startled, Eilidh stopped her horse and listened. It was definitely a man's voice.

"*The Italian fop . . .*" Eilidh pressed her ear to the thin boards of the outbuilding, but the rest of the words were lost.

Another voice. ". . . .*on his last . . .*"

And a third, ". . . .*amned Jacobites . . . kill . . .*"

Eilidh froze, her embarrassment forgotten. Something was going on here, something that involved killing someone. A chill seized her as the fractured words, spoken in secrecy, replayed themselves in her memory. *Jacobites . . . Italian fop . . . kill.*

This was a Jacobite household, known for its unwavering support of Charles Stuart and the rising. So who were these men, meeting in secret and planning treachery against the prince?

Her heart beat with such ferocity that Eilidh was sure it could be heard inside the outbuilding. She clutched the reins and walked her mount back the way she had come for a hundred or so steps, re-mounted, and then rode toward the stable at a brisk pace, making as much noise as possible.

The chill increased as she passed the outbuilding where at least three men planned murder. Three men who were not Jacobites. Who felt comfortable enough to do their plotting in the shadow of the MacLeod stronghold. Strangers.

There was only one stranger at present visiting

Raasay House. A man with flyaway black hair and piercing blue eyes. He could not have been one of the men whispering in the outbuilding, because she had left him behind in the forest. But were they his confederates? Had those men come here to meet Iain MacCrimmon?

A wave of dizziness caused her to sway and almost fall from the horse as another thought gripped her.

Was that even his name?

CHAPTER 23

ISLE OF RAASAY, SCOTLAND - 1746

IAIN

Iain put down his practice sword and wiped the sweat out of his eyes. He bowed to Domnall MacLean and stepped to the side of the enclosure.

What was he doing here, prancing around like some sort of medieval lord? Was this how the wealthy wiled away their time? They should see how a modern army trained for battle. Not so romantic—or so silly—as this jumping around wielding broadswords for no purpose other than to stave off the boredom of not having a real occupation.

He, on the other hand, *did* have a real occupation—and a mission, and so far he was a miserable failure at both. He had discovered nothing at all that would be of value to the British army. It had not been difficult to obtain caché into the household at Raasay, using his contacts on Skye and his cover as a member of the famous musical clan.

They seemed pleased to have a MacCrimmon as their guest, and fortunately Buchanan had been right in that they would not dare ask him to play. *If I took up the pipes, the jig would be up.*

The problem was that, although they accepted him as an honored guest, he sensed he would never be admitted into their confidence. He felt he had made a friend in Hugh MacLeod, but the man did not seem to have a political bone in his body. The others were a mystery.

His attention returned to the field, where Cullen MacLeod faced off against Godfrey Lewis. Cullen's moves were fluid and effortless. He was by far the better swordsman of the two, judging by the other man's more violent swings and two-handed hold. But there was something about that Lewis—almost as if he were holding back, covering a greater skill.

Not for the first time, Iain wondered about Godfrey. He was friendly enough, but his eyes darted everywhere and his movements seemed secretive. Furtive—that was the word. He would have a talk with Rory—see if he knew anything about Cullen's ever-present friend.

As usual when he thought of Rory, his mind wandered to the other MacLean here. He had not spoken to Eilidh since their outing last week. He'd thought their conversation in the woods was the beginning of a friendship, but now . . . when he came across her, he swore she pretended not to see him. It was more than his imagination.

It bothered him for some reason. Had he offended her somehow? Or was he really that much of an oaf that a woman would avoid him like some sort of contagious disease? Worse—had she felt that same shock when he had touched her? He scuffed the toe of his boot in the sand, irritated.

He raised his head, and there she was. She stood alone on the other side of the enclosure, those green eyes riveted on him. When she caught his return stare, she looked away and focused on Cullen and Godfrey--but she'd been watching him, he was sure of it.

All right, enough was enough. It was time to take action. Iain walked around the sides of the field toward Eilidh MacLean, fully aware that he was walking on dangerous ground here. But damned if the woman was going to stare at him and ignore him at the same time! He kept his eyes on the action in the lists and forced himself to maintain a slow pace, the picture of nonchalance. When he got to the other side, he looked up—and she was gone.

Surprise was followed quickly by frustration. Where had she gone? He continued to walk toward the castle and stopped at the main door to pull himself together. Would not do to look too eager.

It didn't matter. She was not in the great hall, or the kitchens, nor was she anywhere in the downstairs gallery. Then he remembered the one place she might be—the place where he had first met her. The library.

Iain stopped on the third stair. What was he doing? This was not why he had been sent here. She was not his to be worried about. He pictured the look on Colonel Buchanan's face should he see him now. He would be hauled back to Edinburgh and probably court-marshaled for dereliction of duty—and he would deserve it.

Still, his mission was to gather information on the Jacobites at Raasay House, and Eilidh MacLean was definitely a Jacobite. If she was not in the library, he could do some reading on Charles Stuart . . . or something. Fortified in his own mind, he moved up the staircase.

She was not in the library. The only inhabitant was Hugh MacLeod, stooped over his books and papers as usual. Iain sighed and pulled up a chair.

"Been practicing in the lists?" Hugh asked him. The young man shivered. "Don't know why you lads want to do that—seems like a ridiculous waste of time to me."

Iain laughed. "You are not alone there. I would rather be doing most anything else. But I was invited by your brother, and I am a guest, so I really felt I should go along. He is good, is he not?"

"The best. Cullen is the active one," Hugh said. "I am the scholar."

There was an odd, strained look on Hugh's pale face.

"What's wrong with being a scholar?" Iain asked.

Hugh shrugged. "Nothing. It is just—" he stopped and wiped at something on the page he was reading.

He took a long breath. "Cullen is Mother's favorite, likely because they are so much alike." There was no self-pity there, just an awareness of the way things were.

"Aye?" Iain liked this young man. Barely twenty, he had the maturity of a much older man, and a kindness that could not be learned.

"I am sick, you know." Hugh looked up. "I will probably not live to see my thirtieth year."

"I—I am so sorry to hear that." Truthfully, he had known that Hugh was not well. The evidence was there for anyone to see. His drawn, pale face, the dark circles under his brown eyes, the rounded shoulders that spoke of constant exhaustion. If appearances served, Hugh would not make it to twenty-five. It was sad, and such a waste. He was ten times the man Cullen was.

"Father will not talk about it. It angers him because he is helpless against time and illness. He avoids me, not because he hates me but because he can do nothing."

Hugh's fists were clenched on the table.

"And your mother? You said Cullen was her favorite, but surely a mother—"

There were tears in the younger man's eyes. "Mother hates weakness." The simple words, uttered in a soft, weary tone, sent chills down Iain's back. He felt a sudden desire to protect this young man.

"Being ill is not weakness," he said.

For a long time it seemed as if Hugh was not going to answer. Then the words began to come, slowly at first, and then gaining in strength.

"I know that. I do. I know that I am smarter than Cullen. But Mother values physical strength, rather than mental acuity." He looked up at Iain. "She has never been in this library. Can you believe that?"

Iain could. The few times he had been in Lady MacLeod's presence, he had felt as if something slimy was crawling up his back. The woman was more than standoffish—she was mean.

Hugh looked up at Iain, his brown eyes clear in the pallor of his face. "Please do not feel sorry for me. I have my books, and this library, and I like my own thoughts. I could not stand to be pitied for something beyond my control."

There were different kinds of strength, and Iain found he much preferred the quiet courage of Hugh MacLeod to the superior bravado of Cullen.

"I do not feel sorry for you," he said. "I admire you. If I had a brother, I would hope he was much like you."

Hugh blushed. "Thank you. I believe I would also like that."

Iain took his leave a few moments later. Absorbed in his thoughts, he almost tripped over a small figure in the hallway. He stepped back, startled. Eilidh MacLean stood in front of him, hands on her hips.

"Who are you?" she asked, her voice low and tense. "Really. Who *are* you?"

CHAPTER 24

INVERNESS, SCOTLAND - PRESENT DAY

. . . in the eyes of love, you can find infinity.
Sorin Cerin

"**D**ad, I think I'm going to need more time." A low chuckle reached Fiona through the phone. "I was waiting for that," William MacLean said. "Does Jeremy know?"

"He suggested it," she said. "He wants me to go up to Raasay Island and check out the castle there—it's open for tours and he won't tell me why, but he's very insistent that it'll help with the mystery."

"Well," her father said, "if Jeremy Brown says it's important, then who am I to disagree? Summer classes are almost over now anyway, so I'll move some people around and free you up for as long as you need. Do you need any money?"

"Not yet. I'm being very frugal—it's the Scot in me. Mrs. MacDonald says I can just add another month onto my stay. She's been a doll."

"Have you heard from Greg?" Her father's voice had lowered, and the lightness was gone.

"Greg? Um . . . no, why?" Fiona pulled the phone away from her ear and stared at it. Truthfully, she hadn't thought about Greg in days. She raised the phone back up and said, "Why—is he all right?"

"He's fine. I just wondered if you two had been in contact."

"No, Dad. It's over between us. Uh—to be honest, I've met someone over here. Early days, but I like him."

"Well, that's good." The relief in her father's voice was obvious.

"What's up, Dad? You never took an interest in my love life before."

"Ahh . . . well, your sister Kirsty and Greg have gone out once or twice, and—"

Fiona burst out laughing. It was a brittle laugh, tinged with the customary irritation she felt at her sister's machinations, but the relief that came with it felt good.

"She didn't waste any time, did she? Nothing new on that front. Well, she can have him. Apparently, he's not too torn up about me being gone, is he?"

"You're sure you're okay with it?" William MacLean asked, his tone anxious. He sighed. "At first I thought your sister only wanted Greg because you had him, but she brought him around for dinner last night and I think she really likes him."

"Well, he's very likable. Seriously, Dad, I'm fine with it."

"I wish you could have been a fly on the wall,"

her father said, his customary humor back in place. "Quietest meal this family's ever had. Brian ignored Greg, and Niall kept sending dagger looks across the table at Kirsty. Your poor mother kept up a running commentary on who knows what—it was a fiasco."

Fiona laughed. "Glad I wasn't there. Anyway, thanks for the added time—I'll let you know what I find out at Raasay."

Her phone buzzed and she checked the display. *Ewan*, it read.

"Dad, I have to go—I'm getting a call."

"Is it the new—?"

"Bye—love you!"

Ewan's grey Mercedes pulled off the single-track road to let an oncoming car pass.

"How do you know when it's your turn to do that?" Fiona asked him.

"There's a highway code."

"Like an honor system?"

"No, a real code for driving single-track roads. If you don't follow the code, you can find yourself in a sticky situation with a very irritated driver."

"So, every driver knows the code?"

"Every Scottish driver. The tourists are another story." Ewan pointed to a sign. "See the sign there that says, 'Passing Place'? If I see a vehicle coming towards me and there's a passing place on the left, I know I have to pull in and wait. If the passing place is on my right, I wait and the other driver knows to pull in. Simple."

"Ahh, simple." Fiona said, her voice sounding dubious. "I'm glad you're doing the driving. I'd be sure to make enemies."

"You'll get used to it. You've been here for a month already—you're almost a native." Ewan glanced over and gave her a smile that caused her heart to slide sideways. She felt heat creeping up her neck and turned to look out her window.

"So . . . how far is it to Raasay?" she asked without turning around.

"About an hour more. After we cross the bridge up ahead, at Kyle of Lochalsh, it's only about twenty-five miles. The problem is that we have to take a ferry to get to the island, so it doubles the time."

"Why would a clan want to stick itself on a little island like that?" Fiona said. "Imagine how long it must have taken to get anywhere in the days before automobiles."

"Aye, the islands of the Hebrides aren't for the faint-hearted." Ewan told her, as he pulled onto the long bridge that led to the Isle of Skye. "Before this bridge was built, the only way to get to Skye was by boat. Your Bonnie Prince Charlie got himself ferried over after the Battle of Culloden, disguised as a woman. Do you know the story?"

"Of course," Fiona said. "I'm a historian, after all—and I come from a long line of fierce Highlanders. Flora MacDonald dressed him up as her maid and took him across to meet the clansmen who still supported him. They hid him in caves until he could arrange his escape to France."

She stared at the island up ahead. "It's hard not to resent him for running away after such a stunning defeat, but there's always more to the story than the legends say. Did you know that Charles was actually a military genius?"

She turned to face Ewan. "You know that Culloden was the only battle he ever lost—and the only one the Butcher ever won, right?"

A smile tugged at the corner of Ewan's mouth. "The Butcher? Tell me how you really feel, my little Jacobite."

Fiona flushed. "Sorry. Not very professional of me, is it? Historians are people too, though, and sometimes they take sides. Besides, I never said I was a *good* historian—I'm way too emotional for that."

"I like the emotional you." Ewan turned the car onto the winding road that would lead to the ferry stop. "I don't think someone who wasn't in touch with her emotions would have been able to handle the weird stuff that's been happening to us."

Us. The word filtered into Fiona's brain and worked its way down to her heart, spreading warmth as it went. Such a tiny word. She rolled it around in her mind. Us.

It was true, though. Before she'd met Ewan MacArthur, the "stuff," as he called it, had frightened her to her core. She'd faced the dreams alone, afraid to tell even her father because it might prove she was insane.

Now, although questions still outnumbered answers, the fear had faded. She realized with a stab of surprise that she hadn't had the dream for a week. Why dream about it when she'd literally met the man of her dreams?

Oh, how cheesy, she thought. But the warmth inside continued to grow.

"What are you grinning about?" Ewan asked. They had reached the ferry park and he turned the car into its boarding lane. Now he turned in his seat, his eyebrows arched in question.

"Nothing," Fiona said, "Just excited because we're almost there."

"Well, we have to wait a few minutes for the ferry. It only makes two crossings a day, and we're booked on the afternoon boat."

"Will it take long to drive to Raasay House from the ferry dock?" Fiona asked.

Ewan smiled. "Not long, since the ferry docks at Raasay House Hotel."

"I read up on it. The hotel was built on the site of the original castle, right?"

"Right. The MacLeod of Raasay was a Jacobite sympathizer and a supporter of Charles Stuart, which as you know didn't work out well for anyone in those days. After Culloden, the government troops went on a rampage and burned the castle to the ground. The hotel is built over the ruins."

Fiona frowned in disappointment. "If that's true, I don't understand what Jeremy Brown thinks I'll find there. There wouldn't be anything left."

"Well," said Ewan, "the family managed to move a lot of their valuables out and hide them before the government pillaged everything that was left. When the house was rebuilt, those original furnishings were returned. Some furniture, almost all of the family portraits, cooking utensils, and some carpets are original. They'll point those out on the tour."

The ferry bumped against the pier, and they drove down the ramp to the hotel that waited for them.

The yellow sandstone structure, with its five gables and turrets, rose up against a backdrop of mountains. To the left, the sea curved back into the island as if it wanted to be a part of this perfect tableau. To the right of the castle the edge of a formal garden completed the picture, and between the pier and the castle stretched a vast manicured lawn.

"Ohh," Fiona breathed. "Oh my."

"Pretty, aye?" Ewan smiled at her delight.

In the front entrance of the hotel, a woman in the distinctive yellow and black Clan MacLeod tartan took their money and gave them their tickets.

"You're just in time for the next tour. Are ye ready?" She gathered the group of about twelve eager tourists into a circle.

"This central section of the castle is the oldest," the guide began. "You can see the difference in the building materials used here. After the government burned the house down in 1746, the family used many of the original stones to rebuild. We'll see some of the MacLeod family's possessions later in the tour. Please do not go behind the ropes—these artifacts are very precious, and human touch is not the friend of time." She waggled a finger at the group. "One might say that humans have never been very good to history."

She took them through the kitchens, the huge dining room, and some of the bedrooms, before leading them to a large room on the second floor.

"Now we're back in the oldest section," their guide said. "Preservation architects followed drawings found after the castle burned; we're fortunate to have had detailed descriptions of the rooms and furniture as they existed in 1746. And this was the family's library."

Fiona glanced around at the floor-to-ceiling bookshelves, covered in mullioned glass to preserve the valuable collections of books and manuscripts.

"I wonder how many of those books are original from that time," she whispered to Ewan. "I wish they'd let me loose in here just for a day."

"Want to sneak in tonight and have a look?" Ewan whispered back. His blue eyes glinted with amusement.

"Many of the portraits on the walls here have been saved from the original collection," their guide was saying. "The man on your left—" she pointed to a large portrait of a distinguished gentleman dressed in the soft blues and greens of the MacLeod hunting tartan "—is Malcolm MacLeod, the last laird to have lived in the original castle. To his right is Lady Lucretia Sutherland MacLeod, a formidable woman by all accounts."

A black-haired woman gazed from the portrait at her audience. The artist had employed the trick of painting the woman's dark grey eyes so that they seemed to follow her observers from any direction. Her expression was haughty, as if she were about to say, "*What are you doing in my house?*"

"And to the laird's left is his son Cullen."

"Oooh, he's gorgeous," a young American voice

said. "He could be in the movies!"

Fiona gave her attention to the picture. He was indeed beautiful, but there was something about the portrait that bothered her.

"I don't like him," she murmured to Ewan.

"Fiona." Ewan's voice was tense. "Look."

She followed his gaze, unsure what she was supposed to be looking for, and then stiffened. The blood drained from her face and she staggered against Ewan. He put an arm around her and held her tight.

The portrait was of a young woman. She sat staring off into the distance, her hands folded on her lap. The woman's hair was tied up except for the chestnut curls that escaped to frame her pale face. The bodice of her gown was cut low in the fashion of the mid-eighteenth century, and an emerald pendant set off startling green eyes.

Fiona felt her stomach heave and nausea rose into her throat.

"Ewan," she whispered, "it's me."

CHAPTER 25
HIGHLANDS, SCOTLAND - PRESENT DAY

Kinship lasts through life and death,
immutable, unchanging, no matter
how great the misdeed or betrayal.
Whitney Otto

Ewan pulled his car into the distillery car park, turned off the engine, and glared at the white building with its distinctive lettering. Wild Thyme, named after the plant badge of clan MacArthur. His father's pride, and now his headache.

He pulled out his cell phone and called Fiona.

"Hi, Ewan. Are you there yet?"

"Hurry," he said. "Talk me out of it. Better yet—come and get me."

Her laugh reached out to him like a blessing. It filled the car and warmed him from the inside out.

"I'll see you tomorrow," Fiona said.

Ewan ended the call and sat still for a moment, torn between the task ahead and the desire to turn around and drive straight to her. He no longer wondered why he had been attracted to Fiona MacLean from the beginning—the portrait at Raasay House had answered that question well enough for him. It was fate, as crazy as that sounded.

The resemblance was uncanny. The chestnut hair, those green eyes. Eilidh MacLean, the guide had told them—betrothed to Cullen MacLeod. She would have become Lady MacLeod when her husband became laird.

Would have become . . .

His memory returned to the library at Raasay House and the discovery of Eilidh MacLean's portrait.

"Mystery surrounds the people you see here before you," the tour guide had told her group in a stage whisper. "People in the family had a bad habit of disappearing. No one knows what happened to Cullen MacLeod after the Battle of Culloden in April of 1746, and his bride-to-be vanished around the same time."

"Didn't noble families keep records?" a grey-haired man raised his hand. "Why don't they know what happened to them?"

"This was not the modern era," the guide said. "No internet databases or DNA services in those days. Everything in the Highlands of Scotland came to a screeching halt on April 16, 1746. Does anyone know why?"

"The Battle of Culloden," announced a young man. "We studied it in school." His girlfriend smiled proudly at him.

The guide beamed at them. "Our schools are doing a good job, I see. Yes, the battle changed life for Highlanders forever. Historical records proved that

Lord Malcolm raised an army of one hundred men and went to fight at Culloden, and it is assumed that Cullen, as an avowed Jacobite like his father, followed him into battle. Whatever happened there, it is known that he did not return from Drumossie Moor with his father.

"It's assumed that he died during the battle, but records from that time are incomplete and no one knows the names of all the Jacobites who lost their lives that day."

"What about Eilidh MacLean?" Fiona's hand trembled as she raised it to gain the guide's attention. "What happened to her?"

"No one knows," the guide said. "She disappeared from historical annals at the same time. There is no register of a marriage, so it's possible she did not become the wife of Cullen MacLeod before the battle." The guide paused to survey her rapt audience.

"Keep in mind that those times were so hectic; a lot of records have been lost. It's just another of the mysteries surrounding clan MacLeod of Raasay. Shall we move on?"

Ewan straightened in the car and sighed. No time for mental wandering—he had to get on with the task at hand, much as he'd rather sign up for multiple root canals. He rolled his shoulders to loosen the tension in his back and stepped into the car park.

Ariadne Beck met him in the outer office. Her smile was bright—too bright, maybe—and her hazel eyes probed his face anxiously.

"Are ye all right, lad?" She placed a hand on his arm. "It's been difficult, aye?"

"Surreal, more like." Ewan patted the hand on his

arm. "Let's get this over with, aye?"

Miss Beck nodded. She led him into the silent inner office and shut the door as she returned to her own desk. Ewan stood for a moment and took in the darkened room, the walnut bookshelves, the framed certificates and awards, and the empty leather chair behind the massive desk.

He walked behind the desk and pulled the chair away, rolling it across the carpeted floor into the corner. Then he fetched one of the armchairs that faced the desk and placed it where his father's chair had been. He sat down and took in the room from the vantage point that had been Duncan MacArthur's.

Okay, he thought. *Mission: get this albatross off my neck so I can get back to my real job.* He glanced at the folders that Ariadne Beck had placed on the desk. On the top was the one with his father's will. The language was clear and simple: he either took over the distillery or lost it. *Damn, there has to be a loophole.*

"Ewan." He looked up to see his sister Iseabail in the doorway.

"Iz-Iseabail."

She moved forward, her walk stiff and her steps measured, as if she had to think where to put her feet. She sat in the chair across from her brother and crossed one slim leg.

"I-I wasn't able to talk to you last week at the reading. How are you?"

Like two strangers. No, like two people who don't like each other.

Ewan's thoughts went back in time, and in his mind's eye he saw a teenage Iseabail—ordering them all around, trying to cook the dishes their mother had made, forcing them to wash their hands and brush their teeth.

She'd kept him out of his father's way, he remembered now. Even in her own grief she had cared enough to protect him. Tears rose in Ewan's eyes as he looked at this rigid, controlled version of the sister he'd known.

"Izzy." The old nickname fell out of his mouth into the tense air. Her eyes snapped up, and suddenly she was crying. The tears ran unchecked down her face and onto her clasped hands, and ragged, choking sounds filled the room.

Ewan sprang out of his chair. He rounded the desk, pulled his sister out of her chair, and folded her into his arms. Time stopped. He could feel the tears running onto his own cheeks as he held this woman who had tried so hard to keep their family together.

"I'm so sorry, Ewan," she sobbed into his shoulder. "I'm so, so sorry. I abandoned you, every bit as much as Dad did."

"Shh, shh," he said, as he patted her back. "You did your best. I never held it against you."

That wasn't true—he'd hated them all for a long time. The child that Ewan was then couldn't understand why his beloved sister had betrayed him. Trapped in his own misery, he hadn't been able to see how much pain she was in.

Kids are selfish, he thought. So, he'd hated her—but that was then and this was now. People grow, they mature and change. Or at least they should.

"It was losing Mom that split us apart," he said. He

held Iseabail by the shoulders and looked into her brown eyes—their mother's eyes. "So it makes sense that losing Father should bring us back together, aye?"

She laughed, a watery giggle that made her seem younger than her thirty years.

"We are a mess, aren't we?" Her smile didn't quite reach her eyes. She stepped back away from him.

"I missed you."

"I missed you too."

They returned to their chairs and sat for a minute, as the silence grew and became awkward.

Ewan was first to speak. "It's hard to believe, isn't it—about Father?"

"Aye, it is. He always seemed invincible."

There have been—incidents.

He paused. "Izzy, did Father ever tell you there was something wrong with his heart?"

"No, never. I was shocked, of course, but the doctor said that a heart attack can happen to anyone, at any time—you know, like those runners that seem so healthy and then just collapse one day."

I think someone is trying to kill me.

"But there was no indication of heart disease—no medication prescribed or anything like that?"

Where was his mind going now? What was happening to him lately? Ever since his fall, and meeting Fiona—and that damned portrait—he'd become fanciful, suspicious of everything. Still, it wouldn't hurt to check with his father's doctor, would it? Ariadne Beck would know if Duncan MacArthur was taking any kind of prescription medicine. He'd start with her.

It was time to get down to business.

"Izzy—I know the distillery was supposed to go to you. I'm trying to figure out a way to make that happen."

She waved a hand. "Ewan, don't worry about it. Yes, I'll admit I was surprised, and a little—okay, a lot—disappointed. Dad always said the distillery would go to me. But it makes sense, in a way. You know what a chauvinist he was, and he never really approved of Aaron. Plus, I think it was his way of apologizing for the way he treated you."

"By making my life more difficult? That sounds like him."

Iseabail laughed, her voice sounding more buoyant than before. "He was a terror, wasn't he?"

Ewan found that he could laugh about his father for the first time in years. "That's putting it mildly. Well, anyway, I don't want the distillery. I'm going to take this stuff home and try to figure out a way to give it to you."

"Thanks." Iseabail stood and smiled at him—a genuine smile.

After his sister let herself out of the office, Ewan tried to go over the files Miss Beck had left for him. After a few minutes he sighed, stretched, and packed everything into his leather backpack. He didn't feel comfortable in this room, and he probably never would. The sight of his father sitting in that chair, staring at nothing, would be in his mind forever.

He stopped to say goodbye to Ariadne Beck. She jumped up and came around to give him a hug.

"Are you all right?" he asked her.

"Getting there, lad," she said. Tears stood in her

grey eyes. "He was a wonderful man. I'm grateful for the time we had together."

She cleared her throat and returned to her place behind the reception desk. "Remember, if you need anything, just call."

"Thanks, Miss Beck," he said. "Same goes for you."

Ewan made his way back to the car, deep in thought. He knew he should be going through those papers, but he wanted to talk to his father's doctor. He also needed to check in with his own business. What he really wanted to do was hit the trail and get in some scrambling. And in the back of his mind was that small voice, saying, "*What you really, really want to do is go see Fiona.*"

When had she become the most important thing in his life? It wasn't fair for a woman to sneak up on you that way and turn your world upside down. He couldn't let his emotions—or anything else—distract him today. Nor could he let those damn distillery papers wreak havoc with his head. It was time for a drive out to the office in Aviemore, from where he ran both of his businesses, and then maybe a pint with Adam. Enough for one day.

As he pulled into town, Ewan congratulated himself again on the decision to locate Wild Scotland in the town most closely associated with the outdoors. The main street was thronged with nature-lovers, attracted to the ski resort, the nature walks, and the outdoor gear shops that lined both sides of the street.

He spent two hours scheduling tours for the next few weeks, and then climbed back into the car for the trip home to Inverness. Tomorrow he had a reenactment tour for Highland Magic—a group of college professors from Maine in the US, and he wanted to be on hand to greet them at the bus station.

Maine was near Canada. Fiona was from Canada. And there he was, right back to thoughts of her. Somehow it seemed the most natural thing in the world to turn to her with his suspicions about his father's death. She would understand. He tried to bring his thoughts back to the road, but it was no use. Ewan could feel the betrayal of his face and knew he was grinning like a fool. He was lost, and he didn't mind it in the least.

He crested a ridge on the A9 and tapped the brakes as he started downhill. His foot went straight to the floor. He tapped them again—nothing. He glanced in the rearview mirror and moved over to the slow lane, which at this time of day was nearly empty, and tried the brakes again. Nothing.

He pushed down a feeling of panic at the knowledge that this road led downhill almost all the way to Inverness. There was no shoulder, and only guard rails to his left.

The car was picking up speed; he had to do something now. There was a turnoff for Tomatin up ahead—his only chance. The exit sign flashed past, and there was the off ramp. He turned the wheel to the left and the car made the turn on two wheels, but at least the change in direction had slowed him down a little.

Up ahead was the thing he'd been hoping for—a field dotted with cylindrical bales of hay. He wrenched the wheel to the right and the car lifted into the air and hit the grass of the field, traveling straight toward the nearest bale.

Hay flew everywhere as the Mercedes nosed into it at forty miles per hour. The car stalled out and he banged his head on the steering wheel, gasping at the agony that ricocheted through his skull. But the car had stopped, and he was alive.

He held on to his head as his father's voice echoed through the pain.

There have been—incidents.

I think someone is trying to kill me.

CHAPTER 26

INVERNESS, SCOTLAND - PRESENT DAY

Evil is unspectacular and always human,
And shares our bed and eats
at our own table . . .
W.H. Auden

The horse responded to her sure touch, cantering between buildings as she made for the stables and safety. She could feel the sweat that slid down her back, the fear that gripped her mind and pushed her onward. The thought that she might be caught here drove her almost senseless with terror.

Fiona jerked awake to find herself in her room on Ardconnell Street. She was clutching the blankets as if they were the reins of a bridle, and her chest pounded from the wild ride.

The dreams were happening again. The circles under her eyes were back, evidence of nights spent tossing and turning, wishing for sleep after a fresh onslaught.

She'd thought they were gone. After she met Ewan, there had been a period of two or three weeks where the past had left her alone. *Funny how you don't appreciate what you have till it's gone.*

Now, since the trip to Raasay Island, the dreams were back. They were changing, too. Not always the battlefield, as before. She was seeing images of the people in the portraits at Raasay House. Sometimes she was in the library; at other times she was walking in the garden.

Of course, people dreamed about things they'd seen—that made sense. The castle and the portrait of Eilidh MacLean had made a huge impression on her. What didn't make sense were the things in the dreams that couldn't be explained—things she hadn't seen.

She hadn't told Ewan about the resurgence of the dreams, and she wasn't sure why. If she told anyone it would be him, but somehow it felt as if keeping them to herself took away their power, made them less frightening. Of course, that didn't seem to be working. She'd have to tell him.

It was only five-thirty, but she forced herself to rise and put some semblance of humanity into her appearance. She crept down the stairs and through the dark front hallway, keeping as quiet as possible. Even Mrs. MacDonald would be too much to take today.

Half an hour later she sat in front of her computer at the university and brought up the webpage for Raasay House. It wasn't an old castle, by Scottish standards; the original structure had been built in the early 1700's as a small hall castle. There was an artist's rendering of the original castle, and she could recognize the architecture of the central tower.

They'd been quite accurate in its reconstruction, all in all. So much so that it would be logical to find images from the castle in her dreams.

She brought up the photographs of the outbuildings. These were original, untouched by the fire of 1746. The stables, a family chapel, and some sort of storage building were clustered close together in the outer courtyard. As she stared at the photo, a chill ran down her back. That storage building had been in her dream last night. There was no doubt.

The outbuildings of Raasay House weren't on the tour. She had never seen them, and yet she stared at them now—and recognized them. Somehow, without her ever having seen these buildings, they had found their way into her dream.

She had been riding a horse. Fiona did not ride horses—she was afraid of them. Back when she was eight, like most girls, she had wanted a horse of her own. She'd pestered her parents until they'd given up and signed her up for riding lessons at a local farm.

Unfortunately, the horse they'd put her on had been huge—sixteen hands high at least—and all she could think about was the great distance she would travel when she fell off. There had not been a second lesson, and her love affair with animals of the equine persuasion had ended abruptly. So why was she dreaming of riding a horse?

Her ringtone broke the stillness of the office. She smiled as she answered.

"Hi, Ewan."

"Mornin.' Want to go for breakfast?"

"I shouldn't. I'm at work."

"Already? It's only 6:30. I know you're an early riser, but isn't this a bit too much? I know the university doesn't set hours like that."

"I couldn't sleep, so I just came in."

His tone changed. "Fiona—what's going on?"

"Noth—"

"Have you been dreaming again?"

Damn.

"Yes." There, it was out. One simple word, and already she felt better. Honesty was so underrated.

"There's something I have to tell you too. I'm on my way." The call ended.

Today Ewan was driving a black Audi. At Fiona's questioning glance, he shook his head.

"It's a rental. Part of the story," he said. "Can you afford to take the morning off?"

"I'm on my own for this project," she said, "so I make my own hours. My boss is my dad."

"Good." He handed her into the car and walked around to the driver's side. "I'm taking you to one of my secret breakfast places."

Thirty minutes later they crested a small hill and drove into a large parking lot with slots for tour buses and a huge area for cars. Public toilets stood off to one side, and a large, free-standing bulletin board fronted the road. Ewan pulled into a space and turned off the engine.

"This is Carrbridge. We walk from here," he said. "The whole of Main Street is only an eighth of a mile long, and there's a wonderful ancient bridge at the end. That's why it's a stop for so many tours."

As they walked along the sidewalk, Ewan reached for Fiona's hand and laced his fingers through hers. A shiver went through her at the touch, and she wondered if she'd ever get over that feeling.

Too soon, Ewan stopped in front of a tiny restaurant with the name "The Kitchen" written on a hanging sign above a white door. Inside, the space held seven small tables and a sales counter. A doorway led to a tiny room full of shelves offering locally made arts and crafts for sale.

"Ahh!" Fiona said. They sat at a table in the corner and a waitress arrived quickly with menus. The food came almost as quickly. Fiona didn't think she could eat, with everything swirling around in her head, but twenty minutes later she found herself staring at an empty plate. She looked up and met Ewan's clear blue eyes.

"Tell me," he said.

So she did, about the changes in the dreams, the connection to Raasay House, the fear that they were more than dreams. He listened without interruption, and when she was finished, he said, "I agree. They're not dreams."

Relief flooded through her. She should have known he'd get it, that he would accept the impossible. He'd done it before.

"So what's next?" she asked.

"Have you thought about hypnosis?" Ewan asked her.

Fiona was startled. "Hypnosis? No!" The vehemence in her words surprised them both. She reached for a ceramic saltshaker shaped like a Highland cow and turned it around and around in her hand. "I mean, I don't want anybody mucking around in my mind, making me agree to do stuff I don't want to do."

"You've watched too much TV," Ewan said, his voice even. "Hypnosis is more than a magic act. It's not about making people bark like dogs or do somersaults for the amusement of an audience. It delves into the memories you've buried in your subconscious and helps you to retrieve them—explain them. It can help you cope with whatever trauma is hiding there."

"How do you know all that?" Fiona said, her eyes wide.

"When I was a kid—after my mother died—I couldn't sleep. When I did, I had nightmares and began sleepwalking. I—even began wetting the bed."

Fiona reached across the table and took his hand in both of hers.

"I tried to hide it, but Miss Beck found out. She got me hooked up with a hypnotherapist." His eyes were moist. "I owe her a lot."

Fiona squeezed his hand. "All right. If you're brave enough to tell me you were a bedwetter, I guess I can't be a coward about this. And I know I have to do something, or I'll go mad."

Ewan grinned at her. "That's my girl. Of course, you do know I was reasonably certain when I first met you that you were mad, right? I mean, walking in front of cars, calling perfectly respectable people names—"

"Oh, shut up, you. I said I'd do it." Fiona released the hand she'd been holding and stood up. "Where's this amazing bridge you were telling me about?"

"One of the first signs of incipient insanity is a

refusal to accept one's failings," Ewan told her, shaking his head. "Very sad."

"Bridge!"

Laughing, they left the restaurant and continued down Main Street. At the end of the street, the shops and the sidewalk came to an abrupt end and the countryside took over. The road crossed over a narrow river and wound up and over another hill, leaving the tiny village of Carrbridge behind.

"And there you have it—the Old Pack Horse Bridge." Ewan leaned his elbows on the railing of the modern bridge over the Duthill River and waved his hand to the left in a sweeping gesture. "It's the oldest stone bridge in the Highlands."

A grey stone arch rose over the river like a humpbacked dinosaur. There were no sidewalls, and the stone blocks were uneven and chipped away by the centuries. Still, it retained a dignity not diminished by time.

"It's not safe, is it?" Fiona looked at the arch dubiously.

"No, not anymore," Ewan said. "Locals used to challenge each other to jump off it not so many years ago, but now it's just Carrbridge's claim to fame, and the reason for the car park."

"How old is it?"

"Glad you asked, my little historian. It was built in 1717 to allow funeral processions to cross the river to the Church of Duthill. The church is still there, but now it's a historic site. Take a picture—everyone does."

They walked back up the street to the parking lot and sat on a bench near the bulletin board.

"Okay, it's your turn," said Fiona. "What was it you wanted to tell me? And does it have anything to do with the rental car you're driving?"

"It does. The Mercedes is in the shop. There's a bit of damage to the front end."

Fiona stared at him, all humor gone. "What? What happened? Are you all right?"

"Luckily, yes. I banged my head pretty hard—" he brushed the hair off his forehead to show her a dark bruise "—but nothing's broken."

He stopped, and when he spoke again his voice had gone serious. "Yesterday, when I was coming home on the A9, my brakes failed and I ended up in a hay bale. They're not as soft as they look."

"Ewan!"

"I had to get towed to the auto shop, and my poor baby will have to stay for a few days to have her kinks ironed out—but that's not the important part."

"Your brakes failing and you almost getting killed isn't the important part?" Fiona felt as if she couldn't catch her breath. "What's the important part?"

"Well, it was odd. The Mercedes is a classic car, so I have her serviced regularly and the last check-up was only a month ago. The brakes were fine then. And they were fine all the way to Aviemore and all the way home, until I hit that long steep hill. Then suddenly they were gone. Just—gone. My foot went all the way to the floor and nothing happened."

Fiona felt a feeling of foreboding begin to spread through her body.

"And?"

"And the mechanic at the shop checked her

over, and he told me that the brake fitting had been loosened."

"What does that mean, exactly?" Fiona asked. "I don't speak auto."

"The brake fitting on a classic car doesn't loosen itself," Ewan told her. His voice had gone tight. "Someone would have to loosen it with a spanner."

Fiona blinked. "And what happens when the brake fitting gets loosened?"

Ewan's blue eyes clouded over and his brows furrowed. "What happens then is that the brake fluid leaks out slowly. When the fluid is gone, the brakes fail."

She stared at him. "So that means—"

"Someone deliberately sabotaged my car," he said. "Someone tried to kill me. And—I don't think it's the first time."

CHAPTER 27

RAASAY HOUSE, SCOTLAND - 1746

EILIDH

"**W**hat are you talking about?"

Eilidh's eyes speared into his. "You heard me. I want to know who you are—before I go to Lord Malcolm and tell him that a snake is residing under his roof."

"A snake?" Iain said. "Is that not a little harsh? You do not even know me."

"I know that you are not a musician. When I asked you last night at dinner if you had ever tried canntaireachd, you said you had not, but you hoped to do so one day."

"Well, must I have tried every dish in the Highlands?"

"Of course not." Eilidh's eyes speared his. "That is not the problem. The problem is that canntaireachd is not a dish. It is the notation system for bagpipes. A *MacCrimmon* would surely know that."

Iain's face went still.

"So, I ask again, who are you?"

Suddenly he took her hand and pulled her into an alcove. She wrested her hand out of his grasp and slapped him across the face.

"Do not touch me. If I scream, someone will come. Answer my question!"

Iain stood still. Then he took a deep breath and let it out.

"Not here. No one can hear. Please."

She stood for a moment, watching him. Something flickered in her eyes, and she nodded.

"Follow me." She turned on her heel and walked away down the hall.

Eilidh led Iain downstairs and outside into the courtyard. Sounds of mock battle could still be heard from the lists, but she did not turn that way. Instead, she headed for the stables.

Rory met them at the doorway. His face lit at the sight of his two favorite people. Eilidh pushed past him and marched down the row of stalls to a tack room.

"In here. You too," she said to her surprised brother. The two men followed her into the small room. She closed the door and turned to face Iain, her face set.

"Now, tell us. Who are you, and why are you here, pretending to be a MacCrimmon from Skye?"

Rory gasped. "What? What are you talking about, El? You are being rude!"

"He is not Iain MacCrimmon," she told him. "And he is going to tell us the truth—now."

Iain sighed. "All right." He walked in a circle and came back to face them. "My name is Iain Campbell, and until a few months ago I was an officer in the British army."

Both MacLeans gaped at him. Then Eilidh spun on her heel and made for the door.

"Wait!"

She stopped. Iain waited, and after a long moment she turned again to face him.

"Please, just listen," he said.

She crossed her arms over her chest and stood motionless.

"I am listening, Iain. Tell me your story." Rory came over and clapped the other man on the shoulder. "I admit I know horses better than people, but I consider you my friend and I do not think I am wrong."

A shadow crossed the Iain's face and was gone. He ignored Eilidh in the doorway and focused on Rory.

"I was a lance corporal in the army," he began. "I believed—still believe—that Scotland and England should remain united. But I do not like the way the clans are being treated. I am a Highlander myself, and I've seen the disdain and the prejudice firsthand.

"My best friend was named Conall MacKenzie—we grew up together in Skye. I joined the army, but he remained behind. He was a Jacobite." Iain sneaked a glance at the doorway where Eilidh stood, immobile. "He came to see me in Edinburgh. When he left, some of the men from my company followed him and cornered him in a close. They were drunk, and they picked a fight. Conall never backed down from anyone, so they beat him—so badly that he will never walk again." Iain looked at Rory. "I left that day. I am a deserter."

Eilidh had edged closer. "Why did you pretend to be a MacCrimmon?" she asked, her voice flat.

"There is a price on my head," Iain said. "If I am caught, I will be court-marshaled. And I want to help here, if I can. I owe it to Conall."

"What do you think you can do here?" Eilidh came up and stood in front of him. "This does not make any sense. Do Lord Malcolm and Cullen know who you are?"

"They do not. But Conall's family knows what I am doing. Now I have to trust you to keep my secret. Please say nothing to them. My life depends on it."

"I am in agreement with Eilidh, though." Until now, Rory had said nothing, simply looked at the floor and listened. Now he raised his head and looked Iain straight in the eye. "What do you think you can do here?"

"I think the government forces have sent spies into the Highlands," Iain said. "I believe they are planning something."

"They would be strangers—these spies." Eilidh's voice was soft. "They might come in the guise of visitors from another area in the Highlands." She paused. "Skye, for example."

Iain raised both hands in a defensive posture, but Eilidh ignored it.

"They might come to a known Jacobite household, posing as guests—hoping to find information on the movements of the Jacobite army. Is that not a greater possibility?"

Iain's shoulders slumped. "You are right—they might. And you are right to be suspicious of me. All I can tell you is, I am here alone, and my motives are the opposite of what you have suggested."

"Well, that is good enough for me, and I for one have work to do," Rory announced. "I will leave you two to your battle of wills, aye?" He made a hasty exit, and a moment later they heard the outer door to the stable close.

Eilidh and Iain stood rooted to the spot.

Iain broke the silence. "I will walk you back."

As they walked through the courtyard in silence, Eilidh's mind went over Iain's story, taking it apart and putting it back together, looking for something out of place. Yes, it could make sense. He could be telling the truth, or—

Suddenly she stumbled on a stone in the yard and felt herself pitching forward. A strong arm went around her waist and she was pulled against Iain's body and held tight.

He held her for what seemed a very long time. She blinked and pushed away from him and whirled to face the man who had saved her from embarrassment or worse. He was staring at her, a shocked expression in the brilliant blue eyes.

"I am—sorry." His voice seemed breathless. "I thought you were going to—I am sorry." He turned without another word and stalked away.

Eilidh stared after Iain Campbell, wondering what was happening. Her face was hot and her breath was coming fast and shallow, as if she'd run for an hour in the hot sun in a woolen gown.

She was not sorry. She did not trust this man, but she had to stay as close as possible to him to ferret out his secrets and make sure he was what he said he was. But how on earth was she going to do that, when his mere touch sent her into a vortex of emotions she could not understand?

CHAPTER 28

RAASAY HOUSE, SCOTLAND - 1746

Iain paced the length of the upstairs hallway, turned, and walked back to the staircase. It was the fifth time he had made this journey, and he was no closer to a solution than he had been when he started.

What am I going to do?

It had been bad enough when she was dogging his footsteps, watching him from the corner of her eye—making it clear that she did not trust him. She sought him out at every opportunity, brought him sweets from the kitchen and books from the library. Did she think he was fooled by the attention?

It was annoying not to be believed, and worse when he deserved it. He was a liar, and in this household a traitor. He had lied about his reason for being here—turned it around and made himself a Jacobite patriot. Disgusting. He sent a prayer to the fictional Conall MacKenzie, asking his forgiveness, but the feeling of disgust only intensified.

In truth, he had found nothing that would justify

his promise to Colonel Buchanan to fulfill his mission, but that did not make his perfidy any the less odious. He would have made his excuses to his hosts and left already—but for Eilidh MacLean.

She had crawled under his skin and into his heart, and the idea of living life without her, of never seeing those eyes again, was as inconceivable as giving up breathing.

The more time they spent together, the worse he felt and the more desperate he became. And yet, when she walked into the room it brightened as if the sun had come down just for him.

He knew she felt something for him, and somehow that knowledge was worse. A part of him hoped it was just a fleeting fancy on her part, the spark of something that he would never see burst into flame. Because the alternative would be to destroy her, and himself in the process.

He would have to tell her. He would tell her the truth, watch her beautiful face fill with loathing where he had begun to think he saw something else—and then he would leave.

To tell her was to lose her. To keep living the lie would twist what they might have had into something rotten, like a strangling vine that has wrapped itself around a young tree.

There was no future for them. So why did he keep holding on, hoping that it could be different— that what they felt for each other would conquer everything?

"Iain." As if he had conjured her, Eilidh stood before him in the hall.

"Aye?" It was all he could muster, and it took everything he had.

"I—I was wondering—would you like a walk in the garden?" She looked at him from under those long, dark lashes.

"Aye." Was he becoming mute? Was "aye" all he was capable of, around her? No matter, she was here. It was all he needed, everything he wanted, and the one thing he should not have.

They walked side by side down the stairs and out of the castle, careful not to touch, not to walk too close in case anyone should be watching. But they were alone.

It was like a dance whose steps had been set long ago and imprinted on the mind. They walked down the garden path, oblivious to the beauty around them, until they reached the arbor where branches hung low and obscured the view.

Iain turned to Eilidh. "I have something I must tell you," he began.

She put her finger to his lips. "Hush. There is nothing I need to hear. I have come to a decision."

Her gaze was luminous, bright with unshed tears. "I do not care, about any of it. I do not care who you are, or where you are from, or why you came here."

Iain stared at her. "How can you not care?"

"I do not know. I only know that you came when I most needed you, and you opened my eyes to a world I never knew existed. I was a shell—an empty vessel, and I did not even know it."

"But—" he began.

"Hush," she said again. "Do you not understand?

Whether you are Iain MacCrimmon, or King George, or Bonnie Prince Charlie—I do not care." She faced him and gave him the full power of those brilliant green eyes.

"I love you. I have loved you from the first moment I laid eyes on you, in the library with Hugh. It is not right, and I do not know what to do with this feeling, but there it is. I love you, and if you leave, I want to go with you."

Iain stared at her in shock. "Eilidh, this is not possible. This cannot be. You know that."

She said nothing, just continued to give him that clear, level gaze that melted his resolve and warmed his heart.

He let his breath out in a long sigh. "I am not a good person. I must tell you—"

"I do not want to know." Her voice was low and the words came in a rush. "Once we are away from this place, once we are free, then you may tell me all that you must. Until then, please—just hold me."

Wordlessly, he took her into his arms and lowered his head until his lips met hers. A force unlike anything he had ever felt before arced through his body and into hers, fusing them together.

This was so wrong. They were playing with fire. She was betrothed to the laird's son, and he was a guest. He was living a lie. Nothing good could come of this—and yet he had never felt better than he did at this moment, holding her in his arms.

A thought came into his mind and emblazoned itself on his consciousness. He would keep this woman safe, no matter what it took. If he had to give up his career, his beliefs, his life—he would do so for Eilidh MacLean. And for the first time, he knew what fate meant.

Iain held Eilidh close, and it felt as if she had been molded to his body. God had made her just for him—surely there could be nothing wrong with honoring his work?

"Eilidh?" he managed.

"Yes, Iain?"

"I love you."

"I know."

INVERNESS, SCOTLAND - PRESENT DAY

The past beats inside me like a second heart.
John Banville

"'m doing this under duress." Fiona gave Dr. Blair a mutinous look. I'm telling you this because it might make whatever it is you want to do harder."

The doctor smiled. "If I listened to every patient who told me that, I'd have quit this practice long ago. Don't think for a minute that your feelings are unique."

"Humph. So . . . what happens first?"

"First is what we're doing right now. I'm getting to know you—learning more about what makes you who you are."

Fiona arched an eyebrow. "And that is supposed to make me trust the process?"

"What do you mean?" Dr. Blair asked, his voice gentle. "Trust the process?"

"I mean—you're going to probe into my life so you'll know what my likes and dislikes are, right? You'll ask me about my family and whether or not I have a boyfriend. Then you'll use it to make suggestions while I'm—in a trance—isn't that what it's called?"

"My, my, aren't you a suspicious lass!" Dr. Blair said. "Why do you think I would want to make suggestions? Suggestions about what?"

"I mean—you saw who I came in with. Isn't that like what fortune tellers do—ask questions so they can tell you you're going to meet the man of your dreams and he's tall, dark, and handsome?"

Dr. Blair laughed. "Whew!" he said. "Thank goodness I hid my crystal ball before you came in." It was his turn to lift an eyebrow. "Lass, you are an absolute delight."

Fiona gave a weak laugh. The doctor sat back in his chair and studied his patient.

"I'm just teasing you. About the crystal ball, that is." He steepled his fingers and leaned forward again. "Hypnotherapists are not fortune tellers, I can assure you. Our job is not to predict your future; it's to help you recover memories you already have—memories that may be buried deep in your subconscious."

"But—"

The doctor sat back in his chair and folded his hands in his lap. He gave Fiona a gentle smile. "Hypnotherapy is many things, but one thing it definitely is *not* is a magic show," he said. "It simply allows you to achieve a deeper state of concentration than your conscious mind allows. You're here to figure out what these dreams of yours may be hiding, aye?"

"O—kay."

"Think of it like this—have you ever seen someone use a magnifying glass to focus the rays of the sun and make them more powerful?"

"Like in the movies, when Indiana Jones uses a piece of glass to start a fire?" Fiona asked.

"Exactly like that. With hypnotherapy, we can help you focus your attention and go deeper into your memories. Experiences your conscious mind has blocked can be recovered and brought to the surface."

"All right. I guess that makes sense." Fiona sat back in her chair and gave the doctor her first genuine smile. This wasn't so bad—so far.

"So, is he?" Dr. Blair said.

"Is who?"

"Is the tall, dark, and handsome lad out in the waiting room the man of your dreams?"

The blush that crept onto her face spoke for itself.

"Well—"

Dr. Blair waited.

The smile faded from Fiona's face. "Well, yes and no. That's the problem—I'm dreaming about a man who looks just like Ewan, but I don't think it's him."

"Hmm. It's pretty common to dream about people you know, though. Tell me why this is so disturbing."

"Because—because I've been having dreams about this man for months now, and I just met Ewan a few weeks ago. It's frightening. Also, the dreams are about places I'd never been until recently—experiences I've never had in my life."

"You know about déjà vu, right? Could it be that?"

Fiona shook her head. "It's not that. Ewan and I

already considered that possibility. I don't know how I know, but we both know that's not it."

Her voice shook. "Can you help me, Dr. Blair? I think I'm going crazy."

He patted her hand. "You're not going crazy. It's not that easy to go crazy, you know." He smiled. "And yes, I think hypnotherapy might help. Shall we give it a go?"

Fiona nodded.

"All right, let me explain the stages of hypnotherapy, so you'll understand what to expect. First, the key is relaxation. You must calm your mind before you can focus on your memories. We use breathing techniques and help you to slow your thoughts and your body."

"Is it like meditation? Something like what I do in yoga class?"

"Very like. Second, you will go deeper into a trance state. I'll know when that is happening because your eyes will move from side to side." He laughed at her expression. "Don't worry, that's good."

"If you say so," Fiona muttered.

"Finally," said Dr. Blair, "will enter what is called the somnambulistic state. Not as scary as it sounds; it's the deepest state, where your unconscious mind will focus on memories that you have repressed, perhaps due to trauma that you may not even be aware of. This is where you want to be."

"I do?"

"You do," he said. Looking at her face, he added, "Don't worry, at any time if you want to wake up, you can do so. It's all up to you. You'll awaken fully alert, although you may find that you do not remember it all consciously. Or then again, you may. It all depends on the individual."

"And no barking or standing on my head?"

"Nothing of the sort, I promise. Ready?"

She sighed. "I suppose so. Let's do this."

"That's the lass," the doctor said. "Just lie down on that couch, and make yourself comfortable."

For the next fifteen minutes, Dr. Blair led Fiona through a series of exercises to relax her mind.

"Now," he said, "I want you to start counting backwards from three hundred . . . three hundred . . . two hundred and ninety-nine . . . two hundred and ninety-eight . . . two hundred and ninety-seven . . . two hundred and ninety-six . . . two hundred and ninety-five . . . two hundred and ninety-four . . ."

Fiona felt as if she were sinking in a warm pool of water. She could feel the ripples as she sank lower and lower, tethered only by the soothing voice of the doctor as she moved further away, down and down in the comforting warmth of the water. She kept her eyes closed and let the current take her.

The voice continued, "Think of someone who loves you . . . a friend . . . relative or . . . someone else. Now, hold onto that person in your mind and don't let go."

Fiona opened her eyes, and Ewan floated before her in the pool, his hair waving about his face with the movement of the water. She fastened onto his face, holding it before her like a talisman.

She studied his eyes, beacons of blue that reached into her very being like an embrace. His generous mouth, lips upturned in the half-smile that had become so familiar. Her mind reached for him, and she felt his arms go about her and hold her close as they descended together.

The water was gone. She was standing alone now, in a field covered by heather and thistle. She heard the wind, felt it against her skin. Ewan was gone, and yet she was not alone.

A woman approached her, walking gracefully through the grass as if she were floating. She was oddly dressed, wearing men's clothing from a long-ago time. A long white blouse had come loose from its kilt and blew in the soft wind. Tendrils of auburn hair curled from under a slouch hat. Black leather boots encased her legs to the knee. Fiona saw that the pattern of the kilt was one she knew well. It was her own—the MacLean tartan.

The woman—no more than a girl, really—approached until she stood no more than three feet away. She said nothing, but her eyes held Fiona spellbound. Mesmerizing eyes, green like a new forest. They held flecks of darker green, as if all the colors of spring had gathered to celebrate.

Fiona knew those eyes. They were the eyes she saw gazing back at her every day in the mirror. Recognition sank into her soul, and she knew without doubt that this was the woman in the portrait at Raasay House. The bride of the future laird of Clan Macleod.

Eilidh MacLean stared back at her. A small smile creased her pale face, and a single tear rolled down her cheek. Then she spoke, her accent strong and musical. "If you are who I think you are," she said, "then you are the me of a future time. I do not know how this is possible, but there are many things in this world that are beyond my ken."

"If you are Eilidh MacLean of Raasay, then I think you're right," Fiona said. "It's impossible, but it must be true."

The woman nodded. She waved a slim hand at the field behind her. "Do you know this place?" she asked. "Does it have a name in your time?"

Fiona forced her eyes away from the woman to look at the landscape. She did know this place. It was different—gone were the paved pathways through the heather and gorse, gone were the engraved boulders placed to honor the Highland clans who had passed here.

They were standing on Drumossie Moor—a vast untouched field that someday would be known as Culloden Battlefield. In her time, a stone monument would be erected in the center—a memorial that read, "*The Battle of Culloden was fought on this moor 16-April-1746. The graves of the gallant Highlanders who fought for Scotland and Prince Charlie are marked by the names of their clans.*"

A visitor's centre would be built, a parking lot constructed for the hordes of tourists who would flow from buses to witness the place where a way of life in the Scottish Highlands had been eradicated in less than an hour.

"My story ended here," said Eilidh MacLean.

Tears rose in Fiona's eyes and she swiped a hand across to clear her vision. The woman in men's Highland clothing raised a slim hand.

"Do not be sad for me—it was my fate. Know that I was happy, if only for a short time. But it can be different for you, if you have courage."

"I don't understand," Fiona said, her voice sounding desperate to her ears. "I don't understand any of it."

"Please—you must listen to me. There is something you must remember when you wake from this dream.

"*Everything repeats.*"

"Everything repeats," Fiona echoed. "What does it mean?"

"The fate in this world is continuing in that world," Eilidh said. "You must protect that man, as I was unable to do."

"Wh-who?" said Fiona. But here, deep in the recesses of her subconscious mind, she knew.

"Protect him against the dangerous ones," Eilidh said again. "They too continue in your time. You must . . ."

"Ten . . . nine. . . .ight. . ."

The scene dimmed. A grey mist rose over the moor, and the woman began to waver and fade. In another moment, darkness had erased the presence of the woman called Eilidh MacLean. Drumossie Moor was gone and Fiona felt herself rising—the water surrounded her again and cradled her in its warmth as she moved upward toward the light.

". . . .even . . . six. . . .ive . . . four. . ." A voice came from far away.

She continued to float upward, toward the sound of the voice.

". . . .hree . . . two . . . one."

Fiona opened her eyes. She lay on the couch in Dr. Blair's office. He was smiling at her.

"I think that we were successful, aye?" the doctor said. "You were gone very far away."

Fiona struggled to a sitting position. Hadn't he said she would wake up refreshed and alert? Her head felt as if it had been packed with wool. She struggled to remember, and through the haze in her mind came a single line. *Everything repeats.*

"Please—" she said. "I need Ewan."

CHAPTER 30

INVERNESS, SCOTLAND - PRESENT DAY

*If I have more than one life, I would definitely
dedicate this one entirely to you.*
Nico J. Genes

"She told me to protect you." Fiona picked up her glass of whisky and downed it in one gulp.

"Ach, watch it, lass!" Ewan took the glass from her hand and put it next to his. "That's all for you."

Her answer was to beckon the waitress over and order another. Ewan sighed and shook his head.

"You'll be sorry later," he warned her. "Don't come crying to me when your head rolls off."

"Ewan," Fiona said, "you should have seen her. She looked exactly like me. I mean, exactly. She *was* me—she said so."

Ewan waited until the waitress had brought another glass of whisky and departed.

"So, what are we thinking here? We're back to

reincarnation, aye? That's what you're telling me."

"I can't believe I'm saying it out loud, but yes. We were right—those are not dreams I'm having. I think they're my memories. Or not mine, exactly. Eilidh's."

Ewan thought for a moment. "So, if she shared her memories with you, that means you are her reincarnation." He looked around the tavern. No one seemed to be paying attention to them, thank goodness. Otherwise, the doctors from New Craig's Psychiatric Hospital up the road could be counted on to show up and cart them both away.

A few weeks ago, he would never have entertained the idea of reincarnation as anything but a movie fantasy. Past lives, ghosts on Culloden Moor warning of danger and intrigue, all that was bizarre and unbelievable. He would have dismissed Fiona MacLean as just another outlander chasing the mythical romance of the Highlands.

But that was before they'd seen the portrait. Before Fiona's experience with hypnotherapy, verified by a respectable professional like Dr. Blair.

Before the accidents.

His fall from the trail at Aonach Eagach could have been dismissed as carelessness on his part—there were no witnesses and the trail was always dangerous.

He had been pushed, though. He knew it now for certain. He hadn't merely fallen—he'd *flown* off that cliff, and only the miracle of that spar of rock and his own conditioning had saved him from certain death.

Even if he could live with the explanation that the fall was all his own fault, there was the brake failure on the A9. He had his beloved Mercedes back; there was nothing to show for his interaction with a bale of hay, but the mechanic was adamant—someone had tampered with his brake line.

And . . . there was his father. No matter how hard he tried, Ewan couldn't shake the feeling that there was more to his father's death than the doctor had allowed. He had no proof, but Duncan MacArthur's words refused to leave his memory.

There have been—incidents.

I think someone is trying to kill me.

"Ewan?" He broke out of his trance to find Fiona staring at him. God, she was beautiful—her green eyes, even slightly unfocused from the effects of the single malt, were like a siren's call. He wanted to fall into them, drown in them.

He opened his mouth, and the words fell out.

"I love you."

"What?" A flush spread over her pale face.

Damn, this wasn't where he had planned to tell her—here in a crowded pub where anyone might hear him.

So, who cares if someone hears? She's the only one that matters.

He was in love with this woman. To be honest, he'd been in love with her from the moment he'd laid eyes—and hands and arms—on her in the car park of Culloden Visitor's Centre. And that was pure dafty.

Love at first sight was stupid. He didn't believe in it for a minute; it was the stuff of romance novels and cheesy movies. He was an adult, for God's sake. He was making a fool of himself over something he knew was ridiculous.

He'd dated before. He'd even thought he was serious about a girl in university, but in the end it hadn't worked out. Nobody's fault; there just wasn't enough to sustain it. They'd parted on good terms and gone their separate ways.

Fiona 's mouth was open in a perfect "O." "I—I—"

"I'm sorry. I didn't—" He'd only had one drink; he couldn't be drunk. He held his breath, hoping this wasn't the part where she cut and ran.

"I love you too." Her voice was so low he had to strain to hear it.

Ewan could feel a roaring in his ears like the sound of wind in a mountain storm. He shook his head to clear it, but the roaring intensified.

He leaned across the table. "I didn't quite get that. Did you just say something?"

"You heard me." She slapped his hand.

"Say it again."

"Nope." Her eyes were bright and luminous. They were the flash of green he'd seen on the Aonach Eagach ridge. Before he'd even met her.

"I'm the one who's had two whiskys, that excuse won't work," Fiona said, laughing. The smile widened and she reached over to take his hand.

"Let's just go with it, okay?"

Ewan took a deep breath. "Aye. Let's just go with it." He stood up, walked a tight circle in the middle of the pub, and sat back down. He knew he was grinning like a fool, and he didn't care. She loved him back. She loved him. He wanted to grab her and kiss her breathless, right in front of all these people. How could no one have noticed the lightning that had struck him just now?

"Um, Ewan . . . there's something we have to talk about." His smile faded at the expression on her face.

"Not here." He got up again and went to the bar, paid their bill and returned to pull her out of her seat. He practically dragged her out of the tavern and into the waning light of the Inverness dusk.

"Whew," he said. "Another minute in there and you would've been in trouble." He gave her a beatific smile and put an arm around her waist. They began to walk down the sidewalk that ran along the river.

"Where are we going?" Fiona asked him.

"My house. It's the only place we can get some privacy."

They walked across the Grieg Street bridge in silence, lost in their own thoughts, until they reached the High Street walkway. Buskers were packing up for the evening, but the street was still thronged with tourists and locals.

At the bottom of the stone staircase that led up to Ardconnell Street, Ewan turned to Fiona. "You know, I saw your car outside your guesthouse—the day we first met. I almost stopped to see you—should've known then there was no hope for me."

Fiona turned. "Why didn't you, then?"

"Two reasons. First, when you left the visitor's centre, your face didn't look as sweet as it does now. I was afraid." He dodged the fist that aimed for his shoulder and laughed. Then the laugh disappeared.

"Second," he said, "my father pulled up in his car. I hadn't seen him in ten years. I was in a right state and I have to admit that you went to the back of my mind. I'm sorry."

Fiona stopped in her tracks and tugged him around to face her.

"Don't be, Ewan," she said. "You might never have seen him again, and you needed to. Whatever happened, he was your father."

Ewan sighed. "I know. I just wish he had come much sooner. Maybe things would've turned out differently. I might have had more time with him."

He looked into her eyes, and suddenly tears were pouring down his face. A sob rose in his throat and he tried to choke it down, but others followed. He sagged against the stone wall and sank to the bottom step, burying his face in his arms.

Fiona knelt beside him. "Let it out, Ewan. It's been a long time coming."

He clutched her arms as if he were drowning and she was his life buoy. Passers-by looked at them curiously, then turned away from the raw pain they saw and hurried on their way.

"Why did I do that? If only I'd given him a chance, heard him out. He apologized, and I walked away from him. He reached out to me—and I was too busy hating him to listen."

Fiona was silent. There was nothing to say at a time like this. She held him, rocked him as he sobbed out his guilt and remorse like the small boy he'd been long ago. It was all she could do; it had to be enough.

After a while, Ewan's ragged breathing steadied. He looked up with watery eyes and summoned a wan smile.

"Sorry."

"What I'm here for." They sat on the stone step for a long time, and then she said, "Ewan, I think your father has something to do with my dreams. Wait, let's call them visions now—that's probably more accurate."

"What do you mean?"

"I can't explain it, but I don't think we're the only ones. It only makes sense that more people have been reincarnated in this time than just us."

"Us?"

"Yes, us. You're a part of this story." She grasped his hand and helped him back to his feet. "Wait till we get to your house. I'll explain there."

Ewan's house was a smaller version of the great guesthouses on Ardconnell Street. Built of local sandstone, it had three dormer windows across the steep roof, and two larger windows flanking the front door. Ivy wound up the chimney and across the front of the house, and two white-painted rocking chairs sat on the patio.

"No one's ever sat in those," Ewan told Fiona. "This used to be a small guest house. I've only had it for a year, and I haven't got around to changing much. I do try to keep up with the back garden—I don't have a green thumb, though, so it fights me all the way."

He led her inside to a charming sitting room with an old stone fireplace and a curved archway between that room and a small dining area.

"It's lovely," Fiona assured him. "Funny—I thought you'd live in an ultra-modern flat. I'm so glad you don't; this is perfect."

Ewan went to an antique sideboard and brought out a bottle of wine. He poured them each a glass and they sat side by side on a black leather sofa. He touched his wineglass to hers.

"To 'us,'" he said. She nodded and took a sip.

"Now, tell me. You said Eilidh MacLean told you to protect me. How did she know? Did she say my name?"

"Well, she wouldn't have known your name, would she?" Fiona said. "She probably didn't even know mine. It's not like I could tell her.

"She said 'everything repeats itself.' And she said that the fate of her time is continuing in ours, and I'm to protect you against 'the dangerous ones'—who also have reincarnated in this time."

"But how do you know she meant me?" Ewan asked again. "You said she just said, 'that man.' Maybe it's someone else."

"She said she was unable to protect him in her time, but I have a chance to change fate. And it has to be you—or why would I keep seeing you in my dreams? Why did I see you dressed in a British Army uniform in the video at Culloden Visitor's Centre—when no one else does?" She stopped, then went on in a rush.

"I think you're the reincarnation of Eilidh's lover. I think something happened to them both, and it has to do with the Battle of Culloden."

"Hmm, okay, let's go with that for a minute," Ewan said. "The tour guide at Raasay House said that Eilidh MacLean disappeared after the battle, and so did Cullen MacLeod. Could I be the reincarnation of

Cullen? After all, they were going to be married."

"Maybe," Fiona said. "The important thing, though, is these 'dangerous ones.' Who could they be?" She took another sip of wine, put the glass down and took Ewan's hands in her own.

"I think some person—maybe more than one—who was dangerous in Eilidh's time is here again in ours—and I think he or she has something to do with your accidents. If we accept reincarnation, then it's not a leap to think that people don't change much over time. People who loved each other deeply then would love again now. Evil people would be evil in this time too."

She looked up, excitement igniting the green in her eyes. "I know I'm right. Don't ask me how I know—I just do."

"I believe you," Ewan said, his voice soft. "And if we accept that, then I think we have to accept that my father may also have been right. He thought someone was trying to kill him—and I can't shake the feeling that maybe someone did."

INVERNESS,
SCOTLAND - PRESENT DAY

If there's one thing I've learned over the eons,
it's that you can't give up on your family,
no matter how tempting they make it."
Rick Riordan

"**P**lease—you have to come with me." Ewan widened his eyes and tried to look frightened. The result was so ridiculous that Fiona dissolved into laughter.

"It's only a family dinner, not an execution," she said. "I wasn't invited, and it would be inappropriate for me to be there. You'll have to man up."

He dropped the beaten puppy face and resorted to pleading. "Please. You said you have to protect me. What kind of protection is this?"

Fiona rolled her eyes. "I don't think Eilidh meant for me to protect you against your own family, Ewan."

Her face stilled and she became reflective. "However, your father *did* suspect someone of trying to kill him, and he *did* will the distillery to you. In a crime novel, it would be a clue."

She turned and faced him. "When did he change his will?"

"I have no idea," Ewan said. "When he met me on your street, he said he *wanted* to make me the heir. I assumed he was just thinking about it, but at the reading I discovered that he was giving me the whole lot. I guess he could have done it at any time."

"So—it was a surprise to everyone, not just you?"

Ewan thought for a moment. "I suppose it could have been. I hadn't seen them for years, and none of them reacted as if they were terribly upset about it, so I just assumed I'd been the only one in the dark."

"So," Fiona said, "maybe they didn't know either. Maybe someone—" she sat up straight on Ewan's couch.

"I'm going to that dinner."

"What?" Ewan stared at her. "What changed your mind?"

"Well, I haven't met any of them yet." She gave him an arch smile. "If we're a couple, I suppose you should be taking me to meet the family—aye?"

Ewan's face lit, and he gathered her into a hug. "Aye. That's my lass." He pursed his lips in a vain attempt to hide the smile that wouldn't go away.

"What?" Fiona said.

"You said we're a couple. We are, aren't we?" The grin widened. "A couple."

She sighed. "I'm too easy. I'll have to work on that. So now that we've settled that problem, what's next?"

"We're going on a tour," Ewan announced. "It's

time you experienced Highland Magic.

"Don't you think I've experienced enough Highland magic for one lifetime?" Fiona asked. "I've had visions, been hypnotized, and found out that I have a doppelgänger in the eighteenth century. I don't know how much more magic I can take."

"Highland Magic is the name of my tour company, ye wee diddy." Ewan ruffled Fiona's hair.

"I thought it was called Wild Scotland. And what's a diddy? Doesn't sound flattering." She gave him her best side-eye.

"It means you're beautiful," he said, but the blue eyes crinkling at the edges told her differently.

"Humph, I'll just ask Jeremy."

Ewan decided it was time for a distraction. "Wild Scotland is my scrambling company. I'll take you scrambling someday, but you're not ready for that yet."

"And what's scrambling? That doesn't sound like much fun."

"Well, fun isn't what scramblers are going for, exactly. It's more to do with the excitement of bagging Munros."

"Wait! I know what Munros are. They're a bunch of mountains, right?"

"Right. You're not such a diddy, after all." He dodged her hand and laughed. "The Munros are a certain group of mountains that are over three thousand feet high. They were listed by Sir Hugh Munro back in 1891—thus the name."

"So, and I hesitate to ask for fear of being called *beautiful*, what is 'Munro bagging'?"

"Munro baggers challenge themselves to climb all

the Munros in Scotland. There are two hundred and eighty-two of them."

"Has anyone actually achieved this lofty goal?" Fiona asked.

"I have," Ewan said. He put his hands on his hips and held his nose in the air. "I am a certified Munroist, along with six thousand others."

"You're messing with me, aren't you? Is that really a thing?"

"Of course it is, young grasshopper. Granted, Munro bagging isn't for everyone, but scrambling is a great way for experienced—and I really do mean experienced—climbers to explore the finest scenery in the Highlands. You'd be surprised how many people sign up for Wild Scotland. I was shocked, honestly—I wasn't sure I could make a living at it, but—"

"But there are a lot of crazy people out there," Fiona nodded. "Got it."

"And that attitude is the reason we're going on a Highland Magic tour instead." Ewan assumed a sad expression. "Trying to deal with the uninitiated . . ." he mumbled under his breath.

"I can hear you, Bagger Man," she said, and danced away from his grasp, laughing.

Fifteen minutes later they were seated in the front seat of a small van with the Highland Magic logo emblazoned on its sides, heading out of Inverness with four other tourists. Two university-aged girls from Germany took the back seats, behind a middle-aged American couple. They introduced themselves in English, and Fiona noticed that the girls' eyes kept straying to Ewan. *Well, they're not immune,* she thought, and her heart did a little flip.

Ewan was oblivious to the admiring glances from the back. "You're in for a treat, lass," he told her, but his look was anxious. Of course, she thought, this was his pride and joy. He had built his unique tour company from scratch, and he wanted to show it off to her.

A wave of affection washed over her. *Even if I hate it, I'd never let him know.*

They crested a rise, and in the distance, on a plateau which rose up and dwarfed the countryside around it, stood a massive stone ruin.

"I don't know this castle," Fiona said in delight. "Whose was it?"

"Bonny, isn't it?" Ewan said. "It's not a castle, though." That's Ruthven Barracks." He refused to enlighten her further, so she gazed out at the countryside and listened to the German students chattering in the rear seat.

They were met at the Barracks by a serious-looking Highlander dressed in the Feileadh Mòr, or great kilt.

"Weel, it's abit time ye showed up. We need aw th' men we can muster if we're tae keep th' damn British aff uir hides," he announced. "Gie oan in an' gie yer muskets. Ye do ken hoo tae shoot a muskit, aye?"

One of the German girls giggled, and the Highlander rounded on her.

"Do ye think thes is fun? We jist took back th' barracks from George's men in Februar, an' lost puckle guid men in th' doin'."

He turned away in feigned disgust and led them to the center of the barracks.

"Aftir ye gie yer weapons, ye need tae ken a wee bit o' th' history ay thes place."

Fiona was struggling to keep up with the man's thick Scots, and she pitied the poor German girls for whom English was a second language. But they seemed thrilled. The American couple was grinning and gesturing to each other.

"Ruthven barracks waur built by George's government atween 1719 an' 1721." He glowered at his 'troops.' "At was efter James, th' king athwart th' water, was defeated. Hard times fur us Jacobites, 't be sure.

"But noo, in 1746, we've taken it back fur Bonnie Prince Charlie, an' we willnae be losin' it again." The Highlander gave the group a triumphant stare.

"But what about the Battle of Culloden?" the American man asked him. "Didn't the Jacobites get defeated there for good?"

Fiona giggled at the look of confused horror on the Highlander's face. She could guess what was coming.

"Whit ur ye yammerin abit? Battle ay Culloden? Ne'er heard sich' drivel. Ye want tae be sent haem packin' tae yer clan?" He clucked his teeth and handed out the muskets, keeping a wary eye on the American.

The audience was entranced. No matter how often they tried to get their guide to break character, he remained firmly planted in his chosen time.

In between teaching and demonstrating the use of a musket, the guide told them that Ruthven Barracks had been built on the site of a medieval castle. He emphasized the strategic location, visible from miles around and dominating the Spey valley.

He pointed out where the guardroom, prison, and bakehouse had been located, as if those rooms were still there. Listening to him, Fiona could almost see the ghost of the old barracks rise up from the past.

"If ye shaw me ye can handle th' muskit, mebbe we'll visit th' brewhoose efter, aye?" He winked at the group.

He glared at the American, to the man's delight. "Nane fur ye, sairrr. Culloden battlefield, n'deed."

On the return trip home, the mood in the van was ecstatic.

"Oh, John," the American woman laughed. "He had your number, didn't he?"

"I have to admit this was the most fun I've ever had on a tour," her husband said. "It's worth the extra expense, and more."

Fiona elbowed Ewan, who gave her a proud smile. *This is his baby—and he's raised it well*, she thought. Pride enveloped her like a warm blanket. *I'm keeping him.*

The dinner was being hosted by Ariadne Beck. Fiona looked around at the substantial apartment and wondered where a secretary had gotten enough money to afford a flat like this. Then again, she'd been Duncan MacArthur's right hand for so many years—he probably had paid her what she was worth.

"So, you're the girlfriend." She gave her attention to the man in front of her. "I'm Aaron. Nice to meet you—you're quite a beauty."

She gave him a polite smile. It was obvious that Aaron Grant had started drinking early. His words were slurred and his eyes glazed.

Despite that, he was an extremely handsome man. *Quite a beauty yourself*, she thought, *though not my type.* An artfully placed lock of wavy dark hair fell over a face that could have come straight from a painting. Large hazel eyes, perfect nose, full mouth spoiled by the leer that twisted his lips. She smiled as she evaded his hand—*and where were you thinking to put that, lad?*

"You must be Fiona." A hand reached out to pull her away from Aaron. She turned a grateful look on the young man who stood before her, brown eyes crinkled in a laugh. "Thought you might need rescuing."

Adam MacArthur was a doll, Fiona decided, and it wasn't just because he'd saved her from an embarrassing situation. Maybe it had something to do with the remarkable resemblance to Ewan. Apart from the difference in eye color, the two could've been twins. Somehow she knew that if Adam let his hair grow longer, it would be just as wild as his brother's.

"Thank you," she said. "I was about to practice some of my favorite self-defense moves, but I could tell he wasn't entirely in possession of his senses. Besides, incapacitating Ewan's brother-in-law wouldn't make for a really good first impression."

Adam laughed. "Well, Aaron probably would've made a pass at you even if he were sober. Thinks he's God's gift to women." He glanced back to where Aaron swayed slightly as he refilled his glass. "To be fair, though, he's not serious about it. Very much in love with my sister, he is. Which is a good thing, because she'll be driving him home tonight."

They were joined by a gorgeous blond girl who reminded Fiona of her sister, Kirsty.

"Sophie, have you met Fiona MacLean?" Adam asked her. "This is the baby of the family," he said. "She's very spoiled, but not so bad when you get to know her."

Sophie punched her brother in the shoulder and then put her arm through his.

"Hello," she said, her voice bright. "I'm glad to meet you—so you're Ewan's bodyguard?"

Fiona stiffened at the words, but the young woman was laughing.

"I mean, Ewan hasn't exactly had an easy time of it. We're a family of numptys, we are. Left him all alone after Mom died. Inexcusable, but we're all trying to make it up to him—although in my defense I was little and didn't really know what was going on."

"Ach, leave me out of it!" Adam waved a finger at her. "I stuck by him."

Tears filled Sophie's eyes. "Aye, you did, and I'm glad one of us had some sense."

"Are you two telling tales on me?" Ewan came up and put an arm around Fiona. "Don't believe either of them. Come on, Miss Beck says it's time for dinner."

Conversation was awkward at first—Fiona noticed covert glances aimed toward Ewan and realized that this was the first time he'd participated in a social event with his family in sixteen years. He pretended not to notice, but her heart ached for him.

She glanced around the table as they ate. Jonah—the studious one, she remembered—gave her a vacant smile and returned to his own thoughts.

Daniel, who seemed to be giving Aaron a run for his money with alcohol, favored her with a practiced smile. The ladies' man, Ewan had told her. Somehow it wasn't offensive coming from him, though. Maybe because his charm was natural and unaffected, unlike the predatory advances of his brother-in-law.

Her eyes went to Iseabail, who kept glancing at her husband with eyes that were half worried, half adoring. Aaron did seem very affectionate toward his wife, Fiona had to admit, and was obviously trying to rein in his inebriation for her sake. Maybe he wasn't all that bad.

She studied him from under her lashes. What was it about Aaron Grant? Had she met him before—maybe on the distillery tour? No, she remembered that horrible day with perfect clarity. Besides, Aaron had the kind of looks that a woman would remember. He was a stranger to her. So why did he seem so familiar?

The words slid into her mind. *Like a painting . . .*

CHAPTER 32

RAASAY HOUSE, SCOTLAND - 1746

IAIN

"Iain," said Eilidh.

"Mmm?" He turned to face her. They were alone in the library. Hugh was ill again and confined to bed, and no one else ever seemed to care where Eilidh was. Iain found that interesting.

They sat at the same table where he'd first seen her, upon his arrival at Raasay House. Eilidh toyed with the pages of the book she'd been reading.

"There's something that's been bothering me," she said. I know you can't talk about your plans, and I respect that. I trust you." She gazed at him, those incredible sea green eyes boring a hole through his soul.

If he had a soul.

"Something happened a week ago. It was the day we—found out who you really are—"

"The day you accused me of being a spy?"

"Which you are," she said, with some asperity. "Don't make me look like the villain here. You just weren't the kind of spy I thought you were."

Iain turned his head away to regain his composure.

He had been lost the moment he saw her, captured by those eyes, by the light that danced through her chestnut hair, but most of all by her spirit.

The spirit of a Jacobite.

He had never felt so good. He had never felt so bad. She trusted him, loved him, and he was the scum of the earth. He could justify, even take pride in, his quick thinking when challenged. How much of it was a need to survive, and how much a desire to have her acceptance, he refused to contemplate.

He could have just run. He hadn't found out anything yet, and he'd been here for a month. He was terrible at this—Iain hated lying even more than he hated Charles Stuart, and he was appalled at how good he was at it.

"Stick to the truth whenever you can," Colonel Buchanan had told him. "Say as little as possible—let your cover do the talking for you. You are there to listen."

And to deceive. He felt sick.

"Iain? What is wrong?" He was jerked back to reality by the concern in Eilidh's voice.

"Oh? Oh, nothing. What did you need to tell me?"

"That day," she began, "we had gone for a ride to the sea, remember?"

How could he forget? "The day you cut and ran and left me alone in the woods?" he said. He schooled his face into a reproachful mask and forced a mocking tone into his voice.

She reddened. "Um, yes, that day. I was—I—never mind. That is not important. That day, I heard something."

Eilidh lowered her voice to a whisper. She told him of the fragmented conversation she had overheard in the outbuilding, and watched concern begin to build on Iain's face.

"These men were talking about Charles Stuart? Are you sure you heard correctly?"

"They called him 'the Italian fop,' Eilidh said. "That's what the government troops call him, isn't it? And they said 'kill.'"

"But why would anyone here at Raasay House want to harm Charles?" Iain scrubbed a hand through his hair. "This is a Jacobite stronghold."

"I know," Eilidh whispered. "That was why I was so frightened. Those men had to be strangers. And it's why I thought—" she snapped her lips shut and studied her clasped hands.

"So that's why you attacked me in the hallway! You thought I was spying for those men!" *You have no idea how close you were to the truth.*

Then Iain's focus sharpened onto what she had just said.

"How did you hear this? How close were you? Could they have seen you?" He felt panic welling up and stood up to walk around the table and clear his head.

"I was outside the building, and there is no way they could have seen me. I sneaked away and made a lot of noise returning, so they would not suspect anyone was there before." Eilidh seemed both proud of her cleverness and surprised at Iain's vehemence.

Her eyes narrowed. "Why are you so angry?"

He came back to stand next to his chair. His next words came out in a hiss of frustration. "If these men were planning the death of your sainted prince, and if they knew you heard them, do you think they would allow you to remain in their way? What does Rory say about this?"

Eilidh's eyes dropped. "I didn't tell Rory yet."

Iain jerked her out of her chair and stood glaring at her. She yanked her hand out of his, but stood her ground.

"If I told him, he would go looking for them. He worries about me more than he needs to. But I worry about him too."

"So why haven't you told Cullen? Do you not think he has a right to know about something like this, so he can protect you?"

It was as if the air had gone out of Eilidh, leaving her visibly deflated. She hung her head and shuffled her foot.

"Would he, though?"

"What?"

"Protect me. Would he even care?"

"You're going to marry him! Of course he would protect you—treasure you. Any man would. I would!"

Iain stopped speaking as the words he had just said reverberated in his ears. Eilidh was staring at him, her green eyes wide.

"I mean—I—"

Eilidh threw her arms around him and pulled him close. His head bent and his lips met hers as if of their own accord, and he kissed her with all the pent-up passion he had not known was stored in his aching heart.

Iain came back from far away and reclaimed his body, moving away from her in a giant step. He stood staring at her, gasping for air.

"I'm sorry," he managed after a moment. "I'm so very sorry."

"I'm not," Eilidh said. Her voice was calm, with only a slight tremor. "I am not in the least sorry." She fisted her hands at her sides.

"I do not care who you are, or what your real name is. I have been wanting to do that ever since I met you. I am not a wanton woman. I will not bother you—I know we have no future—but I wanted you to know. You have given me courage to face the future, and I am grateful."

The distance was bridged again as Iain stepped forward and took her into his arms once more. Their lips met again, and time stopped.

"I will protect you," Iain whispered, his breath soft against her forehead. "No matter what happens, I will protect you."

A soft sound had them springing apart. Iain whirled. Godfrey Lewis stood in the doorway, a smirk on his swarthy features.

CHAPTER 33

RAASAY HOUSE, SCOTLAND - 1746

EILIDH

"Well, this is interesting."

Eilidh stared at Godfrey Lewis. Suddenly she understood how a hare must feel with its shattered foot caught in the trap, facing its hunter for the last time.

"This is not what you think—" Iain began, but Godfrey put up his hand to ward off the words.

"I could not care less." He moved into the room to stand before them. "Shall we sit down?"

Eilidh fell into the chair like a marionette whose strings have been cut. The two men sat, and for long minutes no one said anything. Then Godfrey spoke, almost to himself.

"This might just work out for the best."

Both Eilidh's and Iain's heads snapped up.

Godfrey studied his hands. Then he looked at Eilidh—a reptilian look devoid of emotion. It was almost as if he were seeing her for the first time.

"I thought you would be a complication," he said. "But now I see that it might be best if you know, after all." His eyes glittered.

"It is amusing, really. I only saw you as a nuisance—never figured you for a whore."

"Do not talk to her like that!" Iain's hands fisted and his voice was harsh. "Don't you ever call her that!"

"Calm down," Godfrey said in a bored voice. "I do not care what she is. But she is important."

"What are you talking about?" Eilidh spoke for the first time.

Godfrey looked at her with active dislike. "Did you never wonder why Cullen pays you no attention?" He shook his head in disbelief. "I mean, you are a beautiful woman—were you not at all surprised?"

Eilidh blinked. Had she wondered? Early on, she had wished for more contact from Cullen, more feeling. But she'd assumed that it was just his personality, that love would grow after they were married. And lately, she realized she hadn't much cared. A blush stained her cheeks and she looked across the table.

Godfrey's mouth curled up in a smile of derision. "I have to say, I rather enjoyed watching you trail around after Cullen like a dog waiting for scraps."

"Stop it." Iain's voice was level, but his eyes radiated danger.

"I do not think you are in much of a position to be giving me orders, do you?" Godfrey sent Iain an irritated look. "If I didn't need you, I might take care of that condescending attitude you have.

"Anyway—" he turned his attention back to Eilidh. "Things were going so well here, and then *you* showed up. I know, I know. Not your fault—it had to be done. Cullen had to have a bride, to keep up the family honor and have an heir and all that." He picked up a pen and cleaned a fingernail, giving it all his attention.

"But I find that you have become too much of a distraction. You are not stupid—you would have figured it out sooner or later. So it's probably better if you know. You now have no choice but to keep the secret."

This was like a bad dream, Eilidh thought. She had no idea what this odious person was talking about, but knowing Godfrey it would have to be something awful. She stole a look at Iain, and the dawning horror on his face as he stared at the man across the table made her heart stop. The pieces fell into place, and she felt a rising nausea that had her clutching at the edges of the table with both hands.

"No—" she breathed.

Godfrey sat up and put the pen down. He smiled his pirate's smile. "Well, let us get to it. This is what is going to happen."

Eilidh heard his voice through a growing vortex of sound.

"You will marry Cullen, as arranged. He will not mistreat you—he's not that sort. All that I ask is that you stay out of our way. And of course, your lips will remain sealed."

"You—and Cullen?" Iain's disgust was palpable.

"Don't make it sound so seedy," Godfrey said. "I feel rather insulted by your tone. And after all, you are not exactly a saint, are you?"

"You—expect me to go through with this marriage?" Eilidh managed in a voice barely above a whisper.

"Of course. You will benefit from the arrangement, after all. You will be the beautiful lady of the house, an ornament on your husband's arm—free to move about as will be your due."

Godfrey's face twisted into a semblance of a smile.

"I should apologize for my inappropriate behavior toward you when you first arrived. I find that, when necessary, I can be quite the ladies' man."

He winked at her, and Eilidh felt her blood run cold.

"Did you enjoy your stolen moments with me?" He laughed at the look on her face. "I thought I cut quite a dashing figure, and if you thought I was a lecher you would not have an occasion to suspect anything else. Clever, aye?"

Godfrey turned to Iain. "Mr. MacCrimmon, you will stay on as an honored guest." He leaned back in his chair and stared at the ceiling. "Perhaps you can be prevailed upon to play the bagpipes for the wedding. Then, you will quietly leave and never come back. Does this arrangement suit you, sir?" he asked. His polite words belied the sneer on his face.

Iain spoke, his voice low and venomous. "I am just a visitor at this damned castle. I will be leaving—straightaway—and I will be taking Eilidh with me. I won't leave her alone for a minute in this den of snakes."

Godfrey stood up. "I would not do that if I were you. I will have people watching you. If you try to leave before the wedding, I fear I will have to expose your less than glorious activities. When Lord Malcolm hears how you tried to defile his soon-to-be daughter-in-law, you will be hunted down and brought to justice."

He walked to the door, and turned around to face them again. "Oh, one more thing. I, of course, will go along to make sure the insult to my friend's family is addressed—and to make sure that there is a regrettable accident. I'm afraid that something unfortunate will also happen to Miss MacLean's brothers. Cullen won't like losing Dom, but he is a bit of a fool and he does tend to hang around. I, for one, will not miss his presence." With that, he spun around and left the library, closing the door behind him.

Eilidh and Iain were left in silence. Without a word, he reached for her and pulled her into his arms. She crumpled into his embrace and let the tears flow. Iain held her close, murmuring into her ear.

"It will be all right, lass. He is just a bully. He will do nothing—now that we know his secret, he has too much to lose—as does Cullen."

"But why did he tell us?" Eilidh said. "Why did he take the risk?"

He held her at arm's length and looked into her eyes. "I don't know—perhaps he thinks what he has seen here will insure our silence. But I think there is something bigger going on here—something to do with those men you overheard. I am going to find out what it is, and we will stop it. Trust me?"

Eilidh felt a warmth spread through her body. "I do," she said. "I do trust you."

"When we go—we go together."

He twisted the silver ring off his right hand and pulled the leather cord from his queue. "I have never taken this off. I want you to wear it—as a reminder that I will always be with you." He slipped the cord through the ring and tied it around Eilidh's neck.

She put her arms around him and held on as if she were afraid to let go. When she looked up, her eyes were fierce.

"I promise you this, Iain. I will never let you be hurt because of me. Whatever the cost, I will protect you. Do you understand?"

INVERNESS, SCOTLAND - PRESENT DAY

Love is not an equation, it is not a contract, and it is not a happy ending . . . It is the place you come back to, no matter where you're headed.
Jodi Picoult

"U h . . . Jeremy . . ."

The historian looked up from his laptop. "Aye?"

"What's a diddy?"

A smile tugged at the edges of his mouth. "Someone called you that?"

"It doesn't mean beautiful, does it?" Fiona pursed her lips.

His laugh filled the office. "No. Not even close. It means stupid—a diddy is an eejit, or a numpty, or—"

"I get it," she held up a hand to stop the flow. "He's so dead."

Jeremy Brown returned to his laptop screen. His fingers flew on the keys, but an occasional chuckle told her he was still enjoying the joke.

"So—have you found anything?" Fiona kept her tone as polite as she could. *Someone* had to be professional around here.

He looked up again, and at the look on her face reined in his expression. "Hmm. Your tour guide at Raasay House was correct. There are no records on Cullen MacLeod after mid-April 1746. Malcolm came back from Culloden alone and went into hiding, after deeding the castle to his son Hugh."

He tapped a few more keys. "I did find something interesting, though."

Fiona sat up straight. "About Eilidh?"

"No." He read from the screen. "Did you know that, after the Battle of Culloden, Lady MacLeod left Raasay House and her husband and son?"

"Seriously? That's interesting," Fiona said. "She pulled her chair over beside Jeremy and stared at the screen. It was an article entitled, "The Early History of Raasay House," by Martin Bethune.

"See here," Brown pointed. "According to Bethune, Lucretia MacLeod was a Sutherland. Have you ever seen Castle Dunrobin?"

"Not yet. I've seen pictures, though. Beautiful. The Sutherlands stood for the government, right?"

"Aye. They did not fight at Culloden and backed the government through every rising." He entered "Dunrobin" in the search bar and brought up the images of the castle that had been the Sutherland seat for centuries. "You didn't get to keep a castle like this one if you had been a Jacobite."

Fiona remembered the portrait of Lucretia

MacLeod at Raasay House. The haughty, imperious glare, eyes that followed the observer everywhere.

"She looked like a snob," Fiona said. "Wouldn't surprise me if she left her husband because he was on the losing side."

"It was a strange family," said Brown. "Lots of disappearances. Martin Bethune may know more about what happened to them."

"What are this Bethune's credentials?' asked Fiona.

"He was a distant relative to the MacLeods. The MacLeods were kindred to the family of medical professionals, named Beaton. Later they changed the surname to Bethune."

"And this man is related to them?" Fiona asked.

The professor nodded. "Martin Bethune devoted his professional life to a study of his ancestors. He was at the top of his profession. One of the finest historical investigators in the Highlands."

Fiona noted the repetition of past tense. "Was? He's deceased?"

"No, he's alive," said Brown. "And he lives in Inverness. Shall I track him down?"

She gave him an exasperated look. "That does not deserve an answer—you diddy."

Jeremy Brown laughed and picked his cellphone up off the desk. He made several calls, and fifteen minutes later put the phone down and turned to face her.

"He lives right here in Inverness. But there's a problem."

Fiona's balloon deflated. Of course there was. She had been guilty of too much hope, again. She knew, as a historian, that the failures far outnumbered the successes when it came to tracking down information. Still . . .

"He's ninety-four years old now. He lives in a care facility called Ach-an-Eas. It's on Island Bank Road, very near here."

"That's wonderful! So why's it a problem?"

"I spoke with the director at the facility, and she told me Bethune is scheduled to be moved to another facility soon."

"Why?"

"Because he has dementia. It's worsening, and Ach-an-Eas doesn't provide care for dementia patients. They don't hold out much hope that he'll be able to tell us anything, because he's in and out of reality much of the time and they never know when he'll have a lucid period."

Fiona's shoulders slumped. It was so sad. Such a brilliant mind, reduced to fits and starts of awareness. All that wonderful knowledge gone, like sand with the tide.

Brown's voice broke into her reverie. "Cheer up, lass. You know better than most that we historians never give up. The director said she'll call when he's having a good day, and you can go right over to see him."

For the next hour they worked in comfortable silence—or at least Brown worked. Fiona brought up the website on Raasay House and read the tour information several times. Nothing more was mentioned that hadn't already been imparted by the tour guide, but Fiona's interest wasn't in the words on the screen. She clicked on the photo gallery.

The first photograph was a full front view of the

castle. Having been there, she found it easy to spot the differences in building materials between the central building and the later additions.

Eilidh MacLean walked past this doorway every day, she thought. *She may have touched the same stones that I did.* And then the thought flashed through her mind—*no, I passed by. I touched those stones, in 1746.* She would never be able to wrap her mind around it.

Eilidh, what happened to you? Why were you unable to protect your love?

Fiona returned to the photo gallery and brought up the portraits that she had seen in the library. Malcolm Macleod, resplendent in his clan's hunting tartan, stared back at her from calm dark eyes. *A man to be counted on, a man to trust.* She couldn't believe he could be one of the "dangerous ones," but looks could be deceiving. A portrait painter who wanted to be paid would likely not accentuate any villainous characteristics, after all.

She turned her attention to the portrait of Lady Macleod. Patrician features, maybe a little too strong for beauty. "Aren't we full of ourselves, my lady," Fiona murmured under her breath. Even through the computer screen, the woman's lofty expression dominated the portrait.

Those eyes. Why had the painter made them follow everyone? Was that his subtle way of hiding his opinion of her character within his work? If so, she'd bet Lady Macleod would have approved the result.

I don't like you, Fiona thought. Was she channeling Eilidh's thoughts about her future mother-in-law? She shivered and tore her eyes away from the woman's judgmental glare.

She moved on to the picture of Hugh Macleod. He took after his father—or he would if he gained twenty pounds. The same kind face, the same lovely brown eyes.

She had read that Hugh was sickly. She looked up his biography and found that he had been laird for less than a year, dying of tuberculosis in January 1747. He'd been only twenty-one years old. Sadness welled up at the loss of such a young man. She wished she'd known him.

She saved the portrait of Cullen Macleod for last. This had been Eilidh's betrothed—the man she'd come to Raasay to marry. Had they been happy?

"Jeremy," Fiona said. "Do you know anything about Eilidh MacLean's family? They were from one of the islands, right?"

He tapped a few keys. "Aye, Mull. They were impoverished gentry. A marriage to Macleod of Raasay would have been quite an achievement."

"So, an arranged marriage?"

"Most marriages between members of the nobility were arranged in those days. Travel was difficult, and there would have been few opportunities for a young well-born lady to meet others in her social class. Though clan MacLean had fallen on hard times financially, they were still considered the equal to others in their social strata. It would have been an advantageous match for Eilidh's family."

"But what about Cullen's?" Fiona asked. "What would his family get out of it?"

"Clan Macleod of Raasay had the money, but their

politics put them outside the favor of their better-known branch, the MacLeods of Skye. Because of their strong Jacobite connection, daughters of clans allied with the government would not have been encouraged to marry into Macleod of Raasay."

"So how would a girl living on Mull come to the attention of a clan living two hundred miles away on another island?"

"Good question," Brown said. "I don't want you to think there was no social life during those times, but it *was* harder for young people of the gentry to meet others of a like social status."

He rolled his chair around to face her. "Clan MacLean has, through the centuries, been military allies of clan Macleod. Besides that, clan Macleod of Raasay and clan MacLean of Mull were ardent Jacobites, so their political alliance was strong as well."

He cocked an eyebrow. "Just how many high-born young ladies do you think were wandering around the Highlands? Their lives were, in some ways, harder than those of the lower classes."

Fiona said, "You mean, they were more likely to be political pawns?"

The professor nodded. "Exactly. Where a young man and woman from the village might meet at a ceilidh, fall in love, and become handfasted, someone like Eilidh had no such opportunity. A village woman could even choose not to marry, but that was denied to women like Eilidh too. Her father would have made a match for her."

Fiona turned back to her laptop and the gallery of

portraits.

"Jeremy . . . do you think Cullen is handsome?"

The historian came over and studied the portrait over her shoulder. "Well . . . he's not really my type, ye ken?"

"Pay attention, and stop trying to be funny. I had a feeling about him when I saw this portrait at Raasay House, and I want to verify it—scientifically."

"You want to scientifically prove whether a man is good-looking or not? Oh, aye. That makes sense." She turned and glared at him, and he put his hands up in surrender. "Sorry. You're serious."

He pulled his chair over and nudged her out of the way. "Okay, let me see this paragon." He leaned forward and studied the portraits. "Takes after his mother, doesn't he?"

"That's what I thought," Fiona said. "They really look nothing alike, but there's something—"

"I don't like him," Brown announced. "Aye, he's handsome—beautiful really, almost feminine—but there's something around the eyes."

"So you see it too!" Fiona rounded on Jeremy. "Ewan and I assumed that Cullen was Eilidh's lover, because they were betrothed and—okay, because he's so lovely to look at—but I don't get it."

She looked at the portrait again. "If I'm supposed to be Eilidh's reincarnation, would I have this visceral reaction to the man she was supposed to marry? I don't like him, Jeremy. I didn't like him at Raasay House, and I don't like him now."

"Whoa, lassie," said Brown, "I know you told me about this reincarnation theory, and I'm game for going on with it—in theory." He turned his chair to face hers and put both hands on her arms. "I'm just saying, it's a lot to handle, and I don't want you going and jumping to any conclusions based on some dreams."

"What about the hypnotherapy session?" Fiona demanded. "Doesn't that mean something?"

Jeremy Brown sighed. "Remind me again why I told your father I'd follow through with this insanity?" He ran his hands through his brown hair, a gesture that reminded Fiona of Ewan.

"All right," he said, after a moment, "I can't believe I'm saying this, but let's assume that you are, in fact, the reincarnation of Eilidh MacLean. And let's assume that she really did tell you, through hypnosis, that you were to protect the reincarnation of the man she loved."

"Yes," Fiona said. "Let's assume that." Her crisp tone earned a glare from the professor.

He looked at the portrait again. "If you are seeing the images of Eilidh's lover in dreams, or visions—and I'm particularly interested in the vision you had at the Culloden Visitor's Centre—and if that person looks like Ewan MacArthur—" he broke off and scratched his head.

"Then," he said, holding her gaze, "Eilidh's lover—the one she wanted to protect and couldn't—he probably wasn't Cullen.

"There was another man."

CHAPTER 35

HIGHLANDS, SCOTLAND - PRESENT DAY

*It is the practice of evil, and hence, in a
sense, the inhuman that is the distinctive
mark of the human in the animal kingdom.*
Jean Baudrillard

Ewan sat alone in the office at Wild Thyme Distillery. His words to Fiona played through his memory like a song on repeat—*He thought someone was trying to kill him—and maybe someone did.* At the time, he hadn't meant to say that. Frustration and anger had been building, and the truth was that around Fiona he couldn't think coherently.

He opened his laptop and typed "what poisons can be found easily?" Then he stared at what he'd written and backspaced to delete the query. He sat for a minute longer, and typed it in again.

Was he really doing this? The idea that someone might have murdered his father was ludicrous. It was the stuff of movies and novels. Fantasy.

A month ago, he would never have allowed his mind to go down this road. But a month ago, he hadn't been pushed off a ridge, or had his brakes tampered with. A month ago, he hadn't met and fallen for a woman who was convinced he was the reincarnation of her lost lover. And he wouldn't have seen the proof of that in a portrait painted in 1746.

Ewan sighed and hit the search key.

The list was longer than he'd thought. "Pick Your Poison," "Household Products that Can Kill," "The World's Deadliest Plants." He shook his head in amazement. The ways and means for humans to kill each other were endless. *What a crappy world we live in.*

Aconite, arsenic, potassium chloride, deadly nightshade—*interesting name there*—and ricin. A lot of lethal chemicals were found in household cleaners or gardening supplies.

Who would've guessed that a smoothie could disguise the presence of antifreeze? Or that a little rat poison sprinkled into your cake icing would eventually lead to death?

He changed the phrase to, "What poisons can mimic a heart attack?" and hit the search bar again. Another list came up—shorter but still daunting—and he clicked on the one that said, "Prescription for Murder."

It was a blog for murder mystery writers, and listed several lethal toxins that would ultimately lead to heart failure. There was a case where a woman had killed her husband by injecting him with something called succinylcholine, a muscle relaxant used in hospitals.

But in that case, the murderer had been a nurse.

Not just anyone could get his hands on that stuff. He had learned to respect the supernatural since meeting Fiona MacLean, but the idea of a psychotic nurse or doctor running around Wild Thyme Distillery was beyond anything Ewan could bring himself to imagine. He clicked on another link.

His fingers paused on the keys as a sentence caught his eye. "There is nothing that can kill a person that an autopsy cannot find, in this modern era of science."

Well, there you had it. Duncan MacArthur had been autopsied, so a medical examiner would have found anything suspicious—wouldn't he?

The next sentence brought him up short.

"A few poisons are termed relatively undetectable because one needs unusual methods to detect them in blood. Unless there is a reason for such methods, a general autopsy will not do so."

He pulled up his cell phone and searched for the number of his father's doctor.

"Hello, Dr. Ferguson? It's Ewan MacArthur. I'm doing well, thank you. The thing is—the reason I'm calling . . .

"What do I have to do to have my father's body exhumed?"

"I should have known it would be a problem," Ewan told Fiona later over dinner at the pub. After laying out the details of his request for exhumation, the reality sounded like a lost cause even to his own ears.

"First, legally I would need to establish some sort of proof to support a contention that my father's death might not have been natural."

"And you can't do that?" Fiona asked. "He thought someone was trying to kill him, he had no history of heart disease, and there's the change in his will."

"No one else heard him say those things. Apparently the only one he unburdened himself to was me," Ewan said through his teeth. "After ignoring me for sixteen years, he decided to make me his confidant. And you already know the new will was a secret from all of us." He blew out a frustrated breath. "At every instance, the person who has been throwing roadblocks in my way is my father."

"But his doctor knows his medical history," Fiona said. "Wouldn't it be suspicious if he was in good shape and had none of the signs of heart disease?"

"As to that, Dr. Ferguson just verified what I already knew. There doesn't have to be heart disease for someone to die of a heart attack. Father overworked himself—everyone knew that—and that's one of the prime factors for cardiac problems. His blood pressure wasn't high, but that in itself is not enough to order an exhumation."

He slammed a fist down on the table, nearly upsetting his mug. "It's so frustrating. Who would've thought that digging up a body would be so problematic?"

Fiona choked on her ale. "What did you just say?"

Ewan's eyebrows furrowed, and then his face cleared and he gave a weak laugh. "Aye, I suppose that's not something you hear every day." He took a drink and put the mug down.

"I think we need a change of environment. Let's go for a ride."

"Where?"

"Well, thanks to a certain someone, I've been neglecting my real job lately," he said. "The day I met you, I was at Culloden Battlefield trying to figure out how to incorporate it into Highland Magic."

"But I've already seen the battlefield," Fiona said.

"My lady, there is no such thing as 'I've already seen the battlefield' when it comes to Culloden. "Besides, I'm not thinking of taking you to the part the tourists know."

"There's more?"

"Aye. The National Trust for Scotland owns only a third of the actual battlefield. Because that part is a national graveyard, access is restricted to the pathways and the Visitor's Centre. They won't allow actors portraying Highlanders or government soldiers on the field itself. I respect that, and I would never desecrate the moor to promote tourism—but it occurred to me that there's a different way."

"You've got my attention," Fiona said. "Let's go."

Traffic was light; few cars had passed going toward Inverness, and there was just one white sedan behind them when they reached the entrance to the battlefield. Ewan turned left and continued driving through the countryside.

"This area was all a part of the original battlefield," he said, pointing to the well-tended fields as they passed. "Sadly, Culloden Moor is now under threat again, but this time from a different source."

They passed a group of modern houses, and Ewan pulled the car over. "A few years ago, a group of developers submitted an application to the Highland Parish Council to build luxury homes on this section of the moor. The Council denied the application, so they took it to a government official who had the authority. As you can see, he approved it."

Fiona frowned. "I thought the people of Scotland considered this part of your history sacred," she said. "How could they let this happen?"

"Developers aren't interested in history." Ewan's voice was bitter. "They're interested in money." He gestured to the homes. "There are groups who are fighting, just as they did in 1746, to keep the battlefield from being desecrated. Petitions, websites, demonstrations, and letters to Parliament have been created, but more applications to build are generated every day."

"It's so sad," Fiona said. People in Canada and the US are often criticized for putting development over history—I never realized it was happening here too."

"The worst part," Ewan told her, "is that the developers aren't above using the battle as a selling point. 'Live on the site of the most famous battle in Scotland's history,' the adverts say. They don't mention that your house may be built over the remains of men who lost their lives in that battle."

Ewan started the car and they continued on until they came to a huge red brick mansion surrounded by lush grounds.

"Culloden House," he said. "Not the original, but this one is almost two hundred years old."

"Wasn't Culloden House the place they took the

Jacobite officers after the battle, before executing them?"

"Sometimes I forget you're a historian," Ewan said. "Aye, the original house was used by Charles Stuart as his base of operations before the battle. When it all fell apart, the government forces rounded up the wounded officers and brought them here."

"How close was Culloden House to the actual battlefield?" Fiona asked.

"Not far. There's a wooded area just past this turnoff." He turned into a small gravel car park. They climbed over logs and skirted clumps of gorse and thistle as they walked through the woods, until Ewan stopped at a large, rounded boulder that stood in the center of a small clearing.

"This is where I want to incorporate Highland Magic," he said.

"This rock?" Fiona walked around the boulder, which stood about twelve feet across and six feet high. "You want to make people walk through the woods to see a rock?"

"Not just any rock, my dear." Ewan adopted a lofty tone. "This is the Prisoners' Stone."

"Ahhh," she said. "That means absolutely nothing to me. Pray go on."

"Thought you'd never ask. After the battle, the wounded Jacobite officers were taken, as you said, to Culloden House. Those who didn't die from their wounds were shot. A few—seventeen of them—were held for three days and then put into carts and carried here to Culloden Wood."

Fiona closed her eyes and imagined the fear and

pain that these men had suffered. They had watched their prince run away from the battle, leaving them to carry on the war they had started in his name. Bloodied, many near death, they had been hauled away to languish in the dungeon of Culloden House.

No care had been offered to them—why administer to men who have no future? They would have had only each other in those last days, only their memories of the loved ones they would never see again.

"What happened to them?" she asked, but she already knew. Prince William, the Duke of Cumberland, had made sure that Culloden would be the last battle fought on Scottish soil. "Butcher Cumberland," as he would forever be known by the Highlanders, had ordered no quarter be taken with the wounded Jacobites.

Government soldiers had roamed the moor, listening for moans and cries, and had stabbed any man who was still alive. The officers had been rounded up to endure another few days, knowing what was to come.

"The wounded officers were thrown into the carts like so many sacks of potatoes," Ewan said, "and brought here to this stone. I have no idea how the government troops knew of it, hidden away in the wood like this—but it suited their purpose well.

"The men were pulled from the carts and placed against this stone, where they were shot at point-blank range. Then the soldiers clubbed them with their muskets, smashing the heads of the men they'd just shot to make sure they were dead."

"Wait," said Fiona. "This was obviously something

done in secrecy; otherwise, why drag their prisoners all the way here to the woods? So how did anyone find out about it?"

"Ahh, you are one smart historian," Ewan said. "As you know, truth is sometimes stranger than fiction. One prisoner, a Fraser clansman, survived the brutal attack. He lay horribly wounded until the soldiers left, and then crawled away."

"What? How is that even possible? He was already wounded from the battle, and then shot and his head bashed in. How far did he crawl?"

"Well, historical accounts on that differ," Ewan said. "Some say that a young nobleman was riding by, saw the wounded man, and carried him to a small cottage, where he was treated for several months. Others say he crawled all the way to the cottage by himself. Whatever the truth, it's still an amazing story, aye?"

"And you want to do some sort of reenactment of this story?"

"Aye. What do you think?" Ewan gave her an anxious look.

"I think it's perfect. If you set it up like the experience at Ruthven Barracks, there won't be a dry eye in the house—and maybe you'll be helping to preserve the battlefield."

They walked hand-in-hand through the wood to the car and started back toward Inverness. Fiona turned in her seat for a last look at the endangered battlefield.

"Ewan," she said, "do you remember that white car that was behind us on the way to the battlefield?"

"Aye, I suppose—why?"

"Because there's a white car behind us now, and I think it's the same one. Isn't that odd?"

CHAPTER 36

INVERNESS,
SCOTLAND - PRESENT DAY

Memory is all we are. Moments
and feelings, captured in amber,
strung on filaments of reason.
Mark Lawrence

"ch-an-Eas called. They said if we want to see Mr. Bethune, this might be the best time."

"When?" Fiona jumped up and her fork clattered to the table. Several diners looked up from their plates at the noise. Mrs. MacDonald paused in the doorway and gave her Canadian guest a curious glance.

"Right now, if you're ready," Ewan's smooth brogue came through the phone. "They said he seems quite alert right now, but there's no telling how long it'll last."

"I'm ready." Fiona gave her untouched Full Scottish Breakfast a wistful gaze and then headed for the hallway. Some things were more important than bacon and tattie scones and haggis, and . . . well, actually a lot of things were more important. She took the stairs two at a time and returned with her trusty rain jacket in under a minute.

The drive took less than five. Ach-an-Eas was a stately building of weathered red brick, with a steep slate roof that boasted a row of six chimneys on the main building and three more on a gabled side extension. The elegant picture was finished with a square tower to the left of a red wooden door.

"Oh, it's lovely!" Fiona said. "How sad that Mr. Bethune may have to leave a place like this—there can't be many care homes like it."

"Aye, it has a very good reputation, but they don't have the services for dementia patients. The director told me that they're all very fond of 'our old man,' as she called him, so they're keeping him here as long as they can. Besides, when he's to the point where he doesn't recognize the home or the people, it won't matter so much to him, aye?"

Fiona sighed. "I suppose, but I'd think he would know on some level that he wasn't in the same place anymore, and that would be so frightening."

She turned to Ewan. "Getting old is awful, isn't it?"

He pulled her around to face him and put his arms around her waist. "Oh, I don't know. Getting old with you might not be so bad." He kissed her forehead and looked into her green eyes. "I'm looking forward to the adventure."

Fiona felt the familiar warmth spread through her. How had this man become so important to her in such a short time? They hadn't discussed the future, knowing that real life was thousands of miles away and across the second largest ocean in the world. But now he was talking about growing old together, and adventure, and—*and I want to believe that this is the reality.*

Her arms tightened around him and they stood that way in silence for a moment. Time didn't matter, their quest didn't matter—all that mattered was this man, these arms. Ewan bent his head . . .

"Hello." And the world was back. They sprang apart to see a middle-aged woman in the doorway, a half-smile belying an otherwise severe demeanor. Her brown hair was curled in a neat bun on the top of her head, and she wore a black wool suit with a white button-down blouse. The perfect picture of an efficient administrator, except for the thin tartan tie—and the grin she was trying unsuccessfully to hide.

Ewan cleared his throat. "Oh. Um, yes. Hello. I'm—Ewan MacArthur, and this is Fiona M-MacLean. I believe you called us. About Mr. Bethune." He stuttered to a stop and stood with his hands clasped in front of him like a small boy caught in the act of poaching cookies.

The woman's smile widened. "Ah, yes, welcome. I'm Mrs. Keith, the director of Ach-an-Eas. You're in luck—Mr. Bethune is in fine spirits today. He's been chatting up the ladies and telling them old stories, so we'd better grab him before he runs out of steam."

Mrs. Keith led them through a formal sitting room, which was empty, and past a modern kitchen, also devoid of human activity. She paused at a door and then opened it to show them into a huge community room filled with cheerfully patterned couches, game tables, and bookshelves.

At one end of the room a large television played

an interactive exercise program for four enthusiastic residents who bent and stretched in an attempt to match the instructor. In a corner sat three elderly women with piles of yarn in baskets at their feet. Their fingers churned out rows of stitches as they talked to each other, seemingly all at the same time.

Mrs. Keith stopped to greet a pair of men who were playing checkers near the door, as she led Ewan and Fiona out a French door into the rear garden.

Under a weeping willow sat a very old man in a wheelchair. His white hair stood up all over his head in wisps, and wrinkled hands gestured as he talked to a rapt audience of three old women seated in lawn chairs.

"Good morning," Mrs. Keith said. "Ladies, I came to collect you because it's your turn for aerobics." A groan went up from the audience, but the women smiled and struggled to their feet.

"Mr. Bethune, I've brought you some special guests. Are you up for visitors?" The director ran a practiced eye over her charge.

"Visitors? For me?" The old man seemed surprised and pleased at the idea. "Haven't had visitors in a century or so. Especially not so pretty." He looked Fiona up and down with sharp eyes that belied his advanced age.

Mrs. Keith patted his arm and turned to her guests. "Watch him," she said in a stage whisper, prompting giggles from the ladies gathered around her. "He's quite the flirt." She cocked her head at Ewan. "Be careful that he doesn't steal your girlfriend right away from you. Come on ladies, time to stretch!" She ushered her group away, leaving Ewan and Fiona with Martin Bethune.

"Lovely woman," he told them. "Think she has a crush on me, so I have to be careful not to break her heart, ye ken?" He winked at Fiona.

It was hard to imagine that this old man was suffering from dementia, but she knew this lucid phase could be gone in a moment. Time was the enemy here, in so many ways. Ewan and Fiona took two of the lawn chairs that had been vacated by Martin Bethune's fan club.

Ewan began. "Mr. Bethune, we've read your history of Raasay House, and we are very much impressed by the extent of your expertise. We—"

"Laddie, stop trying to butter me up. I don't have time for it. Just ask what ye want to know, aye?"

Fiona covered her mouth to stifle a laugh. Ewan's face was red and he refused to look at her. She decided to rescue him.

"Mr. Bethune, may I ask you a question?" she asked.

"Ye may ask me anything ye like, lassie." He attempted a courtly bow in her direction, lost his balance and pitched forward. Ewan caught him before he fell out of the chair and resettled him against the backrest, earning himself a nod of gratitude.

"We're interested in the MacLeod family who lived in the castle at the time of the Battle of Culloden," Fiona said.

The old man's face darkened as if a switch had been thrown in a room. His eyes flickered and his lips snapped shut. They waited, but it seemed as if he had gone away somewhere.

"The battle changed everything," he said. "For most, it was bad, but for some it needed to happen."

"What do you mean, sir?" Fiona kept her voice soft. She couldn't be sure if Martin Bethune was still with them, or if he had gone away again in his mind.

The light came back into his face and he smiled at them. "I wasn't there, lass." He waggled an arthritic finger. "I'm old, but I'm not that old." He gave a cackle. "Most of my expertise, as your lad here calls it, came down the way stories have been told for centuries. Way back in the 1700s, one of my ancestors is supposed to have married a MacLean who worked at Raasay House. He was the constable there—you know, in charge of the horses and grooms? Not sure how much of it is truth, mind ye."

Ewan spoke. "Can you tell us about the Raasay MacLeods?"

Bethune sat for a long time, staring off into space. Then he looked at them and said, "It's over, long ago. Why do ye want to know about them?"

Ewan took a breath and glanced at Fiona.

"We think that Miss MacLean is a—descendant— of someone who lived there at that time," he said.

The old man looked at Fiona, and he nodded slowly. "Aye. Eilidh. Ye look just like her. Means you and I are related—it was her brother who was the constable. Welcome to the family, lass."

Fiona stared at him in surprise, then she remembered the portrait at Raasay House. Of course he would be familiar with it.

He gave her a sweet smile, and then his face

darkened.

"Wasn't right what happened to her."

"What happened?" She felt her pulse quicken.

"Don't know." The old man shrugged. "Nobody knew. She disappeared."

The disappointment felt like a weight settling into her heart. He didn't know any more than they did. This was a waste of time.

"But I know about her lover," Bethune said.

"Cullen? What happened to him?" Fiona asked.

"Not Cullen. That one didn't care about her. " Bethune's wrinkled face creased even more in disgust. "He had to marry to provide an heir, that was all."

His lips curled. "It wasn't Eilidh's fault. There was some talk that Mr. Cullen MacLeod wouldn't have liked any woman—if ye ken what I mean."

Fiona's mouth rounded into an "O." She stared at Martin Bethune, at this ancient historian whose mind vacillated from past to present and often went away altogether, and wondered how he had ever come by this juicy piece of Jacobite gossip.

To make matters worse, he treated her to a wink and a leer that would have made any college frat boy proud.

"And he wasn't the one she loved." His look was smug.

Fiona wondered if they were being sold a bill of goods here. Was there any sense in listening to the wandering memories of a lecherous old man descending into dementia? Then again, it did support their theory that Cullen wasn't the man Eilidh wanted to protect.

"Who, then? Hugh?"

"Not Hugh. Hugh MacLeod was a good lad, but he was in love with his books. No, it wasn't one of the family."

"What?" This was the last thing Fiona had expected. "Who then?"

The old man's face became vacant, as if a cloud passed over it and wiped away everything in its path. He looked around, puzzled. The change was startling, and Fiona's heart dropped.

Just as suddenly the glint returned to his eyes and he went on as if he'd never had a lapse.

"There were others at the castle, you know. Eilidh's brother, of course. And Cullen had *friends*." Martin Bethune gave Fiona another sly glance. "They had visitors, of course, as all great families do. Even Charles Stuart stayed there a time or two."

"I didn't know that," Fiona said. But this was getting them nowhere. Eilidh's lover obviously hadn't been Bonnie Prince Charlie.

"Mr. Bethune, can you tell us more about this man Eilidh loved?"

The old man's eyes glazed again, and he reached a frail hand up to scratch the wisps of white hair on his head.

"Mr. Bethune! Please, stay with us." Fiona grabbed his other hand and held it.

The eyes cleared for a moment. "Eh? I don't know—" he mumbled. "Oh. Aye. Him."

He looked at them and smiled his sweet old man's smile.

"Don't know his name." Bethune nodded happily. "But he fought at the Battle of Culloden."

He sat back in his wheelchair and regarded Ewan and Fiona. "Who did you say you were, then? Haven't had visitors in a century or so. Especially not so pretty."

As if summoned by the old man's deteriorating condition, Mrs. Keith appeared beside them.

"I believe you're ready for your morning nap, Mr. Bethune," she said, a cheerful smile pasted on her face. "It's time to say goodbye to our guests."

She took her place behind the wheelchair and turned it to face the house. Fiona and Ewan trailed after her. As they reached the French doors that led to the game room, Martin Bethune turned his head to regard them. A crafty look crossed the wizened features.

"Think she has a crush on me, so I have to be careful not to break her heart, ye ken?"

CHAPTER 37

RAASAY HOUSE, SCOTLAND - 1746

IAIN

Iain backed into the shadows behind the bookshelf. Eilidh had told him about this room off the library and the voices she had heard there, and he had spent hours watching to see what its importance might be.

The room never seemed to be locked. He looked around at the mundane setting. One bookshelf that stood parallel to the wall and about two feet out for access to the other side. One small table and two wooden chairs in the center of the room. No files, no papers, nothing to indicate that the space was used for anything other than reading.

But Eilidh said the room had been locked when she heard whispering coming from behind the door—before Godfrey Lewis had grabbed her and pulled her away. Iain felt his blood boil at the thought of that creature laying a hand on her, and he had to remind himself that this was not the time. He was in a bad situation here.

Waiting behind the bookshelf had seemed like a good idea at the time. If anyone came in, he could stand very still and remain undetected—as long as no one needed something on the shelves.

He was a terrible spy. He did not have the aptitude for sneaking around, and he had not thought this through. So now, here he stood like a deer begging to be slaughtered, while two people locked the door from the inside and took seats at the table not ten feet away from him. He wanted to close his eyes like a child who trusts that no one can see him if he can't see them. He wanted to stop the breathing that seemed thunderous in his own ears.

He could not tell who the people were, only that there seemed to be two. The books and documents concealed him, but they hid anything else in the room from his sight as well. And the voices were whispers, impossible to identify and difficult to hear. They could have been men or women. All he could do was strain, listen, and pray that they were not there for a prolonged length of time.

"*Best chance . . .*" he heard. "*Gathering . . . our source . . . will be here . . .*"

Iain stood still and puzzled at the words. Best chance for what? What, or who, was gathering? Where? This had to be important, else why the secrecy?

There was a rustling of paper. "*Here—the fop—never*

suspect—all over . . . Drumossie . . ."

The fop? The same epithet that the men in the outbuilding had used for Charles Stuart. Were these the same men? But how would government sympathizers find their way into Raasay House?

His blood chilled. *It could only be possible if they were close to the family—or were family themselves.* He held his breath. That meant that someone here, in this household, was a traitor to the Jacobite cause.

Eilidh had been right. The words she had overheard in the outbuilding—*Jacobites . . . Italian fop . . . kill*—now made sense. This was not what Colonel Buchanan had expected when he sent him here, to the Jacobite stronghold of clan MacLeod. He should leave, get back to Edinburgh, and let Buchanan know that his fears were for nothing.

Whoever these people were, they had to be working for the government side. If there was a plan to kill Charles Stuart, all their worries would be over. The Jacobite rising would end as soon as their leader was gone. All he had to do was sit tight and wait for his chance to leave.

To leave Eilidh.

Papers rustled again.

". . . .irst take care . . . girl . . ."

Iain froze. *Girl?* Besides the servants there was only one girl here. Had Eilidh been wrong in thinking she hadn't been seen that day? He felt nausea surge through his gut. This changed everything.

Chairs were pushed back, a lock clicked, and the door opened and then closed again. Silence fell on the tiny room where Iain stood rooted to the spot behind the bookshelf.

He had no idea how long he stood there. He forced his feet to move, and with no real idea what to do next he found them taking him in the direction of Lord Malcolm's chambers. He had to trust someone, and the idea of the laird of clan MacLeod being a traitor to his own cause was so patently ridiculous that it had to be discounted. The chance had to be taken.

He was so far out of his depth that he could feel himself sinking into the confusion in his mind. All he could think about was Eilidh.

"Well, hello, lad," Lord Malcolm greeted him with a smile. "What brings you here so late at night?"

There was no help for it. Iain told him everything from the beginning—his mission, his true name, and the plot he had overheard in the library. He did not mention Eilidh or her part in the story. He was willing to risk his own life, but never hers. It was easy enough to say that it was he who had overheard the speakers in the outbuilding.

Iain was painfully aware that if he was wrong about this man, he was sealing his own doom.

He also knew that he was in the process of committing treason. His life in the British Army was over, his future gone in an instant. And he found that he did not care. At least Eilidh would be safe until he could get her away.

"*When we go—we go together.*" Well, now they would have to go, Godfrey Lewis be damned.

"And you did not recognize the voices?" Lord Malcolm kept his calm demeanor, and Iain realized why he was the head of his clan. He asked questions, made connections, and at no time indicated that he might not believe what Iain was telling him.

"I think you must be wrong about it being someone in or close to the household, though," he said when Iain was finished. "I trust my sons implicitly, and although Godfrey is a bit of a rogue, I've known him since he was a small boy."

Privately Iain disagreed with most of that assessment, but there was no point in arguing.

Lord Malcolm gave Iain a narrow look. "Because you have brought me this information, I feel that I can—no, I must— trust you.

"As we speak, Cumberland's troops are advancing on Inverness. The clans have pulled back and are gathering for a last stand. In a few days, our Bonnie Prince will meet the government troops in a wee altercation."

Lord Malcolm's lip twisted and his brows furrowed.

"I cannot imagine what it must have taken for you to come to me, but I will be honest—as a soldier I am sickened that you would do so. If I were present at your court martial, I would hope to see you convicted. I want you to leave here immediately and return to your company."

Iain nodded, but said nothing.

"If we meet on the field, I will show you no quarter."

Iain nodded again. "I understand, sir."

The laird sighed. "You have done the Jacobite cause a tremendous service, so it seems I must thank you. These lads, whoever they are, have planned harm to the true king, and because of you I know where they will likely strike."

"Where?" Iain said, puzzled. "How do you know that?"

"Something you said," the laird told him. "There is a boggy patch of ground outside Inverness near the town of Culloden, not much use to anybody. It seems a poor place for a battle, but Charles may well be heading there.

"The moor is called Drumossie."

CHAPTER 38

RAASAY HOUSE, SCOTLAND - 1746

EILIDH

"He is gone."

Rory pulled the saddle from the horse and turned at the raw anguish in his sister's voice.

"What?"

"He is gone! Did you not hear me?" Eilidh's hands were fisted at her sides. Tears rolled down her pale cheeks and her breath came in small gasps. "He promised me we would go together, but he is gone! How could he do this?"

Rory caught her in his arms as she sagged. "El—Iain would never abandon you. Never. There is a reason."

"He is gone, Rory. Gone back to his place in the British Army. He left me a note." She spat out the words. "It was all a lie."

Her brother held her close. "No. There is more to this. Iain loves you more than his own life; you know that."

"He lied that he was a deserter. He lied about his reason for being here. He lied about taking me with him—how is that love? I hate him!"

"Do you?" Rory dropped his arms and stepped back. "Do you really? You said you loved him. Was that a lie too? Where is the trust that comes from love?" His voice sharpened.

"Iain would never leave you of his own choice. You must trust me on this. There is more to the story."

Eilidh looked up at her brother from under tear-drenched lashes. "Is there something you are not telling me? Did Iain tell you something?"

Rory turned and picked up the curry brush. He went to work on the horse with vigor, muscles rippling under his woolen shirt.

"El," he said. "Please. You must have faith. He will return to you."

He turned around to face her again. "The MacLeods are leaving here as well. Charles has called, and the clans are mustering and heading for Inverness. They are leaving tomorrow."

"Tomorrow?" Eilidh's mind struggled to wrap itself around this news. "Then what about the wedding? Why has Cullen said nothing to me?"

Rory's lips curled in distaste. "Cullen! Has he ever put you first?"

He stomped a foot in the straw on the stable floor. "Lord Malcolm said that Lady MacLeod told you the wedding would be postponed until we return. She did not?" His features flushed red. "What a witch!"

"I do not care about the wedding; I will go home to Duarte."

"You cannot. Father will be marching with the clan as well. Dom is already gone. You must stay here."

"With Lady MacLeod? I would rather die!" Eilidh's tears had dried up in the flush of anger.

"Hugh will be here. He is not well and will act as laird in Lord Malcolm's absence."

He turned back to the horse. "Besides," he said over his shoulder, "I will be staying as well. You need to be here when Iain returns for you, aye?"

"Humph," Eilidh said. "Why would I want to wait for a British soldier? A man who abandoned me?" She stopped suddenly and tugged Rory around to face her again. "Wait—why are you staying? Should you not join with Father and Dom, if the clans are being called?"

"Someone tasked me to stay, to watch over you." Rory's lips curled in a smile. "Someone you should trust."

He turned his back on her again and began humming as he groomed the horse. Eilidh stared at his back for a moment, and then wandered out to the yard.

Someone you should trust. Was it true? Was he really planning to return for her?

There is something I must tell you.

I am not a good person.

I love you.

In truth, he had never lied, not about the important things. She was the one who had stopped him.

She had told him she did not care who or what he was, that she loved him anyway. So who was she to fall apart like this?

Rory was right—she needed to keep her faith. If she loved Iain, trust came with that love. Yes, he had promised that they would leave together, so something huge must have happened to make him break that promise.

His note had been written in Gaelic. Of the those at Raasay House, only Hugh, Rory, and she were fluent in the language. He was being careful lest his message fall into the wrong hands—whose hands?

She took the paper out of her pocket and read it again. Her name and the date at the top. *Mo gràidh, Feumaidh mi rabhadh a thorn don phrionnsa agad. Na bi earbsa anns na MacLeòid. Bruidhinn ri Ruaraidh.*

"My darling, I must warn your prince. Do not trust anyone here. Speak with Rory."

Speak with Rory. Was that the key? Had he been afraid someone else might see the message? Rory had told her to trust Iain, that he would return for her.

Rory was the message. Shame spread through her body. Iain had not abandoned her. He had entrusted her to her brother, the one other person she knew would give his life to keep her safe. And she had lost her faith in him in the instant. *She* was the one who had abandoned him. The reality cut like a knife.

She made her way back toward the castle, passing the outbuilding from where she had heard the whispered words two weeks ago.

Eilidh stopped in her tracks. Was she imagining things now?

"Think the bastard knows . . . have to stop him before . . . can warn the prince."

No, those were men talking, just as they had before. This must be their meeting place.

"Hate to kill one of His Majesty's own, but . . . traitor . . ."

"Won't matter once Stuart is gone."

A rough laugh sounded loud to Eilidh's ears. Her head filled with a crescendo of roaring sound and she leaned against the building's rough wall for support. She groped for Iain's ring on its leather cord and held it.

Warn the prince. His letter had said the same thing. *Once Stuart is gone. One of His Majesty's own.*

The color drained from her face. *Were they talking about Iain?*

She pushed herself off the wall and started back toward the stable. She needed Rory. A rustling sounded behind her, and her head exploded in pain. She felt herself falling, unable to make her limbs obey. A rough burlap bag, smelling of grain and dirt, was pulled over her head.

"Go! Do what you need to do. I'll take care of this one." A woman's voice, a voice she knew. A cloying scent of lavender seeped through the holes in the burlap bag. Then everything faded away as her body was dragged across the ground.

"Eilidh!" Rory's frantic voice came from far away. The bag was pulled off her head and she felt stale air enter her lungs. She was lying on a dirt floor in the darkness. Rory's hands fumbled with the rope binding her wrists and ankles. He pulled her to a sitting position and pulled her into his embrace.

"El, are you all right? What happened?" he said. "I've been looking everywhere for you. When you did not show up at dinner, I knew something was wrong. Who did this?"

Eilidh struggled to remember: . . . *kill one of His Majesty's own . . .*

She scrabbled for Rory's shirt and managed to pull herself to her knees.

"Rory! They're going to kill Iain and Prince Charles! We have to hurry!"

Her eyes were becoming accustomed to the darkness. She could make out her brother's face, eyes wide and mouth hanging open as he knelt before her.

"El, you've injured your head. I'll take you up to the castle and get you taken care of, just relax."

"Not the castle," she heard the desperation in her own voice. "Lady MacLeod is part of this!"

"Eilidh, listen to yourself. Someone is going to kill Iain—and Prince Charles? Lady MacLeod? Does that even make sense?"

"I don't know how, or where, but that's what I heard! They are probably with the soldiers who are leaving tomorrow. We have to stop them!"

"Eilidh—it *is* tomorrow. Everyone has left. They've gone to join the prince at Inverness."

Eilidh struggled to her feet and stood swaying as the blood rushed in her ears. Her head pounded.

"We have to go!"

"Hush, ghràdhaich. You must stay here and rest. I will go—Hugh can watch over you."

"Ruaridh MacLean, how long have you known me?"

Eilidh glared at him. "I promised Iain I would protect him, and you promised him you would protect me. I am going, and you may come with me if you like." She felt for the ring on its leather cord. "Now, I need a shirt and a kilt! Must I take them off you?"

CHAPTER 39

HIGHLANDS, SCOTLAND - PRESENT DAY

*When all the details fit in perfectly, something
is probably wrong with the story.*
Charles Baxter

It was Scotland, so of course it was raining. A nice, misty rain that was turning to fog in the early dusk. In the movies, it was always raining in a cemetery. Was that so that the ghosts could watch the proceedings comfortably?

As the box containing Duncan MacArthur's body was raised slowly from the soggy earth, Fiona hunched into her raincoat and looked at the people standing around the gravesite.

Ewan's sister Sophie was sobbing, clutching at her brother Daniel's coat sleeve as if it was all that kept her from collapsing. Daniel was the party-boy, Fiona remembered, but today his expression was serious. He patted his sister's hand awkwardly.

Across the muddy hole in the ground, Miss

Beck—Ariadne, wasn't it?— stood alone. She wore a black raincoat and held an umbrella in one hand. Her eyes never left the box as it was pulled slowly from the earth.

On the other side of Sophie, the brother called Jonah shuffled his feet at the muddy earth, head bowed. Iseabail Grant stared across at Ewan with a look of raw anguish.

Her husband Aaron stood next to Iseabail with his feet braced and his fists clenched, his face tight.

"You're not very popular right now," Fiona whispered. Ewan reached for her hand and squeezed it, then let go.

"I didn't expect to be." His voice was bleak. "I'm used to it, though. I've always been the pariah in this family, after all."

The casket was loaded into an ambulance for transportation to the lab, where the medical examiner waited. With nothing left to see, the family began to disperse.

Miss Beck passed without looking at Ewan or Fiona, moving as if she were in a trance. A glare from Daniel as he shepherded the still sniffling Sophie toward the parking lot, a rough shove in his shoulder from Jonah. Ewan stared at the ground.

Iseabail and Aaron came to stand before him. His sister's face softened as she looked at her brother. "I don't understand why you felt you had to do this, Ewan," she said, "but I trust you." She gave him a watery smile.

Aaron clapped him on the shoulder. "You've got guts, I'll say that much." Something flickered in his eyes, and then he smiled. It was not a pleasant smile. "I get that you have some sort of axe to grind, but did you have to go this far? You got the company, isn't that enough?" He shook his head, put his arm around his wife, and ushered her away.

"Don't worry about it, Ewan. They'll sing a different tune if the autopsy turns up something," Fiona said. She put her hand on Ewan's arm and tugged him around to face her. "And it will."

"Why are you so sure?" he asked her. "I'm not sure at all. How are you so fierce?" He gazed into her green eyes, then bent down and kissed her lightly on the forehead. "You have no idea how important you are to me, do you?" he murmured. "I'd have fallen apart by now if it weren't for you, lass."

"Same here," she said. "I guess we'll have to stick together then, eh?" She took his hand and led him from the cemetery.

He has no idea. I'm not sure at all. I only know that I have to protect him this time. And where had that thought come from? But she knew. Eilidh. Her thoughts were merging with those of Eilidh MacLean, and it scared her to death.

Fiona hadn't said anything to Ewan, but for some time now she had realized that things were mixing together in her mind. The visions were more—frantic—than they had been before, and there were times when she lost track of *when* she was. Sometimes she looked into her mirror and saw a face that was hers, yet not hers. Hair that was too long and dressed in a style from a time long ago. A low-cut bodice, a silver ring on a leather cord around her neck.

She recognized the dress. It was the gown that Eilidh MacLean was wearing in the portrait at Raasay House. A normal person would put this down to simple memory of the portrait, but Fiona wasn't normal. Nothing in her life had been normal for a long time.

There were too many anomalies. How did she remember the scent of lavender in the room—an overpowering fragrance that had her head throbbing? You couldn't paint smells into a portrait.

And what about the necklace? At Raasay House she had seen the portrait across the room, from behind a barrier built to hold back over-curious tourists and preserve the artifacts. The necklace in the portrait was an emerald pendant, not a silver ring. Still, she was seeing it, and when she reached a hand up to her neck she could swear she *felt* the ring on its rough leather cord, although there was nothing there.

She had seen a ring like that somewhere else, and recently. The intricate silverwork meant something. But every time she reached for the memory, it eluded her, dancing just on the edge of her senses.

It wasn't always the dress, either. Sometimes her reflection was wearing a rough-spun shirt, streaked with dirt, and a shawl over one shoulder. A shawl of MacLean tartan. How could she know that?

Worst was the pain. Sharp, excruciating—she felt it would kill her. It came without warning and subsided just as fast, leaving her crying and gasping for breath. She had no earthly idea what could cause such agony.

Things were coming to a head. She had been warned to "protect him against the dangerous ones."

Those words haunted her. There was no use in wondering who *he* was. It was Ewan; they both knew it.

"Are you all right, lass?" His voice came to her from far away, and she realized that somehow they had gotten back to the car. He handed her in, slid behind the wheel, and started the engine. All mundane, normal things, part of a life that was slipping away from her.

"Ewan."

"Aye, love?"

"I want to go back to Dr. Blair." Fiona watched him and waited.

He hesitated, then asked, "Why?"

"I need to know, Ewan. I need to know why Eilidh died, why she couldn't protect her love. I think she has more to tell me." Fiona could hear the desperation in her voice.

"I want to know if the story really is repeating now. And this time I want you beside me."

"Then that's what we'll do," he said. He pulled the car into traffic. "I'll call him. Now, how about we pick up some supper?"

"I'm not hungry," she said.

"I am, and you have to eat. It's non-negotiable." She nodded and sat looking out at the rainy landscape as it flashed by.

"Do you mind if we stop by the distillery first?" Ewan asked, as they drew closer to Inverness. "I left my laptop on the desk this morning, and it has all my tour schedules on it."

They pulled into the empty parking lot and took the spot reserved for Duncan MacArthur. No other cars were in the lot; due to the exhumation, even Ariadne Beck's gray sedan was gone. The mist closed in around them as Ewan unlocked the front door. Hand in hand, they walked through the deserted sales room toward the offices.

"Damn it!" Ewan said. "I left the key to the office at home. My mind is turning to mush these days."

Fiona looked around at the dark outer office and mustered a smile. "That's because you're getting old," she said. "You'll probably find the key in the refrigerator."

She thought of the aged historian in his wheelchair at Ach-an-Eas, and her smile faded. "Sorry, that wasn't funny. Once you've known someone like Mr. Bethune, jokes about memory loss aren't funny, are they?"

Ewan squeezed her hand. He found the switch and the room plunged into light.

"I think Miss Beck keeps an extra set of keys here." He went back behind the desk.

"She's a stickler," he said, "and she never lets anyone into her domain. Can't say I blame her, but this is an emergency, aye?" Ewan cracked his knuckles and glanced nervously at the door, as if the desk's owner might appear at any moment.

"Well, let's get this over with. I keep feeling as if Miss Beck is looking over my shoulder." He stole a look behind him.

They studied the piece of furniture before them. A standard office desk, it had a small drawer and a deeper file drawer on each side and a narrow central drawer below a pull-out shelf for a laptop.

Ewan opened drawers and rummaged through office supplies, careful to put everything back the way it had been.

The narrow center drawer held notepads, pens, and pencils. In the top right-side drawer were scissors, a stapler, and a three-hole punch. The drawer on the left held hair spray, a small hairbrush, and a toothbrush in a travel container. A small bottle of perfume, three-quarters gone, read "Yardley's English Lavender."

"Ach, the woman bathes in the stuff," Ewan said. "She never heard the term 'a little goes a long way,' when it comes to perfume."

"Thought I smelled that the last time I was here," Fiona murmured. "I hate the scent of lavender, always have."

"Look," Ewan said. He pointed to two plastic pill bottles for over-the-counter headache medications.

"Our Miss Beck never likes anyone to think she's sick," he said. "She's the first one in and the last out, and always gives the impression that she's invincible. It's nice to see she's human, after all."

The bottom drawers had files placed alphabetically in pristine order. Metal dividers at the back kept the folders in place.

"Ach, nothing here. I was sure I saw her pull the keys out of one of these drawers." He shoved the last one closed.

"Wait," said Fiona, and joined him behind the desk. "Did you hear that?"

"What?"

"There was a rattle of some kind when you closed that one," she said.

Ewan opened the drawer again. "Just files. Nothing that could rattle."

"I know I heard it. Let me at it—men!" She nudged Ewan aside and looked into the drawer. "Look, there's a space behind the file partition."

He looked up at Fiona with a conspiratorial smile. "Well, my little secret agent, your hand's smaller. Reach in there and see what made your rattle, aye? And if it isn't a set of keys, you're fired from MI6."

Fiona laughed and reached behind the metal partition. "There's nothing here—no, wait—there's some kind of round bottle back here."

"No keys? Damn."

Fiona felt around again. "Nope, no keys." She brought her hand out, clutching a small plastic container. "Just this."

Ewan took the container from her and glanced at the label. *Klor Con* M10, with the name of a local pharmacy. He shook the container. Pills of some sort, nearly empty.

"Some sort of prescription. We probably shouldn't be snooping into Miss Beck's medical supplies, aye?" He dropped the pill container back behind the partition. "I guess I'll have to come back in the morning for the laptop."

Ewan closed the drawer again and turned off the light. "I feel as if I should wipe my prints off of everything."

He turned at Fiona's snort. "Go ahead and laugh. Just know that Miss Beck seems like a sweet lady, but she will hunt us down and eviscerate us if she finds out we messed with her desk."

Fiona snorted. "Don't be such a chicken."

"You think I'm kidding? When I was a kid, I swear she could see right through me and knew when I was lying." He gave an exaggerated shudder.

"And you, my lovely, are a co-conspirator, so your lips will remain sealed forever—or else." Ewan dragged his hand across his throat like a knife.

Fiona laughed. "You didn't know that I've seen every single James Bond movie at least three times, did you? I used to imagine myself as 007, fearless super agent, when I was a kid. Bond makes it looks like fun, except when they're shooting at him."

Ewan grinned at her. "If you promise to dress in one of those leather cat-woman suits, I'll support you all the way."

Fiona laughed and followed him from the office. "The reality is different from the movies, isn't it? I never knew being a spy was so exhausting.

"And *now* I'm hungry."

CHAPTER 40
INVERNESS,
SCOTLAND - PRESENT DAY

Love gives you something extra . . .
It makes you limitless . . .
Adam Scythe

"Three hundred . . . two hundred and ninety-nine . . . two hundred and ninety-eight . . . two hundred and ninety-seven . . . two hundred and ninety-six . . . two hundred and ninety-five . . . two hundred and ninety-four . . ."

Once again Fiona focused on Dr. Blair's voice, its cadence soothing and comfortable. "Think of someone who loves you . . . hold onto that person in your mind, and don't let go. Feel yourself drifting down, down . . ."

Someone who loves you. That part was easy. Her person was right beside her, holding her hand and tethering her to the present as she felt the ripples gather around her and sank lower into the warm water. Colors changed from soft grey, to blue, to purple.

Dr. Blair's voice receded into the distance. Fiona stopped floating and found her feet. She was once again standing in a field covered by heather and thistle, but this time she knew exactly where she was. Culloden Battlefield, known in this time as Drumossie Moor.

The scene before her was the same as the one in the video at the Visitor's Center—and yet it was very different.

The black and white of the Visitor's Center video was now flooded with color. The maroon of the heather and the purple of thistle blended with the green of new grass and yellow of gorse bushes just coming into flower.

The sound of bagpipes, harsh and dissonant, rose above the clamor of men's voices and the banging of targes. As the clans lined up to face their enemy, blue and white saltires waved against the early afternoon sky, giving the scene an almost festive air.

The terrain was different too. The Visitor's Center video was a reenactment of the altercation between the Jacobite and government forces on April 16, 1746. It had been staged on the current battlefield, not the one she was looking at now.

Here the field dipped downward in front of her and she could see areas of standing water just beneath the surface of swamp grass. A horrible choice for the clans, who would have to cross that marshy ground to meet their enemy.

As before, she was standing on the Jacobite side, and across the field she watched a sea of red as the British Army lined up and soldiers readied themselves for the coming battle.

She turned to find herself surrounded by Highlanders. Most of the men looked exhausted. Fiona remembered from her studies that they had just returned that morning from a trek over uneven terrain in the dark, in an abortive attempt to carry out an attack on the enemy encampment at Nairn, twelve miles away. Her heart sank at the weariness she saw on the faces of the clansmen, knowing what was about to happen.

Fiona looked for her own clan and saw the MacLeans in the middle of the Jacobite lines. The distinctive red, blue, and green of her clan's tartan filled her with pride, and for a moment she forgot that these proud men, her ancestors, were going to rush to their deaths in a matter of minutes.

Through a sudden film of tears, she looked beyond the MacLeans, and saw that the MacLeods were lining up right next to them. So, that meant she was standing on the right side of the Jacobite lines—and Charles Stuart should be very near.

The loud neighing of a war horse reached her ears, and she turned to her right. Not fifty feet away, dressed in his Stuart great kilt and standing next to his mount, was Charles Edward Stuart, Bonnie Prince Charlie.

He looked so young, Fiona thought. This was the man on whom thousands of proud Highlanders had pinned their hopes, the man known by some as "the Young Pretender" and by others as "the Young Chevalier." To Fiona he exuded that air of power shared by all those in powerful positions throughout history, and she felt awe that she was seeing him in person.

Representatives of the clans approached him, received instructions, and returned to their positions, but for the most part the prince stood alone.

Something moved in the woods behind Charles. As Fiona watched, five men left the trees and mingled with the clans waiting for the call to battle. She strained to see, and identified the yellow and black of clan MacLeod of Raasay.

There was something wrong here. These men were not paying attention to the British army lines across the field, nor were they moving to join the other MacLeods in their position next to the MacLeans. Their attention was riveted on the prince as they moved slowly toward where he stood next to his horse. Their deliberate movements seemed almost furtive.

A cold hand wrapped around Fiona's heart. She stood rigid, but it would not have mattered if she could move. The killers—and she knew that was what they must be—were only feet away from her, but there was nothing she could do. She was not of this time—all she could do was watch.

History told her that Charles Stuart had survived the battle to live in exile, but this was something else. Was it possible for the past to be changed?

A tall man dressed in a black cloak emerged from the trees at a run. He moved to stand next to Charles and bent his head to speak, gesturing urgently with his hands. The prince looked up, startled, and saw the kilted Highlanders moving toward him.

One of the men, his swarthy face contorted with rage, lunged at Charles, dirk extended. The man in the cloak grabbed the assailant's arm and twisted it.

"Go!" he yelled to the prince.

Charles Stuart vaulted into his saddle. "Help him!" he called out and moved away at a gallop. Immediately, other men swarmed the scene. Three of the attackers were overcome and taken to the ground. The fourth struggled in the grip of two burly Highlanders.

"You!" The man with the dirk hissed and swung the weapon at his cloaked adversary, but he was a fraction of a second too slow, and the slice went wide.

"Godfrey!" Fiona heard the cloaked man say. "Of course it would be you."

"Bastard! You've ruined everything!" The weapon slashed forward again, but his target wrenched it from the assailant's grasp. Mad with rage, the attacker lunged forward, his hands reaching for the throat of the man who had dared to destroy his plans.

The cloaked man dodged the thrust again. He tripped over a root and fell backward onto the ground.

The man called Godfrey propelled himself forward and threw himself onto his helpless foe. Fiona watched as the body of the attacker stiffened, then rolled off and to the side, his own dirk planted in his throat. The cloaked man scrambled to his feet and ran to the right, towards the edge of the battlefield.

A howl of rage came from another attacker, held by two Highlanders. He stared in horror at the dead man, then wrenched himself free and raced after the man in the black cloak.

Fiona's eyes followed the prince's savior as he sprinted down the edge of the moor. As he ran, he cast off his dark cloak to reveal the red uniform of a British Army soldier. Minutes later, he had melted into the line on the other side of Culloden Battlefield.

Fiona struggled to understand what she had just seen. A government soldier had just saved Charles Stuart? From his own men? Nothing was making sense.

The bagpipes rose to a crescendo. Without their leader to sound the order to charge, the lines were in disarray. Someone on the far left of where she stood shouted an order and finally the clans burst from their positions, banging their targes and screaming as they rushed across the field.

Fiona's perspective shifted, just as it had in the video room of the Culloden Visitor's Center. Now she was standing at the British lines staring as the Highland clans rushed across the moor toward her.

Shots rang out. Smoke began to fill the landscape, but still the Highlanders came on. More shots, more smoke, and now Fiona could hear the cries of wounded men as the musket fire found its mark.

An entire front row of charging men went down. Howls of agony rose over the bagpipes as the Highland clans continued their mad rush toward the enemy. The screams and the clanging of metal were deafening.

Through the smoke, Fiona could now see individual men, resolution etched on set faces. She stood transfixed as the kilted men met the British soldiers and commenced hand-to-hand fighting. The stench of blood filled the air, and bodies began to cover the boggy ground.

A British soldier turned suddenly, as if he sensed Fiona's presence. He had lost his tricorn; wild black hair flew in the wind. The man's blue eyes stared straight at her—and through her.

Fiona swung around and saw herself. No, not herself—it was a woman dressed in a shirt and kilt two sizes too big for her, with a slouch hat pulled down over chestnut hair that was beginning to escape and fly in the wind.

Eilidh MacLean gazed at the man who stood transfixed in front of her.

"Iain," she whispered.

"Eilidh!"

They might have been alone on the battlefield; everything else had receded into the smoke and clamor. Then he reached out and pulled her into a hard embrace.

Fiona could only watch those intense blue eyes she knew so well. She could see the fear reflected in their depths. It was as if her own hand reached to brush a strand of black hair off his forehead.

"Eilidh. How—"

"Iain, was it you?" Eilidh pushed him away. Her voice was barely above a whisper, but Fiona heard it as clearly as if it had come from her own throat. "Did you warn the prince?"

"There is no time!" His voice was frantic with fear. "You have to go—now!"

Eilidh stepped back. "No, I came to warn you. They are going to kill you! Iain—"

"*You killed him!*"

Fiona turned to see a furious pair of hazel eyes

trained on the man Eilidh had called Iain.

"Do you know what you've done? Who it was that you killed?" The Highlander's voice shook with grief. A man in MacLeod tartan stood before them, tears running down his face.

"I should have killed you when you first set foot in our house!" Men fought and shrieked and died around them, but the three stood together in a tableau, as if they were as much apart from the battle as Fiona was.

"And you—you bitch." The man looked at Eilidh with loathing. "My mother said you were trouble from the moment she saw you. She knew you for a whore."

He turned his back on Eilidh and faced Iain again.

"It was so simple. To kill the Italian fraud and end all of this!" The Highlander spat the words. "A British officer—you should have been on our side!" The man shook his head as if to clear it.

The voice rose to a shriek. "Why did you have to kill Godfrey? Why?" Spittle flew from lips that Fiona had seen before, in a portrait at Raasay House. Lips set in a beautiful face—the face of an angel.

Cullen MacLeod.

There was no beauty in that face now. Hatred and madness had distorted Cullen's features almost beyond recognition. He raised his musket and aimed it at the man called Iain, and the next seconds blurred together.

As the shot rang out, Eilidh jumped in front of Iain and wrapped her arms around him. Fiona felt an excruciating pain in her back, beyond anything she had ever felt before, and watched in helpless agony as Eilidh's body sagged. Iain went to the ground with her and sat cradling her in his arms as tears poured down his face.

"Eilidh, no! Why did you?" His voice was a hoarse groan of anguish.

Her voice was fading, but her green eyes locked on his face and she reached up to touch his lips. "Sshh. It is all right. I promised that—I would protect you." She smiled. "I lov—" Her hand slid down to his shoulder and then fell to her lap as her eyes glazed and she went limp. Immediately the pain left Fiona as if it had never been.

Iain bent over Eilidh's body, heedless of the chaos around them. Great wracking sobs shook him and he rocked her as if they were alone on the vast battlefield.

Cullen's face twisted with hatred. He walked over to the two on the ground and stared down at them, as if he had all the time in the world.

"Mother always hated that bitch," he said, almost to himself. "That was for her. And this one is for Godfrey."

Unable to move, Fiona watched in horror as he reloaded his musket. A shot rang out and Iain's body jerked once. He relaxed into Eilidh's lap and went still, his arms entangled around her.

Cullen stood for a moment gazing down at them, just two more bodies on a field of thousands, and then he turned and melted back into the bedlam that would forever be known as the Battle of Culloden.

Fiona heard the sounds of the fighting begin to lessen around her and the color faded from her vision, as if the battle was returning to the black and white of the video in the Visitor's Center.

"Ten . . . nine . . . eight . . ." she heard, from a great distance. She felt herself floating upward, away from Drumossie Moor and its horrors.

". . . .even . . . six . . . five . . ." Dr. Blair's voice was becoming clearer. She floated on, and up.

" . . . four . . . three . . . two . . . one."

Fiona opened her eyes to find herself lying on the couch in Dr. Blair's office. The doctor watched her closely, concern etched on his kindly face. Ewan sat beside her, holding her hand tightly in his.

"Are you all right?" His voice was hoarse and his eyes looked worried. He looked at her closely. "You were moaning and trying to call out."

"Ewan—" Fiona took a deep shuddering breath. "They died. Both of them." She sat up straight, her eyes wide and glassy.

"We have to stop it," she said, her breath coming fast. "We can't let it repeat this time. We can't." She burst into sobs of grief and loss and collapsed against his chest.

Ewan wrapped his arms around her and rocked her as if she were a baby.

"We won't, *mo ghràidh*," he said. "We won't let it repeat."

CHAPTER 41

HIGHLANDS, SCOTLAND - PRESENT DAY

*Until you realize how easy it is for your
mind to be manipulated, you remain
the puppet of someone else's game.*
Evita Ochel

Ewan stared at the medical examiner, his mind caught on the words he had just heard, like a computer program that has frozen and needs a restart. He had expected this—why else would he have insisted on the autopsy? But the reality was so shocking that he found himself wanting—no, needing—to deny it.

"Potassium chloride is a mineral found in many foods," the doctor told him. "It's needed for several functions of the body, especially the heart, so it doesn't show up in a routine autopsy."

"Why would my father have taken potassium chloride? Was he ill?"

"I would not know that, not being his doctor. It

is prescribed for something called 'hypokalemia,' which is simply the scientific name for 'not enough potassium in your blood.'"

The medical examiner gave Ewan a level stare. "As I said, not enough potassium chloride can cause heart problems. Too much can lead to a heart attack. And there was far too much in your father's system to be natural. I'm afraid this will now be investigated as a possible murder case."

Fiona was waiting when Ewan stumbled into Gellions, white-faced and shaking. Her heart fell.

"Really?" She said, reaching to steady him. She led him to a table at the back and pushed him into the chair. He seemed to be in a zone of his own.

"Tell me," she said.

"He was right," he said. "Someone was trying to kill him. Someone did kill him. What am I supposed to do?" His eyes begged for answers.

"Ewan, let the police handle this. You can't be involved, especially if someone is after you too. Please, be careful." The fear was back in Fiona's eyes—remnants of the terror that had been hiding there since her hypnotherapy session two days ago. It killed him to see her like this, but there was nothing he could do—except try his damnedest to stay alive.

"I will, *mo ghràidh.* I won't go scrambling for a while, and I'll check the brakes before driving anywhere. Promise."

Fiona raised anxious eyes to his. "If someone wants to hurt you badly enough, sooner or later they'll succeed. You can't anticipate everything."

He hesitated. "That's why I think we need to

be proactive—" he put up a hand to stall her next words—"and think this through."

"What do you mean by 'proactive'?" she asked. Her eyes narrowed. "You don't mean 'sneak around and investigate by yourself,' do you?"

Ewan tried his most convincing laugh. "Of course not! But I do have a job, you know. I can't hide in my house waiting to see if someone's lurking outside in a black trench coat with a dastardly gleam in his eyes."

The joke fell flat. Fiona grimaced. "I do know that, Mr. Braveheart. But when you're not working or sleeping, I'm going to stick by your side, understand?"

"Fair enough," Ewan said. "That's actually a pretty good deal, from where I stand." He gave her a horrible imitation of a leer and put his hands up to ward off the blow he knew he deserved. Then he sobered.

"I can't just sit around doing nothing, though. I cleared my schedule for today, so let's go back to my house and make some lists. We don't have to go anywhere to do that, right?"

"Oh-kay," Fiona said. "I guess that's safe enough." She wagged a finger at him. "Just know, I'm watching you like a hawk."

"Aye, ma'am." Ewan saluted her and was gratified to see her relax a little. He felt a very strong urge to find whoever was behind this and throttle him—not just for his father, but for putting that fear in her eyes.

They picked up a pizza and walked up Ardconnell Street. Nothing had changed—except for the haunted look in Fiona's eyes, and the covert glances she cast around them as they walked. Nothing—and everything. He reached for her hand, taking comfort in the feel of something so simple, yet so profound.

Things could not be repeating. God would not allow such a thing. There was a human being behind this, just a sick individual with an agenda that could be stopped.

Ewan tightened his grip on Fiona's hand and picked up the pace, nearly dragging her up the street toward his house.

"S-slow down!" Fiona's voice came on a gasp. "Why are you in such a rush?"

"I don't know," Ewan said. He slowed his pace but didn't let go of her hand. "I just feel that if I don't get to the bottom of this soon, I'll go crazy."

"Well," she said, "you're not alone in this. There are two of us, and one of us is an intrepid secret agent, remember?"

Ewan stopped in his tracks. Fiona bumped into his back and stared at him, eyes wide.

"Fiona, what you just said—"

"Well, I was just trying to lighten the mood, y—"

He turned and began to run again, pulling her along in his wake. Inside the house, he sat down beside her on the couch, pulled his laptop over, and opened it.

"Something's been bothering me. Just listen—I'll walk you through what the medical examiner said, and you tell me if you spot anything—just anything. All right?"

She nodded.

"He said that potassium chloride is naturally present in the human body, but sometimes a person's blood doesn't contain enough, so a doctor will prescribe a supplement to make up the deficit. The condition is called 'hypokalemia.'"

"Okay, but—"

"He also said that hypokalemia, left untreated, can cause heart problems.

"So he thinks that your father had this 'hypo—kalemia?'"

"He couldn't say," Ewan said. "But he said my father had four times the normal amount of potassium chloride in his blood."

"Four times?" Fiona gaped at him. "And what does that do?"

"Too much potassium chloride can cause a heart attack."

Ewan's eyes met Fiona's. "There is no way the body would produce that much naturally. Someone gave it to him."

"So it really was murder." Fiona shook her head in disbelief. "I hear it, I'm taking it in, but a part of my brain just won't compute that. It's too much like the movies."

"Movies take their stories from real life." Ewan's eyes were bleak. "Potassium chloride can be injected or taken orally. No injection site was discovered in either autopsy, so—" He returned to the laptop and typed in "potassium chloride."

Several sites popped up immediately. The first seemed to be a simple explanation of the mineral, instructions on how to take it when prescribed, and a poison control number in case of accidental overdose.

"Fiona." Ewan's finger went to the top of the page.

Under the heading "potassium chloride" were the following words:

Generic Name: potassium chloride. **Brand Name:** *Kal Potassium 99, Klor-Con, K-Tab*

His finger stilled.

"I knew it," he said softly. "When you said 'secret agent,' I remembered the bottle you found in Miss Beck's drawer. I wondered why it was hidden away behind the files, when she had other pill bottles in the top drawer in plain sight."

"Maybe she's embarrassed because it was a prescription," Fiona said. "You did say she didn't want anyone to think she ever got sick."

"The prescription label on that bottle was for 'Klor-Con 10,'" Ewan said softly. Fiona blinked.

"And look here." His finger continued down the page and stopped at a section under the heading "Medications That Should Never be Taken in Combination with Potassium Chloride."

"Look at the one in the middle," Ewan said.

"NSAIDs," Fiona read. "Like aspirin or Advil."

"Here it's called Nurofen. And that was what was in one of the pill bottles in that top drawer."

Fiona stared at him. "Why would Miss Beck have a prescription that interacts with Nurofen?"

Ewan's eyes hardened. "Let's go find out."

"What do you mean?" Fiona asked. "How?"

"I mean, let's ask her."

The salesroom at Wild Thyme Distillery was crowded when they arrived. They threaded their way through the horde of eager tourists and past the sign-up counter for tours. As soon as they closed the door marked "Private" behind them, silence fell on the hallway to the inner offices.

Ariadne Beck was at her desk, on the phone. She looked up and her face broke into a welcoming smile. She spoke rapidly and hung up the phone.

"Ewan! Miss MacLean. It's good to see you here. I've been meaning to call you, to see how you're managing to juggle all your jobs." Her voice was teasing, friendly—the same voice that had consoled a young boy after his mother's death. She was family—more so than the people who were actually related to him.

"Hi, Miss Beck," Ewan kept his voice light. "I wanted to show Fiona something in Father's office."

"It's your office now," she said, and laughed. "Until you figure out what to do with it, that is. Let me know if there's anything you need." She picked up the phone again.

"Well," Ewan said, "there is one thing I'm curious about."

"Aye?" Miss Beck looked up again.

"Are you ill?"

"What? Of course not. Why would you ask that?" The voice was puzzled, and the secretary seemed honestly confused by the question.

"I just wondered. You see," Ewan kept his voice level. "The other day I was here to pick up my laptop, and I'd forgotten my keys. I knew you kept a set in your desk, so I—"

Miss Beck's knuckles whitened on the phone receiver. "You looked through my desk? You know how I feel about that, Ewan."

Was there something besides irritation in her

voice, or was it his imagination?

"I do, I do." He put his hands up as if in self-defense and made his voice light. "I would have had to go all the way home, though, and I knew you'd take pity on me."

The secretary put the phone down slowly. "I don't keep the extra keys in my desk anymore. Anyway, why this confession? And what does it have to do with my health?"

Ewan felt cold sweat break out on the back of his neck. He felt Fiona's hand slide into his.

"I know. I couldn't find them, but I did come across something that worried me a little. In your bottom drawer."

Miss Beck sighed and folded her hands together on the desk.

"Ahh," she said softly. Her face clouded. "I was afraid that's where you were going with this. The pills."

Fiona's fingers gouged into his hand, and he winced.

"Well—yes. It seemed like a serious prescription, and I was worried—"

"They're not mine." The hazel eyes filled with tears. "They were your father's."

"Father's?" Ewan kept his voice even. "What were they for? His heart?"

"Yes, dear. He didn't want me to tell you, but he hadn't been feeling well for a long time. He was under so much stress."

Her voice broke and she reached for a tissue from the box on her desk. After a moment she spoke again.

"He had something called hypokalemia. It means

his blood wasn't producing enough potassium. That prescription was for potassium chloride, to regulate the amounts."

She began to cry, quietly. Ewan stared at this woman he'd known most of his life. Never, not when his mother had died, not even at his father's funeral, had he seen her cry.

"It's my fault," she said, her voice low. "I should have watched him, checked to see if he was taking it correctly. I should have been there when he needed me. I hoped you would never find out, but I knew you would when you had him exhumed."

She was sobbing now, hands covering her eyes. Her voice rose into a wail. "Why did you have to do that? Couldn't you let him rest? Couldn't you let him keep his pride?"

Ewan gaped at her. She was telling him his father had overdosed accidentally? Was it possible? Guilt gripped him.

"I'm sorry, Miss Beck. I'm so sorry to have upset you." He stumbled back and away from the desk. "I—I think it's best if we leave for now."

"Yes. Yes, please leave. I hate you seeing me like this." The secretary waved a hand toward the door and covered her face with another tissue.

Ewan ushered Fiona quickly out the door and down the hallway. They sat in the car in silence for several minutes.

"I feel like shite," Ewan said. "I've known her all my life—how could I forget how much my father meant to her?"

Fiona said nothing. Ewan turned to look at her

and saw furrowed brows and a set mouth.

"What?" he said.

She stared out the windscreen for a moment.

"Maybe it's because you've known her all your life. Please don't be angry with me—I don't know her at all, but I didn't think her story rang true. Don't you think you should start by calling your father's doctor to see if he had hypokalemia?"

Down the hall, Ariadne Beck threw the tissue into the waste bin next to her desk. She picked up the phone and dialed a number.

"We can't wait any longer," she said. "It has to be now."

CHAPTER 42

INVERNESS,
SCOTLAND - PRESENT DAY

So it's true, when all is said and done,
grief is the price we pay for love.
E.A. Bucchianeri

Ewan hung up the phone and started the car. "Since it's after hours, Dr. Graham's answering service picked up and promised me they'll try to reach him, but I couldn't tell them anything so I just said it was an emergency."

He rubbed his temples and grimaced. "They didn't sound terribly impressed. I'm sure they're used to people calling and saying it's an emergency—after all, that's what they're there for, aye?" He pounded the wheel in frustration. "I wonder how many of his patients say that just to get him to call for some minor ailment?"

"They'll get him, Ewan. I could hear the tension in your voice, and I'm sure they could too." Fiona knew her words weren't making much of an impact. She wasn't even sure he was listening.

"I can't believe it," he said. "You must be wrong. Miss Beck has been with Father since she was a girl. She practically started the business with him. For that year after Mam died, she was the only thing that held me together in that house."

Ewan's hands on the wheel were tense, his knuckles white. He turned tormented blue eyes on her, and then pulled out onto the road. They drove in silence through the hazy sunlight of a Scottish spring afternoon.

Fiona's heart ached for him, for the small boy who had depended on this woman at the worst time of his life, and for the loss of innocence and trust that would surely haunt him if her story did in fact turn out to be the lie of a cold-blooded murderer.

"Well, when Dr. Graham calls back, he'll tell us if he prescribed Klor-Con. Then we'll know." They lapsed into silence again, each lost in thoughts they could never have imagined before.

"Where are we going?" Fiona asked, after a while.

"I don't know. Just—anywhere. I can't think straight waiting for the doctor to call. Any ideas?"

"Could you take me to Urquhart Castle? I haven't been there yet."

"It's very crowded, especially this time of year. One of the main tour stops."

"Exactly. Lots of people. No one can hurt you there."

Ewan glanced over at her, opened his mouth and closed it again at the look on her face.

"Aye, love," he said, and turned the car around.

The car park at Urquhart Castle was crowded with tour buses of all sizes. Languages from all over the world mingled together in a cacophony of sound.

The visitor's centre had been set up to herd tourists into the gift shop, and from there to the castle grounds themselves. It was a triumph of marketing, and exactly the thing Ewan had fought to avoid for his own tours.

Ewan and Fiona stood on the patio of the visitor's centre, looking out at the grounds and the castle ruins. Couples strolled around the grounds, children ran about under their parents' feet, and the waters of Loch Ness sparkled in the distance.

"There is simply no time that this place isn't overrun by tourists. Did you know that there were over half a million visitors last year?"

"Well," Fiona said, "I doubt the original builders anticipated that the A82 would run right past the back door, or that the tour buses would be continuing down the road to visit the Loch Ness monster."

Ewan laughed. "Aye, they'd be quite surprised at the way things turned out."

He swung away from the stone wall and took her hand.

"Shall we go join the masses?"

The doctor had not called by the time they returned to the car and made their way out of the crowded park and back onto the A82 for the return trip to Inverness. As they wound around curves behind two camper vans and a tour bus, Ewan pointed to the right.

"This is one of the most scenic roads in Scotland,

and we're not enjoying any of it," he said. He pulled into an overlook and parked behind a brown camper.

Loch Ness seemed intent on giving them the best of herself today. Maybe the ancient waters, home to a fantastic beast out of folklore and legend, wanted to tell them that nothing was impossible, that their story was not the only one of its kind.

People were born, fell in love, and left the stage. If love was strong enough, they never truly died, but were reborn to love again. *It can happen—it has happened many times,* the water spoke to them. *Trust in the love. Trust in each other.*

They returned to the Mercedes and turned toward Inverness. Behind them, a white car pulled out from behind a van and fell in behind.

On Charles Street, Ewan found a spot across from his house and parked.

"Stay here, I'll just grab the laptop, then we can walk down to the Castle Tavern. I think I need a whisky—or two." He jogged across the street to his door.

Fiona felt her own nerves jangling. She opened the car door and stood on the sidewalk, rocking back and forth from one foot to the other.

Ewan appeared on the sidewalk, laptop bag over his shoulder, and started across the street.

A single engine suddenly roared into life. Startled, Fiona looked up the street to see a white car traveling much too fast, racing toward Ewan where he stood on the curb. An alarm bell went off in her head.

"*Protect him,*" Eilidh MacLean's voice drowned out all other thoughts, and Fiona found herself running. She reached Ewan and pushed him out of the way as the car jumped the curb and reached the spot in which he'd been standing not a moment before.

She felt an excruciating pain arc through her body. In the next second she was thrown over the top of the vehicle and onto the pavement behind. The car's tires screamed as it pulled back into the road and disappeared around the corner.

"No!" Ewan howled. He picked himself up and ran to where Fiona lay in the middle of Charles Street, unmoving. He gathered her up in his arms and looked up at the small gathering of people who were responding to the sound of screeching tires.

"Call 119, damn it!" he screamed. He turned back to see Fiona's green eyes, open and filled with pain, watching him.

"Stay with me," Ewan begged her. "Help is coming—please, love, please stay with me!"

She smiled.

"I—did it." Her words were the softest of whispers.

"Don't talk, *mo ghràidh*," Ewan said softly. Tears ran down his face and onto his shirt. He took her hand in his and held tight. "I'm here. I'm here."

"I protected you this time." The words came on a hitch of breath. Fiona's hand clutched his, and she smiled. "The story—it didn't repeat itself."

Her eyes closed and her hand slipped out of his grasp. Ewan was left alone in the street, holding the tattered remnants of his heart.

CHAPTER 43
INVERNESS,
SCOTLAND – PRESENT DAY

Do you think the universe fights
for souls to be together?
Some things are too strange and
strong to be coincidences.
Emery Allen

The darkness was absolute, like a night with no moon or stars. Something cold had slithered across her arm and fixed its teeth into her hand, and she was helpless to chase it away. A monotonous beeping filled her ears, driving conscious thought away. Fiona huddled deeper into the darkness and waited.

The world lightened to a dull grey, like clouds before a winter storm. The grey swirled and parted and teased at her eyelids. The beeping continued without cessation.

She opened her eyes and shut them again to avoid the brightness reflecting off the white walls that surrounded her. She was tethered to a tube that ran from the back of her hand to somewhere behind her. She turned her head to follow the pathway of the tube and saw an IV cart next to the bed. The beeping came from a monitor behind and almost out of sight, and around her sat her entire family, grinning like loons.

This would have been a very nice dream, except for the pain. Not the horrible wrenching agony she'd felt before, this was a dull, throbbing ache that intensified when she moved. Maybe she shouldn't do that, then.

"She's awake!" A shriek like a crow's call, followed by a shushing sound that seemed familiar and comfortable. She felt tears welling and didn't know why.

"Honey," her mother's voice was the rippling water of Baddeck Bay, the coo of the mourning doves outside her bedroom—the sound of home. The tears overflowed and slid down her cheeks.

They were all here in the dream. Fiona took in their faces like a starved child. Dad, new lines etched under his eyes. Brian, green eyes clouded with fatigue. Niall, perched on the edge of her father's chair, his brown hair slicked back from his forehead in an attempt to look civilized. And Kirsty—why was Kirsty wearing a hospital gown, and whoa—where was the mascara and the lipstick? This dream was becoming ridiculous.

She heard her own voice, cracked as if from disuse. "Wh—why are you all here? Kirsty—where are your clothes? And you're not wearing makeup." Somehow that last part seemed incredibly important.

Kirsty sniffed. "Well, don't think for a minute—"

"Kirsty gave you a piece of her liver!" Niall crowed.

"She didn't want to 'cause now she has a scar, but she was the only one who could and I guess she doesn't want you to die, after all."

Fiona gaped at him. Slowly it began to dawn on her that this was not a dream. She was in a hospital, and her family was truly here.

Her father took over. "Fiona, you were in an accident. You had a concussion, and your liver—well, it was pretty bad for a while. We all got tested and Kirsty was a match. Your surgery was day before yesterday, and everything went well. You're going to be fine."

"Where am I?" In this Alice-down-the-rabbit-hole world, she had forgotten to wonder about that. Her thoughts drifted, solidified and a sudden fear gripped her heart like a vise. "Ewan! Where's Ewan?"

"He's right outside, dear," her mother said. "He's been here the whole time. We've gotten to know him quite well during the week you've been here in the hospital, and he seems such a lovely man." Tears stood in her mother's eyes. "He graciously gave up his spot for us for a little while, but I don't think we'll be able to keep him out for long."

Her father fixed her with a gimlet eye. "I'm thinking I might be looking for a new teacher at Gaelic College, eh?"

Fiona blushed and turned to her sister.

"Um—Kirsty? Thanks. I guess you saved my life."

"Well, yeah, I guess I did." Kirsty eyed her sister from under her lashes. "Does that make up for stealing your boyfriend?"

Fiona laughed—a bad idea. She winced and said, "Mom—Dad—please tell me she hasn't gone after

Ewan yet. Please."

At Kirsty's outraged gasp, William MacLean rolled his eyes and stood up. "No worries there. And now that we've made sure you're all right, let's get out and let him in before he paces a groove in the hallway, okay?" He herded them all out and paused in the doorway. "Get some rest, sweetie. We'll be back tomorrow, and you can tell us all your adventures."

Fiona lay back and closed her eyes. When she opened them again, Ewan was sitting in the chair by her bed, holding her hand. His eyes were soot-rimmed holes in his head, his lips were cracked from biting, and his hair straggled over his forehead. Gone was the handsome Highlander who had walked out of the pages of a Scottish romance novel—this man was a wreck. He was the most beautiful thing she'd ever seen.

"I—thought I'd lost you." Ewan's voice trembled like that of a man twice his age. "The way you flew—" haunted eyes fixed on hers. "You. I will never forgive you."

Fiona's lips curled upwards and she raised the hand that clutched hers. "So, I was supposed to let you be killed, and spend the rest of my miserable life suffering? That's not very nice of you. You'll have to suck it up, because I'm never letting you go."

His answer was to bend over the bed and deposit a soft, sweet kiss on her lips. The kiss deepened, and Fiona's mind deserted her. Every cell in her body responded to that kiss; even those in her new liver gave up their complaining and sighed in contentment. As far as lack of forgiveness went, this was pretty good.

Eventually Ewan forced himself to sit back in the chair. "So," he said, "are you up to hearing what's been going on in the world while you were lying around for a week doing nothing?"

Fiona nodded. "Tell me everything."

"First of all, Dr. Graham called while you were in the emergency room. He never prescribed Klor-Con—was appalled at the idea." The pain in Ewan's eyes at the idea of Ariadne Beck's betrayal had been replaced by a deep anger that Fiona suspected would be a long time leaving. He straightened his shoulders and attempted a smile.

"She was arrested three days ago—gave it all up with hardly a struggle. It was like a TV crime show—dedicated secretary, secretly in a one-sided love with the boss, love turns to hate, she gets revenge by killing him."

Fiona stared at him. "That was it? But wait—why did she go after you?"

"Ahh, my little secret agent, even when you're poorly you're pretty sharp," Ewan said. "It gets even weirder. Guess who Miss Beck's son is?"

"She has a son? Come on, just tell me! My head hurts."

A sudden pain clouded his face, and his fists clenched. "Aaron Grant." He gritted the words through his teeth. "Miss Beck had an affair in college, and he was the result. She had a cousin raise him, and all his life she told him he was Father's son and that the company should go to him as the oldest."

Fiona's mouth fell open. Ewan reached out and

closed it gently, and then went on with his story.

"She killed Father, but it was Aaron who pushed me off the ridge and tampered with my brakes. He knew that the distillery would go to Izzy if something were to happen to me."

Ewan shook his head. "Murder and multiple attempted murders—the two of them will be going away for a long, long time."

"Oh God, your poor sister!" Fiona's eyes flashed. "How despicable."

Ewan nodded. "She'll be okay. Izzy's strong."

"Was Aaron the one who tried to run you down?"

"Aye. He abandoned the car just out of town in the Tesco car park. It was stolen, of course, but forensics being what they are these days, it was traced back to him pretty quickly. Not smart—just desperate. Miss Beck called him, and he responded like a trained hound."

"Something interesting came up, though." Ewan twined his fingers through hers. "Something only you would understand." He looked into her eyes.

"Beck was her mother's maiden name." He paused. " Her real name was Sutherland." He waited for the pieces to fall into place.

Fiona gave him a confused look, and then her eyes widened. "Lucretia MacLeod was a Sutherland." She stared at Ewan. "Could it be?"

Ewan shrugged. "There are a lot of Sutherlands. But is it really reasonable to assume that our past story was just ours? Eilidh told you that there were others whose stories were repeating, and you said yourself that evil probably doesn't change through time."

"Well," Fiona said, "maybe evil doesn't, but our story changed, thanks to Eilidh. I wonder . . ."

"Aye?"

"I wonder what happened to Cullen, in the end."

"Don't know, don't care." Ewan navigated the tubes and put his arms around her. "I can't stand not to touch you. Tell me if I'm causing you pain."

She reached up and pushed a lock of hair out of the blue eyes—eyes that had followed her through history.

"You've never caused me pain. Not then, and not now. I think we've proven that the world isn't wide enough to keep our souls apart. Looks like you're stuck with me."

Ewan kissed her again. "We never had a choice, did we?" he whispered against her ear. "It was fate."

Half an hour later a nurse opened the door. She took a look at the two sleeping figures, hands clutched tightly and tousled heads close together, and smiled as she backed out again. It wouldn't hurt to wait a few more minutes. Sometimes the best healing had nothing to do with science.

19 APRIL 1746

The air was crisp with the promise of new growth. Rays of sunlight arced through the trees like hopeful beacons, promising another glorious day in the Highlands of Scotland. Dew sparkled like fine jewels on the ferns that lined the path, and a cool breeze rustled the leaves high overhead.

The forest had already forgotten the battle. Men came, destroyed each other, and were replaced by others like them. They strutted their moment on the stage and were gone in the space of a heartbeat, but the trees watched, and waited, and lived on.

A cart rumbled along the path, disturbing the peace of the quiet woods. Moans rose above the sounds of birds and the creaking of wheels and were lost in the forest air, ignored by the stoic guards who accompanied the cart on its gruesome journey.

A man cringed away from the filthy body next to him, trying to avoid the stench of blood. This was a mistake—a nightmare that would end when they realized who he was. And then he would make them pay for treating him so carelessly.

It had been so satisfying at first. He had failed his mission but destroyed his enemy, watched him join the thousands of pathetic dreamers lying dead on that murderous field, and walked away unscathed. It was time to go home, to take what was rightfully his, and to forget . . .

The bayonet pointed at his back seemed a momentary roadblock at first. His red-coated captors simply did not understand what he had tried to accomplish for them, that was all. When he explained, he would be hailed as a hero.

But they were not of a mind to listen. Filled with blood lust and hatred for anyone wearing tartan, they herded him into a foul-smelling outbuilding and threw him down amongst the injured Jacobite officers. He cringed away from them in disgust and bided his time.

One by one, his fellow prisoners had been marched away, none to return. And every time, he begged his captors to listen, to understand that it was all a horrible mistake. He was not like these fools. His pleas fell on deaf ears—they were simply too stupid to listen.

On the third day, he and the sixteen other officers who were left were bound and dragged outside to where a rough farm cart waited. And now here he lay amidst the wounded, like a trussed pig. It was almost laughable, but he no longer felt like laughing.

The trees parted to reveal a clearing, at the center of which sat a huge boulder. The men were dragged out of the cart and forced to march to the boulder, where they were lined up to face their captors.

So, more humiliation. He could endure this—the revenge he would have on these arrogant pricks would be worth the discomfort. He studied the faces before him, memorizing them for the future.

"Present arms!" A voice rang out, and muskets were raised to red-coated shoulders.

Horror stole his thoughts. This could not be happening! It was not supposed to end this way. He extended a shaking hand in supplication.

"Fire!"

He felt something burst in his chest. White-faced in shock, he sank to his knees, clutching at his filthy shirt. As if watching from a distance, he saw the others fall around him to lie like broken dolls at the foot of the boulder.

The soldiers stepped forward and turned the butts of their muskets around. Without hesitation, they began to club the dying men, watching without expression as blood and brain matter seeped from ruined skulls.

Cullen MacLeod stared up at his executioner with dimming eyes. How had it come to this? It was all so unfair. He was to be laird, he—

The musket descended, and his world exploded.

Without a word, the soldiers turned back to the cart and left Culloden Woods to its secrets. Silence returned to the clearing. The day passed and dusk came, bringing a grey mist that swirled around the boulder like wraiths.

A man in Fraser tartan stirred and opened one eye. Next to him lay the body of a MacLeod clansman, empty eyes staring at the sky. He turned away from the sight in horror and revulsion. His eyes fastened on the blood smeared rock behind him and he collapsed, his head a raging well of pain. He lay still for a time, and then forced himself to gaze upon his dead companion for another moment.

He struggled to his hands and knees and stared around him in disbelief. The others lay scattered at the foot of the great stone, battered and bloody. Dead, all of them. He rocked back and forth, lost in his grief.

Thoughts swirled like the mist. It was over. The dream that had sustained him, sent him rushing onto the killing field of Drumossie Moor—it was gone like the mist over the lochs. The pain was a wild thing, clawing at his body and telling him to give in, to let death carry him away. But he was a Highlander, and defeat was not in his nature. He owed it to his comrades to live.

Slowly, an inch at a time, he began to crawl away from the Prisoner's Stone, toward freedom.

ACKNOWLEDGEMENTS

Carl Dannenberger, my tireless husband and agent extraordinaire. You allowed me to concentrate on writing while you handled the business end of the project, which is always a mystery to me. Love you, dear!

Màiri MacKinnon, my Inverness kinswoman and keeper of the Scots language. Your help in translating Canadian/American to Invernessian Scottish kept my characters true to their heritage. I canna thank ye enough!

Steve and Mary Maclennon. You were so much more than my Highlanders for Hire. You shared your history and introduced me to the Prisoners' Stone and Ruthven Barracks, and in the process became dear friends.

Kenny Tomasso, my law enforcement ally and source of mayhem. You were my resource for all the best ways to kill people, an invaluable friend to have! Therefore I will keep you alive in my books.

According to local tradition, the Prisoners' Stone in Culloden Wood marks the spot where seventeen wounded prisoners were executed three days after the battle. The prisoners were placed against the conglomerate boulder, then shot and clubbed to death. The boulder measures about 5.5 meters in diameter.

Information from Martin Briscoe and Historic Environment Scotland (AKK) 30 September 2016.

ABOUT THE AUTHOR

MacKinnon has always been a writer. When she was eight, she began her career with a story called "Princess Zelda", a heavily plagiarized mixture of Moses and Cinderella. It was so good (in the author's humble opinion) that she begged her mother to take it to the local library and get them to publish it. A gentle refusal to do so, while seen as a betrayal of the highest order, did not stop MacKinnon from continuing her writing, although she has since learned that there are a few more steps between pencil copy and library.

MacKinnon writes emotions: love, hate, fear, redemption, second chances. Her writing is primarily historical paranormal romance with modern mystery thrown in for spice, and a little horror to stir the senses. And humor. Always humor.

MacKinnon lives in New Jersey with her husband. Two months each year are spent in the Scottish Highlands, her happy place and the source of her inspiration.

Learn more about M MacKinnon by visiting her website: www.mmackinnonwriter.com.

Or connect with her on social media:

Facebook: https://www.facebook.com/M-MacKinnon-539689769771150

Twitter: @MMacKinnon8

Instagram: www.instagram.com/mmackinnon_author

If you've enjoyed *Drumossie*, please consider giving the novel some visibility by reviewing on Amazon or Goodreads. A review doesn't have to be a long, critical essay—just a few words expressing your thoughts, which could help potential readers decide whether they would enjoy it, too. *Tapadh leat!* (Thank you!)